CONFESSION WITH BLUE HORSES

SOPHIE HARDACH

HEAD
of ZEUS

An Apollo Book

This is an Apollo book, first published in the UK in 2019 by Head of Zeus Ltd

9 7 5 3   2 4 6 8

A catalogue record for this book is available from
the British Library.

ISBN (HB): 9781788548762
ISBN (XTPB): 9781788548779
ISBN (E): 9781788548755

Typeset by Adrian McLaughlin

Printed and bound in Great Britain by
CPI Group (UK) Ltd, Croydon CR0 4YY

Head of Zeus Ltd
First Floor East
5–8 Hardwick Street
London EC1R 4RG

WWW.HEADOFZEUS.COM

CONFESSION WITH BLUE HORSES

This book is dedicated to my son, Aaron

I

The Model Migrants

The barbed wire fence across Potsdamer Platz – that barbed wire fence has disappeared and given way to a worse, more permanent obstacle. What we're seeing here on the corner of Potsdamer Straße and Potsdamer Platz right on the edge of the pavement is a concrete wall of a height of about 70 or 80 centimetres, topped by two layers of hollow bricks. Eye-witnesses report that the work began last night at 1.30 a.m., when six lorries turned up with building material, and five vans with bricklayers. They have built a new stone border right through Berlin.

RIAS Berlin, Broadcasting in the American Sector,
18 August 1961, Reporter: Rainer Höynck

Prologue

Summer 1987

M Y BROTHERS FELL ASLEEP after drinking Mama's tea. Heiko lay slumped against her shoulder, his mouth half open. Papa carried Tobi in his arms. The afternoon was fading, and our lengthening shadows merged with the shadows of leaves and swaying corn stalks. A meadow stretched out in front of us. Two storks were picking their way through it, twisting their white necks and clicking their beaks.

Beyond the meadow loomed a forest, dense with brambles and conifers. We would cross the meadow, enter the forest on the other side, slip through the barbed wire and keep walking until we saw houses. There, we would be safe.

I gripped the hem of Mama's jumper and whispered: 'What if they shoot at us?'

'They don't do that here.' She looked away.

'It's not dangerous' – my father, now – 'lots of people have done it.' He paused. 'Or at least some.'

'Look.' Mama squatted down next to me, awkwardly because she was holding Heiko. His arms flopped about, limp and heavy with sleep. 'It's not like Berlin, you can see it for yourself. There isn't a wall here.'

'I don't want to go,' I said. Just then, the storks took off. They drew a wide circle over the corn field and vanished into the distance, away from the forest.

Mama stood up. My brother Heiko slipped from her grip. Just a little: she caught him, snuggled him against her chest, cupped his bottom with her hand. It was the last time I saw her do that, holding him with the jagged nervousness that was typical of both my parents, who were never quite sure how to handle us. It was my grandmother who raised us mostly, and I wished she was with us to tell us all what to do.

Mama and Papa turned towards the meadow. My two little brothers were all they carried. We did not need suitcases, tickets, passports, keys. The door to our old flat in Berlin would be opened by other people, long after we were gone. Our Trabant, which was parked on the other side of the corn field, would be found by the local villagers in the morning, with the key left in the ignition.

Mama shifted Heiko's weight to her hip, held out her hand and said:

'Come, Ella.'

The light was fading quickly. This was the right time, my father said. Dark enough to be hidden, light enough to see where we were going. Very safe, nothing to fear, but we had to go now. I took my mother's hand and followed her into the meadow.

Ella

My Mother Was Afraid of the Dark

London 2010

A YEAR OR SO after my mother died, I received an unexpected inheritance. At the time I was living on a boat in South London, underneath an elevated railway line; not a proper houseboat, just an old fishing boat that had been dumped into Deptford Creek. Empty crisp bags littered the towpath and blew into the water when the trains rumbled past.

I had been stuck on the boat for almost a year. Initially it had seemed like a good solution: independent, cheap and self-contained. Not quite on land, not quite in the water. An in-between life that had suited me well, at least at first, during the warm summer months. Autumn had still felt romantic, in a creaking and storm-tossed way, but now it was spring and I had lost my last shreds of enthusiasm somewhere between February and March. When it rained, water trickled down the inside walls of the cabin. Slugs left trails across the windows.

The bathroom was in a cupboard, with the shower head suspended right above the ridged footprints of the squatting loo. My most precious possession was a photo of all of us on Oma's allotment back in Berlin. She was standing among some sunflowers and waving a little flag, probably for a Socialist holiday; my grandmother loved official holidays and never missed a march. Next to her was Mama with baby Heiko in her arms, and Tobi clinging on to her skirt. And there was Papa, dangling me by my feet so that my hair swept the grass. It was our favourite game: 'How do the bats sleep?' he'd ask – 'Upside downnn!' I'd scream and run into his arms, and he'd pick me up and turn me upside down. *This is how the bats sleep!*

—

Every evening, I cycled over to Canary Wharf, where I worked as a cleaner at an investment bank. My shift started just before midnight. The banks were beautiful at that time, tall lightboxes in the dark. Often a few traders were still tapping away on their keyboards, striking frantic deals with New York. They lifted their feet, I mopped the floor under their desks, they put their feet back down and thanked me, all with their eyes fixed on the screen. My shift ended just as the earliest traders came in to catch up with their colleagues in Singapore and Hong Kong.

My mother had also worked as a cleaner for a while, after she'd been released from prison. Later, in London, she left most of the chores to us, especially the things she couldn't bring herself to do, like fetching bottles of fizzy water from the cellar.

Mama did not like the cellar. There was no proper light in it and she was afraid of the dark.

—

One morning I came home from my night shift, shouldered my bike and carried it across the narrow wooden plank to my boat, when I heard someone cry out behind me: 'Ella Valentin? Hey! Ella Valentin?'

A postman in a hi-vis jacket jogged up to me, his crown of coiled black dreadlocks wobbling dangerously with every step. 'Parcel for you.' He stopped and passed me the box across the water.

I smiled at him. 'Well done for finding me.'

'Yeah, well, tell them to put a postcode on it next time. This almost went back to the sender.' He paused to fix his hair, then nodded at the boat with amused curiosity. 'Not too damp in there?'

'It's all right.' I wanted to say something else, to stretch out the conversation, because I rarely spoke to anyone in those days, and he was being friendly. But I could not think of anything, and so I just wished him a nice day and he walked back to his wheelie bag.

I went into the cabin, kicked off my shoes and lit the stove. It was a heavy parcel, solid and well packed, like the ones we used to get from West Germany when I was a child. Inside were brightly coloured art books, and a note from the new owner of my mother's flat in Finsbury Park. He was converting the attic and had found a bunch of her art books there. Tobi and I must have overlooked them when we cleared out the place. One by one I spread them out on my mattress, letting them light up my cabin with their saturated cheerfulness. German Expressionism, the Bauhaus, Dada, but also more obscure East German movements. A slim, worn paperback celebrated the programme of the Bitterfelder Weg, which encouraged artists to go and work in the factories, feel the weight of a spanner and learn about 'real life'. I was surprised Mama had kept that one. An envelope fell out, and crumpled bills and bits of paper. How typical of my mother, who had always used makeshift bookmarks, to leave these little traces of herself behind. I found a hair band between the pages of the Bauhaus book, and a notebook wedged into the back of the Dada catalogue.

The notebook was filled with long lists in her familiar, rushed handwriting:

> *Barking dogs: that never used to be a problem, it is now.*
> *'Privileg' (the smell)*
> *That accent from Dresden, I heard it on the tube this morning, had to get off and walk.*

Ach, Mama! I put the notebook aside and went through the other scraps, the bills and the envelope. They were nothing special, just utility bills and an admin-type letter from some office in Germany, but it touched me to read her name on them. The envelope contained a photograph, of a painting of three blue horses. They were standing in a meadow, massing against a storm, necks curved, hind legs tucked under. There was a dark shape at the edge of the meadow, a curled-up body in the grass. No, it was only a shadow, the shadow of a cloud.

So it really had existed, the painting of the blue horses, even though Oma had tried to convince me otherwise.

I picked up the German letter. The phrasing was complex, bureaucratic, and I had to read it several times before I understood the gist of it. Apparently my mother had corresponded with an archive in Berlin; I could guess what this was about.

The door to the deck swung open and let in a gust of wind and water, a fishy tang, a smell of chip shop and wet metal. I stepped outside and looked up at the brightening London sky, at the grey weeds that clung to the cracks in the concrete. On the other side of the canal loomed the old Deptford sewage pump, its windows smashed, its loading dock abandoned.

I climbed onto the roof of my cabin to get a better signal, and then I called my brother Tobi.

OUT OF ALL OF us, Tobi truly was the model migrant. We had all hoped for a fresh start when we moved to London in the early nineties, sponsored by Mama's supporters, but Tobi was the only one who really seized the opportunity. He assimilated to the point of sprouting freckles. Whenever I spoke in German to him, he replied in English. He even spoke English to Mama. And we let him, because we were proud, I think, that at least one of us had really made it.

I had to call twice before Tobi answered the phone, sounding cross and sleepy. 'It's six in the morning.'

'Time to get up and lay some turf!'

'I don't actually lay turf, Ellz, I have people who do that for me.' He yawned. 'Mind calling me again a bit later?'

'I'm about to go to sleep.'

'Speak at the weekend, then?'

'It's kind of urgent. Well, not urgent, but…' I told him about the notebook, the photo, the letter. The more I talked, the more excited I became, and the more certain that these documents were meaningful and important.

'Or they could just be bookmarks,' Tobi pointed out.

'Even so, they're worth looking into. Why don't you come

over for dinner? And then you can take the books home with you. I don't want to keep them here, everything's damp.'

'You can always stay with me, you know.'

'I know.'

'OK, I'll come over.' He paused. 'What did you say the notebook was? A diary?'

'Something like that.'

We hung up. I went back into the cabin and put on the woolly hat I wore to bed. The photo of the blue horses I placed on an upturned crate, with a circle of salt around it to keep the slugs at bay.

I N THE AFTERNOON I got up and tidied the boat for Tobi. I washed the plastic windows, emptied a bucket of soapy water over the deck, banged against the clogged stove pipe with a frying pan until it puffed more freely. Last, I aired the old green gaberdine coat that I inherited from my grandmother, Oma Trude. It was shiny with age and hung on me like a wet sail, but I liked to wear it anyway. At art school I had used it for a performance in which I dressed in a blue boiler suit and the old gaberdine coat, then piled broken bricks on top of each other. The tutor asked if it was a comment on 9/11, and I said no, it was a piece about my grandmother.

Oma always proudly referred to the coat as her 'OdF coat'. OdF stood for *Opfer des Faschismus,* or Victim of Fascism. Many of Oma's friends were fellow OdFs, elderly people who liked to start sentences with 'When I was in Buchenwald...'

They formed a little aristocracy, so it seemed to me at the time, these men and women who had proved their worth in the fight against Hitler. But there was also something lonely about them, or perhaps I see this only now, how mistrustful they must have been of the people around us, the same people who in the old days had hounded them. They gathered around the samovar in Oma's living room, warmed their hands on

significant about the notebook, the photo, the letter; that these had to be clues of some sort.

Popping balloons
Loud voices
Cushion covers embroidered with little flowers

When I was a child, my mother sometimes broke into a sweat for no apparent reason. We were at a birthday party, and suddenly, we had to leave. Or we were on the tube, and Mama's hand gripped mine; she rushed me out and back up to the street. There we waited for the bus in the rain, my hand crushed by her fingers, until we got on, found a seat and she collapsed into it, damp with fear. They were so vivid, those moments, as if every single one of my fingers had stored the memory of her hands.

Gunshots (also, slamming doors; the bang! of an exhaust pipe)

I looked at the trolley again. The little fish were gone. There was one thing I had not told Tobi, and perhaps I should have: when my mother was already very ill, she made me promise I would not go looking for my brother Heiko. We had been looking for him for years, it was our only real activity together, and I had expected her last request to be the exact opposite: that I would spend the rest of my days searching for him.

I asked her what she meant, but she refused to explain, and as so often, we left it at that. By then she was in constant pain.

Sometimes it was even harder than usual to tell when she was lucid, and when she was off into one of her fantasies. She said, for example, that it no longer mattered who betrayed us, that she had wasted so much energy on trying to find out who it was, and now realised it was of no importance, and had never been of any importance.

'What do you mean, betrayed us?' I asked, and held her hand. She was in bed, her bony head propped up on the white pillow.

'Someone told them about us.' She closed her eyes. 'It doesn't matter.'

'How do you know?'

She shook her head. 'I looked into things. I shouldn't have. Let's talk about something else, Ellachen, let's talk about your paintings. Are you still working on those mushroom paintings?' She opened her eyes and smiled. 'I wish I could go and see them. What are they like?'

I described them to her: the large canvases inoculated with a special fungus that changed colour as it aged, from brown to deep greens and even blues, creating a cycle of growing, living paintings, unpredictable and rather beautiful. It was only partly a lie. I really had experimented with canvases and colour-changing fungi, but the result had looked like a collection of damp rags. I was no longer making anything, really, but I did not want to tell her that. It was easier to invent imaginary paintings that were exactly as I wanted them to be. She listened with great interest, and said they sounded wonderful.

That was the sort of thing we talked about in those final

months: paintings, sculptures, artists we both admired, exhibitions I had seen. She only mentioned the past one more time.

'Remember when we saw that balcony fall off?' She laughed quietly to herself. 'We were lucky it didn't hit us.'

'I didn't see it fall off, you were on your own that day.'

'No, no, I can see it right before my eyes, it whooshed right past us, it missed us by *this* much.' She showed me with her index finger and thumb, marvelling at our narrow escape. '*This* much. And you held on to my hand for dear life.'

'Maybe.' I pressed an ice cube from its tray. My mother liked sucking on them. A falling balcony, a flat with a magical bathtub, two little girls sticking out their tongues at a concrete wall. Some of the stories from my childhood sounded like fairy tales, but they were no less true than this ice cube I was holding right now, this cool soaked flannel, this thin hand poking out from a pyjama sleeve.

'Mama, do you remember my friend Sandy?' I asked. But she had already fallen asleep.

I MADE BOILED EGGS in mustard sauce for Tobi, a recipe from Oma. We sat down on two wooden crates, but Tobi's was too low for his long legs. He stretched them out and pulled them back towards him, all the while trying to balance the plate on his knees. He leaned against the damp wall, winced, discreetly sat up again. Maybe he'd hit a slug trail.

'Is it OK?' I gestured at the eggs.

'Delicious.' I'd never heard my brother describe a meal as anything but delicious, or a person's house as anything but lovely.

'Do you ever wonder what he's like?' I asked.

Tobi had picked up our mother's journal, about to open it, but now he paused.

'Is that why you asked me over?'

'I'm just thinking, I hope he's charming. It's such an asset in life. I hope he knows how to make people like him.'

'It's hard work, is what it is.' Tobi massaged his legs. 'I thought this was about Mama.'

'You used to be so close, you two. Don't you remember? You'd stand there, hugging each other, and all the grown-ups would be like, aww, and then one of you'd scream – *He bit me! He bit me!*'

'I'm not a biter.'

'Maybe it was him then.' I could see them very clearly, squeezing each other so tightly.

'The things you remember.' Tobi shook his head. 'I don't remember anything. I suppose I'm lucky that way.'

'You must wonder, though? Is he happy, is he safe? Even the small things: does he like dogs, what's his favourite food, has he got a girlfriend...'

'Or a boyfriend.'

'Or a boyfriend.' And I tried not to smile because I thought, of course Tobi thinks about him, of course he tries to imagine what he's like, and he probably pictures him as a charming garden designer with a nice boyfriend, just like I picture him as a somewhat lost artist obsessed with the past. Where else could we start but with ourselves?

'He might even be really sporty,' I said, and Tobi said: 'Highly unlikely', and we laughed, having finally hit that point of connection. Team sports: never a Valentin strength.

Tobi opened the journal. His lips moved as he tried to read Mama's handwriting.

'*Privileg?* What's *Privileg?*'

I leaned over the page with him. We were both left-handed, which was not something I thought about except when we sat close together, and didn't have to worry about things like clashing elbows. 'It's a kind of aftershave. Really, you don't even remember that? Papa used to wear it.'

'*Privileg.*' He shook his head, pointed at the next line. 'No, nothing. And this? *Cushion covers embroidered with little flowers. Not as bad as the rest; slightly unpleasant.*'

'I don't know. Maybe they put a cushion over her head?'

'Ella! Please.' He closed the notebook.

'What do you expect? It's a trigger diary,' I said.

'What's a trigger diary?'

'A diary of things that frightened her. Come on Tobi, you know what a trigger diary is.'

'You say that as if it's common knowledge.'

'It is.'

'In your world, maybe.'

'What do you mean, in my world?'

He ignored me and picked up the photograph of the blue horses.

'Tobi, what do you mean?' I repeated.

'I mean that you've always been obsessed with that sort of thing, lists and codes and stuff.'

'That's so not true.'

'I don't blame you, it's not like Mama ever gave you a choice.'

'I'm not obsessed. I just notice things.' I could hear the frustration in my voice, the impatience. 'This painting, don't you remember this painting?'

'No.'

'Well, I do.' I snatched the photo away from him.

'What is this, an interrogation?'

'I wasn't an only child, Tobi, that's all I'm saying. You were there, too.'

'And Heiko.'

'And Heiko.'

'I'm not saying I wasn't there, I'm just saying – I can't really see why you're bringing him into this, or why we're sitting here talking about Papa's aftershave, or why it matters how Mama felt about embroidered cushions.'

The visit wasn't going at all as I had hoped. It shouldn't have surprised me. We'd had this conversation before, and he'd blocked and derailed it before. I'd just thought that having something tangible to show him would make it different.

'Look at this letter.' I unfolded the typed letter I had found among her books. 'It's from an archive.'

He frowned. 'It's a bit dense.'

'You're a bit dense.' Line by line I translated the letter for Tobi, which I had to admit was rather satisfying. He was better at life, but I was better at German.

OFFICE OF THE FEDERAL COMMISSIONER FOR THE
RECORDS OF THE STATE SECURITY SERVICE OF
THE FORMER GERMAN DEMOCRATIC REPUBLIC

SUBJECT: Request to view personal file

Dear Frau Dr Valentin,

Further to your application to view your personal State Security file, we can confirm that such a file exists here at the Office of the Federal Commissioner for the Records of the State Security Service. Unfortunately, much of the file appears to be missing. Even the pages we have succeeded in recovering are mostly incomplete.

I would of course be more than happy to show them to you, should you be interested in viewing them anyway.

I am sorry, Frau Valentin, that there is so little we can do to assist your search.

Yours faithfully,

Dr Reinhardt Licht

Archivist

My mother had regularly travelled back to Berlin, each trip one of her many futile efforts to reunite our scattered family. I tried to recall if she had ever mentioned an archive, but all I could remember from her last trip was some sort of school reunion. I hadn't asked her about it; it hadn't seemed important at the time. But I hadn't asked her about plenty of really important things, either, and now desperately wished I had. Talking is a habit like any other, it needs to be sustained through practice. If you never talk about the small things, it feels weird to suddenly launch into a heart-to-heart. 'Of course I never asked him about that,' my father once said about his own father, who had been a member of the Nazi party. 'We didn't even talk about the weather. How could I suddenly ask him why he'd joined the Nazi party?'

We had often trawled websites together, my mother and I; had posted search ads and dates of birth in the usual desperate threads and depressing forums; had fielded dubious replies from strangers who were quick to mention finder's fees. *I am looking for my son, Heiko, who was taken from us,* she had typed again and again.

We had put in official requests to various German ministries, only to be told that in cases like ours, there was nothing to be done. The separation had been legal under the old law, the GDR's law. The details of the case fell under the Data Protection Act, including Heiko's new address, if he had one, and his new name, if he had one, or even the basic question of whether he was still alive. It turned out that the question of whether my brother was alive was a very private matter, one that could not be shared with his family; because legally speaking, we were of course no longer his family.

'You mean our politicians were able to hammer out a deal about nuclear bombs, and borders, and the privatisation of an entire economy, but not about what should happen to little boys who were stolen from their families,' my mother said to a senior official during one of those visits back to Berlin. 'You mean they were able to agree on how quickly Moscow would pull out its troops, and which weapons our country should be allowed to have, and how to value a collective pig farm – but not whether mothers like me would ever see our children again, no, that didn't enter their heads, did it? To figure out how I might one day see my son again.'

Upon which the official patiently explained again that while he understood our frustration…

'I know,' my mother said. 'I know, I know. I know.'

And yet she'd never mentioned this archive.

'I've looked it up,' I said to Tobi. 'Check this out.'

I opened my laptop, but the connection had frozen.

'We'll try the roof,' I said.

'I don't believe this.' He groaned. 'Every time, Ella, every time I come to visit you…'

'… we have such a lovely time, right?' I nudged him. 'I know. It's wonderful.'

I climbed onto the roof of my cabin and opened my laptop. Tobi followed, making a great show of wiping down a corner before he sat down. Which was ridiculous: surely he worked in places much dirtier than my roof.

'Should have brought my gloves and overalls,' Tobi said, as if he'd read my mind.

———

The archive's website had seemed a little overwhelming at first, filled with pictures of looted Stasi offices and archivists painstakingly reconstructing old files. But there was a friendly sidebar for people like me: *Are you a victim, or the descendant of a victim, of the State Security Service of the former German Democratic Republic? Here is how the archive can help.*

'That's us!' I swivelled the laptop so Tobi could see. 'Victims and their descendants. That's us, right there.'

'You say that as if it's something to be proud of.'

'It's certainly nothing to be ashamed of. We *are* victims.'

'*I'm* not a victim, I'm a garden designer.'

'They're not mutually exclusive.'

I clicked on the link in the sidebar. A new page opened up with a contact form.

Please tick one of the following four options:

I want to research...
 • the activities of the State Security Service
 • the rulership mechanisms of the GDR
 • the rulership mechanisms of the Soviet-Occupied Zone
 • the National Socialist past.

'That's so German,' Tobi said. 'Like a menu, or multiple choice. *Which of our twentieth-century atrocities are you most interested in? For genocide, dial one...*' I noticed a link at the bottom of the page: *Viewing files for near relatives of missing or deceased persons.*

This was very different from the dire online forums we had wasted so much time in. Much more legitimate, more official, more promising. If there was a surveillance file on my parents, then surely it would include details on our family, and our separation. And we had the right, it seemed, to view that file. Even if it was incomplete, it was at least *something*.

Who knew what else my mother had discovered in Berlin? Were we not perhaps doing exactly what she had wanted us to do, walking in her tracks, following the little trail she had laid for us? If she had truly wanted me to stop looking for Heiko, she would have destroyed the letter from the archive. Instead, she had left it there for us to find.

I took the laptop back from Tobi and started filling in the contact form. We could get a cheap flight, go for just a few days, visit the archive, see what we could find. Already I could picture us going through the records, noting down addresses and leads, finally getting somewhere.

'What are you doing?' Tobi craned his neck to see.

'Could you take time off next week, do you think? A couple of days should be enough.'

'To do what?'

'To meet this guy, this archivist who wrote to Mama. He sounds helpful.'

'Ellz…'

I sighed. 'I know what you're thinking. You're thinking that this is just one of my crazy ideas, and you'll have to bail me out in the end.'

'Who says I'll bail you out?'

'She went to Berlin to visit that archive.' I could hear myself getting louder. 'She must have thought they could help her find Heiko.'

'So what? She also thought the lady in the corner shop was spying on her.'

'You can't discount everything she did because of a few isolated incidents.' For a moment I wasn't sure if I was talking about our mother or myself. 'Come on, give her some credit. She wasn't stupid, she knew more about the world than you and I ever will. And you can say what you like, but that corner shop woman *was* a bit weird. Remember the time she asked Mama where we were from?'

'That wasn't weird,' Tobi said wearily. 'What's weird is that Mama replied, "From Canada."'

'It's no one's business where we're from.'

He shook his head. 'Don't you think it might be better to leave him in peace?'

'You can't mean that.'

'All those years she spent looking for him, and not a single trace, not a single sign. If he wanted to be found, he'd have let us know.'

'Why would he not want us to find him?' I said, suddenly feeling a bit deflated.

'Because he doesn't even know we exist, maybe? Because he's fine with the way things are?'

'I have a friendly disposition and tolerate all known foods. My hearing is above average and I have a fine creative mind. Why would anyone not want me for a sister?'

'Ach, Ella.' He put his arm around me. 'Don't run off to Berlin. Stay here and…'

'… get a proper job.'

'Exactly.'

'I'm the worst cleaner in London. My clients' desks actually look dirtier after I've been there. I think I'm about to get fired.'

'How about teaching art?'

'I'm terrible with children.'

'That's not true.'

'They make me sad. I look at them and I think, that's how small he was.'

'Take a year off and focus on your art then. You can stay with me. I loved your show, I thought it was brilliant.'

'No one came to that show.'

'I did.'

'OK, one person came to that show.'

'You'll have thousands of shows. Look at Picasso, it took him decades to make his mark.'

'No it didn't. Picasso was a child prodigy.'

'You could pass for a child prodigy.'

'Thanks.'

'With a bit of Botox.'

'Oh Tobi.' I laughed.

'That's better.'

We went down onto the deck to watch the rain-swollen creek. The dark water rushed past carrying with it all sorts of urban swag. Broken barbecues, bicycle pumps, plastic bottles. Another shopping trolley.

'Look.' Tobi pointed at the trolley. 'That one's from Waitrose.'

I smiled. 'We're gentrifying.'

He caught a passing branch from a tree, let go of it, caught another branch.

'I think I need to at least give it a go,' I said. 'I'll visit this archive, I'll check what she saw, and I'll come right back. And I'll pay you back, of course, as soon as I can.'

'I like how you elegantly slipped in the issue of funding there.'

'It's just the flight and a room somewhere.'

'This isn't about the money. I just think you're in for more pain, and more disappointment, and more time wasted chasing someone we'll never find.'

'I have no choice, Tobi. I have no choice.'

Often when I stood on the deck I had to fight the urge to jump into the water, not out of a death wish but because it would be so refreshing, so mentally cleansing. I would dive in and come out as new, with all the old Ella washed off.

'I miss him,' I said. 'Don't you?'

A few moments passed, and then he said: 'Can you show me that photograph again, the one with the horses?' I gave it to him and he looked at it for some time. Eventually, he nodded. 'There was a story you used to tell me…'

I shook my head. 'That was Mama. She told us a story about the three blue horses.'

'No, it was you.'

'Really?'

'Once upon a time, there were three children who lived in a bathtub. Then one day, the sorcerer came and…' His voice was half drowned by the noise of the creek, but it did not matter, I knew the story so well.

'… and took the children away,' I continued. 'And he carried them off to his castle, and there he turned them into three horses, into three blue horses.'

'But their grandmother went after them. She killed the sorcerer, she lifted the spell, and she brought the children home.'

'Except she didn't bring all three of them home, did she?' I reached down and dipped my hand into the water. 'She only brought two.'

Berlin 1987: Spring

'STICK OUT YOUR TONGUE,' Sandy said and handed me
the binoculars. 'Go on.'

'You first.'

She stuck out her tongue. Sandy was not afraid of anything.
'Now you.'

I leaned out of the window as far as I could. There, just
beyond the wall that closed off the end of Sandy's street, was a
viewing platform with tourists on it. Through the binoculars
I could see them quite clearly. They huddled together to allow
the rest of the group onto the platform. There was even a little
queue on the steps.

I looked at the street below, the shabby front doors with the
flaking paint, the car parked on the corner, the guard by the
wall, the women queuing outside the grocery.

'Must be a slow day over there,' I said, 'if they're queuing up
to look at queues.'

'Let's make it more exciting then.' Sandy waved her hands
over her head. 'Hello poo-poo-heads!'

'Don't!' I jumped back, certain the guard must have heard
her. But when I peeked, he was still in the same spot, staring
into space.

'You think they'll come over here and complain?'

She was right, of course, and this was quite a nice feeling: that the people over there couldn't do anything to us, couldn't reach us, couldn't even complain to the guard, because he was *our* guard, not their guard.

Sandy had only joined my class a few weeks before, but I already liked her more than anyone. Every day we played in the empty lots and abandoned basements of our neighbourhoods, slipped through rusted doors marked DANGER NO ENTRY and dug out old bullet casings and Red Army badges from underneath piles of rubble. Sandy was the one who told me that the holes in the wall of my building were bullet holes from the war. We fought endless street battles in which I often forgot that we were only playing, and would hide in the shadow of a building with my heart racing as her steps drew nearer. It was in one of the piles of rubble that we had found the heavy old pair of binoculars. The leather strap had snapped but once we'd wiped the lenses clean, the rest of it worked fine.

'Go on,' Sandy said. 'Honestly, I do it all the time.'

I popped my head through the window and stuck my tongue out.

'Are you crazy?' Sandy grabbed me and pulled me to the floor. 'Not like that!'

'Like what?'

'Didn't you see? The guard looked up! Now we're in big trouble.'

'Seriously?'

Sandy was making strange grunting noises. I looked at her. She burst out laughing.

'Haaa! Got you!'

'You gave me a heart attack.'

'It was fun though, wasn't it?' She peeked out, and added almost casually, as if in an aside: 'My mum's over there.'

'In West Berlin?'

'In Hamburg. She's going to send for me really soon, though.' She drew back and closed the window.

This was one of Sandy's more obvious lies. If her mother were really in the West, Sandy would never be allowed to live so close to the wall. Not that her lies bothered me. I lied quite a lot myself, mostly to make things seem more interesting than they were. Ultimately, it didn't matter where exactly Sandy's mother was. Sandy seemed to mostly raise herself. Her dad always put an apple next to her placemat before he went to work in the morning, and then Sandy did all the shopping, all the cooking, and no cleaning at all, which was why their place looked terrible.

She was putting on her shoes now, restless as usual, always on to the next thing: 'Come, I'll show you something else.'

We left the flat and walked a few blocks to the Bösebrücke. The bridge was closed off by a border post, with allotments to the right and flats to the left. Sandy's father grew vegetables on one of the allotments. We squatted under some redcurrant bushes there, and she told me her latest secret in hurried, conspiratorial whispers:

A few weeks ago she had looked out of her window and

noticed that the viewing platform was closed, and the street filled with police. She'd gone to the allotment to ask her father about it, but the allotments had been cordoned off too, with more guards and policemen patrolling the bridge. She'd managed to slip into the allotments through the back, and had hid under the bushes, right here, and been quiet as a mouse, with her ears wide open, and she'd heard everything. A man had been shot on the bridge.

'He nicked a ladder from one of the sheds over there,' she whispered dramatically. 'And then he used that to try and climb into the border post, and then he was shot.' She pointed through the twigs. 'Right over there.'

'Did you see the body?' I whispered back. She shook her head. I was in awe of her courage. Then it occurred to me that this might be another lie. I would ask Oma Trude about it later, because she usually knew what went on in the neighbourhood. And Oma was not like other grown-ups; she never said that she was busy or that my questions were giving her a headache or that I should go and ask someone else.

'I'll show you where he tried to climb over,' Sandy said, and pulled at my sleeve. 'There might still be footprints.'

But I'd had enough. Already I was regretting our stupid game with the people on the platform. And it was almost dinnertime.

Sandy walked with me to my corner, rather quiet now. That morning our art teacher, Frau Obst, had asked us to close our eyes and draw the shape of happiness, and Sandy had just sat there with her crayon in her lap, and then Frau Obst had asked if she wasn't going to draw anything, and Sandy had said that this was the shape of happiness: nothing. Frau Obst had said that Sandy had done something very profound and lovely, because happiness was invisible, wasn't it? But I knew she hadn't meant it like that.

To cheer her up, I told her about the yellow parcel we had received the other day, with chocolate and a doll from my dad's cousin in West Germany. I would bring the doll to school and we could play with her, I said; then I remembered Sandy's mother was supposedly in the West, and wished I hadn't said anything.

She looked a little sad when we said goodbye at the corner. Her dad was on a late shift again. It was only when I walked through the front door of our building, which was much nicer than hers and always smelled a little of floor polish and cake, that I realised I should have asked her if she wanted to have dinner at my house, with all of us.

—

Like most buildings in Berlin, ours was divided into a front-facing *Vorderhaus* and a shabbier, darker, back-facing *Hinterhaus*, with a gloomy courtyard between them. The *Hinterhaus* was mainly occupied by students, and this was my one trump card against Sandy's endless supply of drama and adventure, because there were no students at all in Sandy's street. She shared my fascination with them and noticed things I never had, like how one of them, whom we came to call sock man, always dried his socks on the window sill. Sock man and his friends slept all day and sat on the roof drinking beer at night. They fought and kissed and walked around their flats naked. Once, one of the girls threw her lover's clothes out of the window, and he had to rush around the courtyard with a towel around his waist and pick them out of the flower beds. Sandy and I re-enacted this scene endlessly, one of us standing on the bed and flinging things across the room, the other running around to collect them:

'Forgive me, Beate!'

'Never! Here are your stinky trousers, take them and go!'

—

I let myself into the clean, bright, well-mannered *Vorderhaus* where we lived, and knocked on Oma Trude's door on the ground floor. No response. Oma was the only one in the building who had a telephone, which was impressive but a bit useless as a telephone only really makes sense when other people have one too, and can call you. Instead we left messages on her 'door telephone' – a notepad made of scrap paper that was taped to her door, with a pen dangling beside it – and she left messages on ours.

Liebe Oma! I scribbled on her notepad, high up on my tiptoes to reach the paper, *I will see you upstairs! Love, Ella.*

I had a rule for walking up the stairs to our flat on the fifth floor: one flight backwards, one flight forwards, one flight backwards, and so on. This was satisfying because it meant I always faced in the same direction. My ambition was to spend an entire day without turning my head, walking backwards, sideways and so on, but that would have to wait until the holidays since there was no way I would get away with it at school.

—

I walked backwards past the door of Frau Rachmann, who was about the same age as Oma but very forgetful. Sometimes we had to go out and look for her, and she would be wandering the streets in her rose-patterned nightie. Oma revered Frau Rachmann, who in her time had taught literature classes in Moscow and translated the greatest Russian poets. She was, Oma said, 'a true woman of culture', someone who had devoted her brilliance to the good of the country, not like today's intellectuals who were only thinking about how to become head of department and move to a big house in the suburbs with more room for their books. ('Just use the library,' Oma muttered whenever my father paced the flat with a stack of books in his arms, looking for somewhere to store them. 'Frau Rachmann used libraries, Gogol used libraries, Pushkin used libraries all his life.' To which my father would tetchily reply that Pushkin had certainly *not* used libraries, Pushkin had had his own private library with gilded bookcases; and then he would wedge the new books into the last remaining little space between the old books and the ceiling, just to make a point.)

I stepped sideways on the landing and continued up the stairs, facing forwards, passing Frau Pietsch, who was on her knees, washing the stairs in her green housecoat. I stopped to greet her and play with her little dog, Schnauzi, whose paw prints were all over the wet stairs. Frau Pietsch often accompanied Oma to party meetings and marches. From Oma I knew that she had married a man who was nice enough but hadn't wanted children, and when Frau Pietsch was too old to have children he left her for a younger woman and started a family. This, Oma said, happened quite often, and I should keep it in mind when I got older so it would not happen to me. The other thing to keep in mind was not to become like Frau Minsky on the third floor, whom Oma called 'die Minsky' or simply 'Minsky'.

Die Minsky was a round and rosy woman who had stolen old Herr Minsky from his previous wife. Not long after their wedding Herr Minsky suffered a stroke and now Minsky was his carer. Walking backwards again, I passed her open doorway. She was leaning on her mop and looking bored, a cigarette in her mouth, her pert bottom sticking out.

'Watch where you're going,' she said crossly, which was silly because the whole point of walking backwards was that you could not see where you were going. Still, I quite liked Frau Minsky, even though Oma did not. Die Minsky was the kind of person, Oma said, who broke the only hacksaw in the factory and then blamed the brigade. Frau Pietsch, on the other hand, was the kind of person who would stay behind after everyone else in the brigade had gone home, just to fix the hacksaw. Frau Rachmann had never touched a hacksaw in her life, but that could not be held against her as she was a great woman of culture. (Oma had worked in a fridge factory for many years, and that had shaped her view of things.)

All the women in our buildings had stories like that, and Oma knew them in detail: who had trouble in her brigade, who had lost three little babies before they were born, who had been a big Nazi and now thought no one knew, who was making eyes at both Dr Kaminsky, who lived on the fourth floor, and the postman. The men in our building didn't have any stories. Or if they did, they did not tell them to Oma. Herr Minsky had almost lost a leg in the war, that was all. And Opa Horst had been at Stalingrad but that was not talked about.

—

I stopped at our own front door and read a message my father must have scribbled on his way out:

We don't have eggs, we don't have cheese,
Can somebody go shopping, please?

Underneath, my mother had added in her own small, sharp handwriting:

How about YOU go shopping, for a change?

Which broke the rules: when somebody left a message in rhyme, your reply was supposed to rhyme, too. I tore off the message because I hated it when my parents argued on the notepad, in front of all the neighbours, or at least in front of anyone who made it all the way to the top floor. The door swung open. Heiko ran into my arms: 'Eyya! Eyya!' He slapped my face, which he always did when he was too full of love.

'El-la! Say El-la!'

'Eyya!' Heiko poked me in the eye with his fat finger. *'Auge.'*

'Aua!'

'Aua! *Auge putt.'* He poked my eye again.

'That's right, now my eye is broken. I'll have to go to the shop and buy a new one.'

He slapped my face again and laughed. Tobi came out into the corridor, chewing on a piece of bread, and told me that Heiko had tried to flush his glasses down the toilet. Heiko grabbed the bread and drove it along the wall, making engine noises. Then he ran back into the kitchen.

Mama was sitting at the kitchen table, her foot in a bucket of ice. She was still in her work clothes, a brown skirt and a beige jumper with the sleeves pushed up, her dark hair gathered up into a bun. Oma sat next to her, dressed in a purple housecoat with small orange snails on it, brooding over a crossword. I went up to Mama and gave her a hug. 'What happened?'

'Nothing, Ellachen,' Oma said. 'Your mother stubbed her toe.'

Mama sighed. 'That's one way of putting it.'

'A type of shelter, five letters. Any ideas?' Oma squinted at her crossword.

'How did you stub your toe?'

'I went to buy you some trousers.'

She stretched her arms, leaned back and began:

One of Mama's colleagues at the university had heard that a shop down the road had a new supply of children's trousers, and they went out to buy some. Only the shop turned out to be not down the road at all but in an entirely different neighbourhood. They had to take the tram. Along the way they met another art historian, who asked my mother how her chapter was coming along. Which was a mistake, of course; Mama did not like to be asked about her chapters.

Eventually they found the shop, spent the afternoon queuing, reached the front of the line, and were told there were no more trousers left, or indeed any children's clothes left. All that was left were some women's blouses with a flower pattern and ruffles, which Mama said looked like baby clothes in adult sizes. She bought one anyway since she'd come all that way.

'Well done,' Oma said. 'Leave it with me, I'll swap it. There's always someone who needs a blouse.'

Oma was an alchemist: she could turn blouses into bottles of vodka, and bottles of vodka into tyres, and tyres into spare parts for the love seat on her allotment, her *Hollywoodschaukel*, where she liked to sit and read biographies of great women of culture.

'Yes, that's the moral of this story. There's always someone who needs a blouse.' Mama took off her glasses and rubbed her eyes. Her face looked naked and tired. 'There were no men in that queue, you know. No men at all. I suppose they were busy building the Socialist dream.'

'But how did you stub your toe?' I asked.

'Ah. Yes.'

After the failed shopping trip Mama had taken the tram back to our neighbourhood, where she queued at one shop that was selling bruised apples and green oranges, and at another that was selling soft carrots and tins of *solyanka*. At a third shop she bought a chicken, and was about to pack it into her bag when she heard a loud crashing sound. Dust and debris flew into the shop. Everyone screamed. When the dust settled, they saw that a balcony, an entire stone balcony, had hit the pavement right in front of the shop. There were bits of stone everywhere, and broken flower pots, soil, dirt, a chair even. Everyone in the shop started laughing, and this infuriated my mother, because she could not see what was funny about a balcony breaking off the side of a house and almost killing her. So when she left the shop, she kicked a big chunk of carved stone.

'And that's how I broke my toe,' she concluded.

'I don't think it's broken, I think you just stubbed it,' Oma said. 'A kind of shelter, five letters. Any ideas?'

'Was anyone actually *under* the balcony?' Tobi asked, intrigued. 'Did you check?'

Oma tapped her pen on her crossword. 'One, two, three, four, five. But I think the word should be *Dach*. That's four.' She crossed out the last box and wrote in the remaining ones: D-A-C-H.

'From now on I'm always going to walk in the middle of the road,' I said.

'I'm going to walk even more in the middle of the road,' Tobi said.

'You can't be more in the middle than the actual middle.'

'*Auto*,' Heiko said. I took a pen and a piece of paper and drew two circles. That was enough to get him excited: '*Auto! Auto! Auto!*'

I drew the rest of the car. No one else in the entire world appreciated my drawings as much as he did. No one. It was as if I could do magic, could conjure actual cars from nothing but ink and paper. He snatched the pen from me and ran it back and forth across the whole page, all over the car, until you could barely see it.

'Heiko, don't cross out Ella's car!' Mama said. 'That's not nice.'

'He's not crossing it out.' I put myself between them. 'He's drawing.'

When we were alone, I often let Heiko draw on the walls under our beds, or behind the bench in the kitchen, or in the corner by the rubbish bins. What a stupid grown-up rule that was, not to let children draw on the walls of their own home.

'Anyway, the balcony fell off, and I kicked it, and that's how I broke, or stubbed, or anyway injured my toe. The End. It was right on Lychener Straße.' My mother said this as if it was the most disappointing detail of them all, that even the houses on Lychener Straße could no longer be trusted. 'The shopkeeper said there's an official word for it now, *Balkonsturz*, that's how common it is. It's like a biblical curse. Frogs, hailstones and balconies.'

'Done!' Satisfied, Oma folded her crossword and stood up.

'Mutti, did you hear what I just said?'

Oma sighed. 'What do you want me to say? You think I made the balcony fall off? You think Marx made it fall off?'

'It's a scandal that they're letting us live like this.'

'You think Lenin made the balcony fall off?'

'I said, it's a scandal.' My mother took a deep breath. 'That they're letting us live.' Another deep breath. 'Like.' She thumped the table. 'This.'

'Mama loud,' Heiko said and started to cry. Oma picked him up. He wiped his nose on her housecoat. Mama, too, started to sniffle. Heiko quietly whispered '*Auto*,' his comfort word, which he liked to mutter to himself in times of distress.

'Ach, Reginchen,' Oma said in a surprisingly gentle voice. 'It's just a balcony. Come on, we're tougher than that. Imagine if it had been the whole house! Then you'd have something to complain about.'

'Or if it had been the whole street,' I said.

'Or the whole universe!' – Tobi, now, with his mouth full of bread again.

Mama laughed, despite herself. 'I'm not like you, Mutti, I'm not tough at all. Look at what they gave me at the shop. That's probably not even a chicken.'

'Of course it's a chicken! It's just right for soup, it's perfect, it's *exactly* what I had in mind.'

I loved my grandmother very much just then, the way she made everything a little better, the way she saved the ruined afternoon by pointing out what was good about it: we had brought her a chicken, a chicken that was *exactly* what she had had in mind.

—

43

Oma was looking after us that evening; my father was at one of his university meetings, which usually ended in a *Kneipe*, and Mama had some mysterious opening party to go to. Oma tried and tried to find out what it was, but all Mama would say was that it was a little exhibition in someone's attic, just a small display of some paintings organised by a friend.

While my mother was getting ready for her party, I helped Oma change Heiko's nappy. The bathroom in our flat was tiny, just a loo and sink behind a door in the corner of the kitchen. If you wanted to have a bath or shower, you had to pull out an enormous orange drawer with the tub inside it from underneath the kitchen counter. It was all very clever, and it never quite worked.

Heiko was gripping the toilet lid. He lifted one foot, then the other as Oma put his trousers back on. I dropped his cloth nappy in a bucket to soak. Tobi sat perched on the kitchen bench, watching and commenting.

'I was potty-trained at one,' I said proudly.

'I was potty-trained forever,' Tobi said and pulled a face at me.

'Everyone has different talents,' Oma said, patted Heiko's bottom and stood up.

'Don't they make him use the potty at nursery?' I asked.

'He's refusing.' Oma carefully washed her hands, then lifted Heiko to wash his.

'He can't just refuse!'

'*Nass*,' Heiko said and splashed with the water.

'Oma *nass*.' Oma gently pulled him away from the tap. My mother came in, dressed in a black skirt and a glittery jumper.

'Has anyone seen my black handbag?'

Oma handed her the bag. 'Are you sure you want to go?'

'Thank you for helping out, Mutti.'

'I'm just thinking, who would throw a party in an *attic*?' Oma frowned. 'All that dust...'

'Perfume, Ellachen?' My mother sprayed scent on my wrists. She opened her little compact blush, sucked in her cheeks and brushed pink powder on her cheekbones. I was glad I did not have to go with her. I liked drawing and painting, but I found exhibitions painfully boring, the pictures all above my head height, the adults standing around and talking.

'Who'll be there?' my grandmother asked suspiciously.

'Just the usual bores.' My mother inspected herself in the mirror. 'Don't worry, I won't be late.'

I sniffed my wrists. A heavy, flowery scent. The perfume had arrived in the yellow parcel from the West, along with the chocolate, coffee, plastic nappies for Heiko, a toy car for Tobi and the doll for me. Mama and Papa had been very happy. The whole flat smelled of coffee. The doll was called Sabrina. She closed her eyes when I put her to bed, and opened them when I stood her up on her little feet in their white cotton shoes. Best of all, Heiko slept through the night in his new nappies, and we were all in the generous mood of the well rested.

'Oma, smell.' I held out my wrist.

'Yes, it's nice, it's nice.' She shrugged. 'I'm not against these things.'

Because Oma and Opa were pensioners, they could travel to West Germany, drink hectolitres of coffee, try out every single perfume in the universe. Yet they never did. Oma didn't see the point of visiting the West to stare at other people's houses, when she could go to her lovely allotment on the outskirts of Berlin instead and relax in her *Hollywoodschaukel*. The *Datsche*, a little shed that had grown into a Russian-style summer house, was where she and Opa spent all their free time, harvesting gooseberries, making jam and sitting in the shade of their big cherry tree.

Oma brushed a bit of fluff off my mother's shoulder. 'Maybe you misheard, and they meant a gallery called "Attic"? That would make more sense, wouldn't it? "The Attic". That would be a good name for a gallery.'

'Goodbye, Mutti.' Mama kissed her. 'Thank you.'

She hurried off before Oma could ask her any more questions. Heiko cried a little when she left. He hated it when people came back and then went out again; it confused him.

—

Oma took some eggs from the fridge and showed us how to crack them. She had two particular talents that fascinated me: she could peel a potato using only one hand, and she could crack and separate an egg, also using only one hand. She had learned this when she was a young servant girl on Gut Czarnikau, a big estate in East Prussia. She liked to say, with a small, hard laugh, that all the girls there learned to cook with one hand because they needed the other to fight off the master.

The estate featured in many of Oma's stories, sometimes as

a place of terrible hardship and at other times of simple joys, of celebrating the harvest, and picking berries and mushrooms in the forest. Oma had started out working in the fields, like her siblings, but when she was fourteen she was taken into the house, and that, she said, changed everything. The *gnädige Frau*, who was *sehr sozial*, as Oma said, very socially conscious, taught her to read. A stablehand, who was even more *sozial*, taught her about Communism. As soon as she could, Oma hitched a ride to Berlin, stayed with one comrade and then another, and never curtseyed again.

I was great at cracking eggs; my brothers were rubbish. I was great at so many things they were rubbish at, but no one ever seemed to notice.

Oma let us have a go at separating the eggs.

'Why is Mama's friend having a party in an attic?' I asked. 'Aren't there cobwebs?'

My egg yolk slipped through my fingers, and as if she had seen this coming, Oma caught it with a bowl. Then she separated six eggs with lightning speed using only one hand. Tobi insisted on separating an egg just to let the yolk slip through his fingers and watch Oma catch it with the bowl.

I beat the yolks with sugar, flour and milk, while Oma whipped the whites. Then Oma showed me how to fold my mixture into the whites. She was the only person I knew who made pancakes like that, foaming East Prussian pancakes that puffed up in the hot pan.

She talked about the estate again, which she had been doing more and more lately. She talked about the big forests and frozen lakes, and watching her father and the other men chip off big blocks of ice from the lake for the cellar. She talked about the cook, Big Hanne, who could make foaming pancakes for twenty, thirty people. In the winter, guests from other estates arrived at Czarnikau in horse-drawn sledges, and the servants gathered the fur blankets from the seats, brushed off the snow and laid them out in a warm room behind the kitchen until the evening was over, and the guests ready to leave.

Even my brothers went quiet when Oma talked about her childhood. The white and grey horses snorting in the cold, the silver cutlery and white china plates on the table, the day some of the silver went missing and a spirit medium was called in.

'She was called Frau Günther Gefferts,' my grandmother said. 'We had to lay her place with a china plate and a special set of wooden cutlery, because whenever she touched metal, her hands went like this.' She clenched her hands. 'They were magnetic, you see.'

I clenched my hands. How wonderful it would be to be a spirit medium, and have magnetic hands.

'And just as Frau Günther Gefferts was sitting there and eating her pancake,' my grandmother said and slid the first pancake onto a plate, 'she stopped and rolled her eyes, and we thought she was having a fit. But no, it was a vision. She said, "The next person to come through the door is the thief." And the door opened, and it was the estate manager, and when he was confronted with the facts, he burst into tears and confessed everything.'

When he was confronted with the facts was a phrase Oma used every time she told us this story. I liked it almost as much as the bit about the wooden cutlery.

'It was all superstition, of course,' she said, and took the chicken out of its bag. 'Silly, silly superstition. People were very ignorant back then.'

She put on the chicken soup for the next day, and we sat down to eat pancakes. I wanted to ask her about the man at the Bösebrücke, but it would have to wait until my brothers were in bed.

After dinner, we moved the chairs out of the kitchen and into the corridor. It was bathtime. Oma and I gripped the heavy orange drawer under the counter. I pulled, and my grandmother pulled. Nothing happened. My shoulders hurt.

'I wish we had a proper bathtub,' I said. 'I saw one in Sandy's flat. It has feet.'

'A proper bathtub?' My grandmother wiped her forehead. 'When I was a child, we didn't even have running water. You have your own bathtub, you have your own bed, you have your own towel *with your own name on it*, and still you complain!'

Even though I knew it would be better to be quiet now, I could not help blurting out: 'But it's stuck!'

'It's not stuck!' my grandmother shouted. 'IT'S – NOT – STUCK!'

And with that last 'stuck', she put one foot against the side of the counter and yanked the reluctant drawer out of its hiding place. Then she fished the hose from the cavity behind the tub and prepared a bath for us while I helped Tobi and Heiko out of their clothes.

'What a nice hot soup of Valentins,' she said when we were all inside.

Tobi splashed around with his hands: 'Stir us! Go on, stir us!'

Oma took a big wooden spoon from the counter and stirred us. There was water all over the floor, but that kind of thing never seemed to bother her. When we were done, I pressed a button and a hidden pump sucked the water out of the tub.

It was when my brothers were finally in bed, and I had Oma all to myself, that I decided to ask her. We were brushing our teeth over the kitchen sink.

'Oma?'

'Yes?'

'Is it true that someone was shot at the Bösebrücke?'

She stopped brushing her teeth and stood there, her lips flecked with foam. Then she continued brushing, but more slowly than before.

'Who told you that?' she mumbled through the foam.

'People at school,' I said cautiously.

'Ah.' She spat out white blobs of toothpaste. 'People at school!'

'Is it true though?' I asked.

We rinsed our mouths. My grandmother sat down, her hands in her lap. She looked at me for a long time before she answered:

'I don't know. But it's true that sometimes people do try and cross, and then the guards have to shoot.'

I sat down, too, with my hands in my lap.

'Why?'

'It's their order. They have to protect our border.'

'But he wasn't coming over from the West. He was running away.'

I dangled my legs back and forth.

'Well, imagine if everyone ran away.' Oma put her arm around me. 'Then the country would be empty. That's how it used to be, you know, you couldn't move for traffickers and smugglers and gangsters talking people into leaving. Every day someone else went over, they just downed their tools and to hell with solidarity. I showed up at work one morning and the whole factory floor was empty, the entire brigade had left. The entire brigade!' She shook her head. 'We didn't make any fridges that day.'

I pushed my tongue against a loose tooth. It had been bothering me for days. Tomorrow I would tie a string around it, tie the other end to the door handle and ask Sandy to open the door. I could already taste a bit of blood. I did not want our country to be empty. Why hadn't the man just stayed here?

Oma stroked my hair.

'If only someone had told his parents. They could have talked him out of it,' she said quietly. 'He'd still be alive, that boy.'

'So he *was* shot?'

'Ach, Ellachen.' Oma closed her eyes.

⁓

When I finally crept under my duvet, I could not sleep. Something dark and frightening was lurking under my bed. I counted the stones on the amber necklace under my pillow. All three of us had worn these necklaces as babies; they were meant to soothe teething pains and ward off evil. I counted three or four rounds, then I lay there and listened to the familiar sounds. Tobi tossed and turned in his sleep. Heiko snuffled and snored. Occasionally he stirred and said in his high, clear voice: 'Auto', or 'Bus', and then went back to snoring.

I could not stop thinking about the man at the Bösebrücke.

I had taken Sabrina to bed, my new doll from the West, but she was too hard and plasticky to cuddle. I reached for Nucka-butz instead, my floppy old bear.

A key turned in the lock. I heard my father's heavy footsteps. He exchanged a few whispered words with Oma, then they grew louder.

'She's not back yet?' He sounded worried. 'I'll go and look for her.'

'I told her, Jochen! I told her it was a daft idea, but she just laughed, she laughed and said…'

The front door opened again. A low crashing sound came from the corridor, then a curse and the rattle of dropped keys.

'Regine!' My father sounded both angry and relieved.

'I'm sorry! Oops!' She giggled. 'I'm so, so sorry – I completely lost track of the time! It was *such* a great exhibition, Jochen, you should have seen the paintings – and the whole atmosphere, everything just felt so…'

Oma interjected: 'We were *sick* with worry.'

'… so *alive*. So alive.' There was a silence. 'And now I'm back. Sorry.'

'Well, I'm glad you had a nice time,' Oma said sourly.

Mama opened the door to our bedroom. She looked lovely in the sliver of light, her face flushed and happy, her eyes shining. She was even carrying herself differently, more upright, with her head high and shoulders back. She tiptoed over to me.

'You're awake, how come you're still awake?' She stroked my hair. Her breath smelled of wine.

'I can't sleep.' I took her hand. 'I was scared.'

'Why were you scared, my darling?'

'Because you were gone.'

'But I was only looking at some paintings, Ellachen! I was only looking at some lovely, lovely paintings.'

'Someone shot a man at the bridge,' I mumbled sleepily, but it did not feel that frightening any more, because Mama was back now. I held her hand and fell asleep.

I N THE DAYS AND weeks that followed, Mama often talked about the exhibition in the attic. She thought the paintings were good enough to be shown in a proper gallery. Perhaps she could introduce the painter to some of her friends at the artists' association. Maybe my father could help?

'I'd love to,' Papa said when she brought it up over dinner one night. 'I can think of nothing more thrilling. It's just that I'm really busy marking papers right now.'

'You're always marking papers.' My mother gently pricked his arm with her fork. 'How about Gerhard? Don't you think Gerhard could help?'

'Gerhard is also busy marking papers.'

'Gerhard doesn't even teach!' She shook her head. 'I wish you'd at least look at his work. It's fresh, it's different, it's worth supporting. Think of it as our gift to the art historians of the future. I don't want them to look at our country and think it all began and ended with *The Polytechnical Classroom*.'

'I like *The Polytechnical Classroom*,' Oma said brightly. 'I find it uplifting.'

'Of course.' My mother leaned back and closed her eyes, just like Oma did when she wanted to end a conversation.

Oma lifted the lid off the soup tureen. 'More goulash?'

'Thank you, I'm fine. That was delicious.' My father sat back and folded his napkin. 'I suppose it can't hurt to take a look at what he's doing. If it means that much to you, Regine.'

'It does. He said we could visit his studio out in the country-side. Wouldn't that be fun? The children would love it.'

I would have preferred going to the park, but no one asked me. It was decided that we would visit the painter the follow-ing weekend.

⁓

Sven lived in a lakeside *Datsche*, a wooden cabin with an over-grown garden where rabbits and hedgehogs roamed. It looked like a page in my book of fairy tales: weeping willows, a pier with a bobbing boat, daffodils along the shore. The painter himself was sitting on the veranda, a big, grey-haired man with a beer bottle in one hand and a cigarette in the other. When he saw us, he jumped up, smiled and opened his arms wide.

'Welcome to Villa Sven!'

He had bits of cigarette ash in his moustache, and reeked of paint and turps. Mama hugged him like an old friend. Papa gave him a frosty handshake. Tobi, Heiko and I set about exploring the garden. Within minutes, Heiko had pulled a worm out of the compost bin and was stuffing it into his mouth. Tobi had climbed up one of the willows and was swing-ing from a branch. I sat down on an upturned plastic bucket and opened a textbook I had brought, *Our Spelling Book*, to show that I had more important things to do than eat worms.

Heiko came over and reached for my book with his muddy hands.

'Go away.' I pushed him a little. 'I'm busy.'

'Are they always this loud?' Sven tugged at his moustache.

'They're just overtired,' Mama replied with a nervous laugh. 'Tobi, can you come down from that tree, please? How about a nap, boys? Sven, where would be a good place for them to nap?'

'The boat, maybe?' Sven scratched his beard. 'That's where I nap, anyway.'

'Tobi, I'm going to count to three. One…'

'Are those tanks?'

Everyone went quiet. Sven, who had been peeking at my book, repeated: 'Are those tanks? They're making five-year-olds count tanks?'

'I'm eight,' I said.

Sven took the book from me and read out: '*Today we are waiting for Helga's big brother. He is a soldier in the people's army. He and his comrades are making sure that we can all live in peace.*'

He shook his head.

'Good God. Have you seen this? *Soldier Heinz says: "Our job is hard. But we do it willingly so you can learn and play without worrying. No enemy shall dare attack our German Democratic Republic."*'

'It's impressive, isn't it?' Papa said quickly. 'Such a long text, and Ella can read it all by herself. She's well ahead of her age, you see.'

Sven looked up. He was going to say more, but something in Papa's face stopped him.

'Very impressive.' Sven closed the book and gave it a pat.

It started to rain. We went inside, my mother with a wary eye on my brothers. My father tapped his finger on the frame of a painting of a red tiger.

'Neo-Expressionism, is it?'

'I don't believe in categories,' said Sven.

'Well, an art historian would certainly categorise this as neo-Expressionism.'

'I think it's wonderful.' My mother nudged my father away from the red tiger. 'It's so refreshing to see something other than – Tobi! Don't do that! – other than workers and factories.'

Sven looked pleased. 'I completed this entire series when I went to Hungary. I was completely possessed; I slept out in the fields and painted like a madman.'

My father smiled. 'Red tigers? In Hungary?'

'Jochen is more of a realist.' Mama's apologetic tone was new to me. 'I used to paint – I think I told you? Before I had children...'

'A painter has to throw himself at life.'

'Absolutely.' My mother turned towards a painting of a flock of black birds. My father looked at it, too, and for a moment they were both quiet in the way of people who were trying to think of something to say.

'Wingless birds.' Sven broke the silence. 'I'm not afraid to paint what's on my mind.'

'Hm.' My father shifted uncomfortably from one foot to the other. 'Some birds are of course flightless by nature.'

'Jochen!' My mother nudged him again.

'Like kiwi birds, for example,' my father continued. 'Kiwi birds are flightless by nature.'

Sven smiled. 'It's up to you to interpret the painting as you wish.'

My mother was still talking in her strange, slightly apologetic voice. 'It's such a treat to see someone's work in progress. We don't do that enough; we're always so stuck in our boring little circle.'

'We went to see Barbara's exhibition only last week,' Papa said defensively.

'Well, yes. But Barbara is Barbara.'

'*Barbara is Barbara*,' Papa imitated her. 'That's not what you said at the time.'

'No, because Barbara knows she is Barbara, so I don't need to tell her, do I?'

They started to bicker in their usual way.

Sven pulled me aside and whispered that he had something for me. He opened the large, flat side pocket of his baggy jacket. In it was a set of black pens, and my spelling book.

'Look at the bit about Soldier Heinz,' he said.

I flicked through the pages, and almost dropped the book in shock.

Someone had drawn all over the pictures of Heinz and Helga with a black pen. Soldier Heinz had sprouted two black antennae, like a Martian. His nose had grown into a long elephant's trunk that wrapped itself around the next tree. His sister Helga had been defaced, too. Instead of a normal nose and arms, she now had a snout and batlike wings. I rubbed at the black lines, but they were dry and solid. My stomach hurt. The book belonged to the school; I could not even imagine what the punishment for this would be.

'What's that?' My father grabbed the book from me, furious, and swivelled towards Sven. 'Are you out of your mind?'

'Oh, Sven.' Mama looked anxious. 'That wasn't really... I mean, it's funny, of course, but...'

'We'll have to say that she lost the book.' Papa took a deep breath.

Just then, Heiko fell off a chair, right into a wet palette, and burst into tears.

'That wasn't me!' Tobi shouted. 'That wasn't me!'

Heiko waddled towards my mother, eyes squinting and little arms outstretched. His hands were smeared with fresh paint. Before Mama could stop him, he brushed against a canvas on an easel, a big canvas that showed a landscape with three blue horses.

'Careful!' Sven shouted.

'An eye for an eye,' my father mumbled.

'Sven, I'm so, so sorry.' My mother scooped up Heiko, but it was too late. A fresh red streak ran all the way across the bottom of the painting.

Sven crouched down and inspected the damage.

'Let me buy it.' Mama squirmed with embarrassment. 'Please, Sven, I've been wanting to buy one of your paintings anyway – please, let me buy this one, please!'

Heiko was wriggling and protesting in her arms, Tobi was smearing more paint across the floor. Mama looked close to tears. I realised how much this visit had meant to her, how much she had wanted to sit in this cabin, drink beer, talk about paintings and remember the days when she used to paint, too.

'It's just a bit of red,' my father said. 'Just a tiny touch of paint. It's not like permanently defacing a book, for example.'

But my mother was already asking the price and counting out the money. This seemed to soften Sven. He cracked open more beer bottles. The tension in the room eased a little. Heiko put an empty tin over his head and shouted, 'HAT! HAT! HAT!' I found a comfy armchair by the window, stared out at the lake and wondered what it would be like to row across it.

We stayed until the rain stopped. The garden was filled with puddles. My brothers raced through them to the car, all wild hair and muddy faces. Without taking the cigarette from his mouth, Sven wrapped up the painting and handed it to my father.

'We had such fun.' My mother took both his hands and shook them.

'If you ever want to get back into painting, I'd be happy to put up an extra easel,' he said. 'It's always nice to see a beautiful woman paint.'

My mother let out a shy little laugh.

'Why not? I guess it's never too late.'

—

Back in the car, Papa imitated Sven's rough voice.

'*It's always nice to see a beautiful woman paint. It's even nicer to see her open her wallet.*'

'What's so ridiculous about encouraging me a bit?' She crossed her arms. 'Anyway, we're lucky to own one of his paintings.'

'Lucky? That man hasn't sold a painting in years!'

'That's not his fault.'

'Yes, it is. It's the end of the twentieth century, and he's painting like people did before the world war. Before the *first* world war.'

'I thought we could hang it in the kitchen.'

'I thought we could hang it in the bin.'

'You're being very mean,' my mother said. 'And spiteful.'

'I'm actually just glad you didn't buy the one with the wingless birds.' Again my father imitated the painter: '*I created this to symbolise the universal state of winglessness in this country. And also, to give the children nightmares.*'

It was warm in the little car. Tobi and Heiko had already fallen asleep, as always when we drove back from somewhere, and I snuggled against the door and closed my eyes.

'What are we going to do about Ella's book?' my mother said, with a hint of contrition in her voice. 'He didn't mean it, you know, he's just impulsive like that.'

'I guess we'll say I lost it.' My father shrugged. '*I'm terribly sorry, but I took it to work the other day by accident, and then I must have left it on the tram.*'

'Not on the tram, or they'll tell you to call the tram office. Just say you lost it. They think you're a bit batty anyway.'

'Batty? Who thinks I'm batty?'

'Ella's teachers.' My mother started to laugh. 'Because you're always losing things.'

'Hang on a minute! How many lost books have you pinned on me?'

'Oh, not just books. Homework, trainers, lunchboxes... we always say it's you, that you just take stuff to the library and leave it in strange places because you're absent-minded, and all you think about is old art.' She put her arm around his shoulders, and he rubbed his face against it.

'Silly wife.'

'Silly husband.'

I nodded off, and only woke up when we reached our street. It was almost dark. We climbed out of the little car.

'Next time, can we go in the boat?' I asked.

My mother clicked her tongue. 'There won't be a next time, not after the way you've all behaved.'

'Ah, what a shame,' my father said and smiled.

—

Despite my mother's threat, we visited Sven many more times that spring, sometimes with other friends, sometimes with Oma Trude and Opa Horst. My father took to calling him Maestro Sven-dinsky. Oma used that nickname, too, and once asked Sven if there were production targets for artists, and if not, why not?

Only my mother loyally defended Sven and praised his talent. When the weather was warm, they set up two easels by the shore of the lake and painted. Mama was very shy about her paintings. She never brought them home. I think she feared that my father would make fun of her. As much as my parents loved art, they had always joked about 'Sunday painters', 'retirement painters', people who painted fruit bowls and sunsets as a hobby. Now my mother was a Sunday painter, and while Papa did not comment on this directly, he never missed an opportunity to take a swipe at Sven:

'The Maestro is not very original, is he?' He nodded at the painting of the blue horses, which now hung in the kitchen. 'A poor man's Franz Marc, really. And decades too late.'

Since my father and my grandparents were indifferent to the painting, my mother tried to interest us children in it, me especially. The blue horses, she said, were really three little children who had been cursed by an evil sorcerer and held as prisoners in his dungeon:

'But then their mother flew over on her fairy wings and waved her magic wand, abracadabra, and just like that, she lifted the spell and the horses were turned back into children.'

'And what happened to the sorcerer after the mother freed her children?'

'He turned himself into a tree and hid in the forest.'

'You mean he got away with it?'

'Not at all. They found him and chopped him up for firewood.'

'And made a nice bonfire.' I giggled.

'Absolutely.' She pulled me close. 'And then they toasted sausages over the flames.'

M Y FATHER WAS OFTEN away during that time. His work was going well. People all over our country invited him to give lectures and seminars. On one rare evening, he took over the cooking because Oma was at some committee meeting and Mama had to attend another opening.

'Do you know what we're going to make tonight?' he asked with a grand flourish of the wooden spoon.

'Fried eggs.'

'Fried eggs! Pah! Far from it. Today I'm going to make...' – he twirled the spoon again – '*Painter's Potatoes.*'

'Do I have to peel the potatoes?'

'The potatoes are already peeled, young lady, but that's not the question you were meant to ask. You were meant to ask: What are Painter's Potatoes?'

'What are Painter's Potatoes?'

'Now that's a question many, many people have asked over the centuries.'

'It's fried potatoes with eggs, isn't it?'

'It's certainly not fried potatoes with eggs!'

'It's boiled potatoes with pickled herring,' I guessed.

'Boiled potatoes with pickled...' Papa gripped his head. 'No, and no! And again no! Would I protect the recipe for something as boring as boiled potatoes with my life? Would I protect fried eggs with my life?'

'Why do you need to protect it with your life anyway?'

'Because it's a very secret recipe and I am only allowed to pass it on to one person in the entire world.'

'Me!'

'Well, yes, you because you are my daughter, and then one other person. Namely, a truly remarkable painter who deserves a good dinner of Painter's Potatoes.'

'What does "remarkable" mean?'

'It's when someone is such a good painter that everyone remarks on him.'

'You could give the recipe to Sven.'

A dismissive snort – 'I said "truly remarkable" though, didn't I?'

Before I could think about what he meant by this, he pulled me over to the stove to show me how to make Painter's Potatoes. It was easy. We mixed onion soup powder with sour cream, poured it over pieces of chicken in an ovenproof dish, and put the dish in the oven. The potatoes we set to boil on the hob as usual.

'It's not really Painter's Potatoes, is it?' I licked the stirring spoon. 'It's chicken.'

'And that's the real secret of Painter's Potatoes.'

'That it's actually chicken?'

'That it's actually chicken. With boiled potatoes.'

'Papa, why is Sven always here?'

'That's an excellent question. He's not *always* here though, is he? He's not here right now, for example.'

'He's always here when you're away.'

My father froze. I wished I hadn't said anything, but the question had been on my tongue for weeks. Why *was* Sven always here? Why did he turn up at our flat as soon as my father was off on one of his research trips? Why did he put his feet on our kitchen table, his dirty feet in socks with holes in them?

I was still thinking of a way to take back my words when my brothers came in and saved me. Tobi jumped up and down and said he was hungry and would continue jumping until he was fed.

Papa picked up Heiko and carried him around the kitchen on his shoulders: 'I am Pazuzu, son of Hanbu, terror of the ancient world!'

'Pa-Zoo-Zoo!' shouted Heiko. 'Pa-Zoo-Zoo!'

'Watch out!' Mama came in. 'His head!'

I hadn't even heard her key in the lock. Her hair was wet from the rain. She reached up to steady Heiko, who was shrieking with delight.

'I am Pazuzu!' My father trotted around in a circle. 'I wreak havoc!'

My mother sighed, but she was smiling. 'What's got into you?'

'I can't help it. I've been possessed by an ancient demon.' He put Heiko down, winced and rubbed his back. 'An ancient and surprisingly heavy demon.'

'Something smells nice.' Mama opened the oven door. My father glanced at her. There was an odd shadow in his expression, as if he was assessing her, or searching for something.

Heiko squatted down and stared at the bubbling dish of cream and chicken. He held on to his waistband with both hands. His face was bright with happiness and wonder:

'Eyya made it!'

I stroked his hair, so soft and wispy. 'Say: *Ella* made it.'

'Ella made it.'

THE LAST TIME I saw Sven was on another Sunday afternoon. Tobi and Heiko were downstairs with Opa Horst. I was polishing shoes in the corridor. Oma Trude was dragging the hoover around our flat, pointing the nozzle at the ceiling to vacuum up spiders and flies.

From the kitchen came the angry voices of Sven and my parents, and I moved closer so I could hear what they were saying.

Two men had visited Sven's *Datsche*. They had inspected his paintings and decided they were not good enough for a member of the professional artists' association. He would have to paint differently or lose his membership.

'Paint differently?' my mother asked him. 'How? What did they say?'

'What did they say? Come on, Regine, you can guess what they said!' Sven switched to a Saxonian accent: *'Comrade Painter, the real question here is, why paint blue horses? Why not paint a combine harvester instead? Horses are pre-revolutionary, horses are frankly feudal. There's something downtrodden about a horse, if you think about it, something lacking in class consciousness, or indeed any consciousness. Has a horse ever led the workers into battle? Has a horse ever sabotaged a capitalist factory? Has a horse ever done a single thing for our state of workers and farmers? Who wrote* Das Kapital, *a man or a horse? "The horse is Tsarist by nature," that was Lenin, write that down for future reference. In fact, who has ever seen a blue horse, comrade? Who has ever seen a red tiger? Why lose yourself in indulgent fantasies that ignore the reality of our society? Why chase romantic daydreams when you have the honour of living right among the great clashing forces of revolutionary change, not to mention the thrust and drive of modern collective farming?'*

Sven threw his heavy body around the kitchen as he talked. He crashed into the table and the chairs, sent the wall calendar swinging back and forth, elbowed his painting of the blue horses.

'Now hear me out, Comrade Painter, how about a portrait series of the men who make history? "The Frame-Manufacturing Brigade at Dawn", "The Steel Workers at Dusk"… No, not dusk, dusk is defeatist.'

Sven gave a magnificent performance. He ranted and sneered and imitated the leaden, monotone drawl that even I recognised as typical of our leaders, and finally, returning to his own rich and rounded voice, spread his arms to declare that art was not – and would never be – a mere illustration of this miserable little half-country, this joke, this pseudo-state that took itself so seriously when it was really just a fart emitted by the Soviet empire, not even a powerful fart but a mere *pffft* after another hearty ladleful of Mother Moscow's cabbage soup.

'Now, now, Maestro,' my father said and patted Sven's shoulder. 'Let's not get carried away.'

My mother lowered her voice. 'What if you don't do what they say? What if you just go on painting quietly in your *Datsche*?'

'And live off what? No more commissions, no more sales, no more exhibitions, no more money, no more food on the table, no more roof over my head. If I want to eat, I'll have to do as I'm told.' Sven turned to my father. 'It's what you always do, isn't it, Jochen? You always do as you're told.'

'I have no idea what you mean.' My father crossed his arms.

'You write what they want you to write. *Down with decadence, long live Socialist Realism.* You might as well be taking dictation from Moscow.'

'Sven, you asked for my advice, and I'll give you my advice,' my father said coolly. 'If you want to be part of the association, you have to follow their guidelines.'

Waving the hoover's nozzle, Oma cried: 'And if you don't, then go and get a real job!'

Everyone looked at her, shocked. Undeterred, she went on: 'It's true though! If you don't want to paint properly, then get another job. I can't see what all this fuss is about, it's only a painting.'

'You!' Sven jabbed his finger at Oma. 'You're Stalin in a housecoat!'

'And you, you've never known hardship! You've never known suffering! When I was in Buchenwald...'

'Oh please, not Buchenwald again.' Sven took a last swig and tossed the bottle in the bin.

'Don't talk to her like that,' said my father in a surprising moment of solidarity with Oma.

Sven turned to my mother: 'Regine, not a word in my defence?'

'What can I say? Maybe you could paint tractors by day, and...' My mother was searching for the right phrase, and settled on: '... and pursue the rest as a hobby?'

Sven stared at her with an expression of utter disgust. He pushed her away and stormed out of the flat. My mother looked as if she was about to run after him, but my father grabbed her arm.

'Let him go, Regine.'

'We shouldn't have been so harsh.'

'He's crazy. He'll get himself into trouble, and he'll drag down everyone who knows him.'

My mother hesitated. I was afraid that she would walk out anyway, leaving us behind, because Sven painted as he pleased, Sven didn't do as he was told, Sven was utterly reckless, and she liked him for that. But then my mother said: 'It's fine, Jochen. I'm not going anywhere. I'm as much of a coward as you are.'

That night, I heard my parents argue in low voices. It was all the painter's fault. He had brought unhappiness and anger into our home. I hoped he would never show his face again.

FOR THE NEXT FEW weeks, no one mentioned Sven. Mama grew irritable and withdrawn. Papa told me to be nice to her. She was struggling at work, he said. Her book would not be published after all. It was tough, he said, but eventually she would come to terms with it, and then everything would be as it was before.

I felt a little remorseful for wishing Sven away. When my father was away at his seminars and retreats and conferences, Mama lay on their bed, fully clothed, a cigarette in her hand, and listened to songs by Wolf Biermann.

Du, laß dich nicht verhärten
In dieser harten Zeit…

'Don't let yourself be hardened / in these hard times…'

I brought her a cup of rosehip tea, because she seemed ill. Maybe she had the flu. Standing by her bed, I waited for her to sit up and talk to me, but she only mumbled, 'Thanks, Ellachen,' and closed her eyes. Oma came into the room and switched the music off.

'What's this? Biermann? You want to invite trouble into your home?'

Mama lazily reached out and switched the music back on.

'*You* listen to *your* music,' she said to Oma and lit a cigarette, 'and I listen to mine.'

'It's three o'clock in the afternoon, Regine. Don't you have any work to do?'

'I'm sick. I've got a terrible flu. I've got the plague. Cough, cough. It's very subversive, isn't it? Bunking off work, being lazy, that's our only revenge. What's a worker's state worth if its workers won't work? Ha, what a tongue twister!'

'Suit yourself.' Oma picked up the full ash tray. 'You're not a worker anyway, you're the *Intelligenz*. Unlikely as this may seem.'

'Right. Of course. Have you heard the one about the parking ticket?'

'I'm not interested.'

'How many members of the *Volkspolizei* does it take to write out a parking ticket?'

'I don't know.'

'Three. One writes, the other two keep an eye on the *Intelligenz*.'

I laughed. My grandmother grabbed my hand.

'Come, Ellachen. Mama is being silly.'

'What, you think she's too young for this? You think she doesn't know? You think she hasn't noticed that half of her friends haven't come back from their holidays?'

'That's ridiculous.'

'Everyone with half a brain is leaving.'

'Regine! Enough!'

My mother looked at me. 'And do you know why they're leaving, Ella? Because life is better over there. It's that simple.'

Oma tried to talk over her: 'Mama doesn't mean that, she's just sulking over her book.'

'Sulking? I'm about to lose my job! They want to sack me over one book, a modest little book praising the genius of the German avant-garde, just because I was hinting, merely hinting, that the avant-garde was better and bolder and more *revolutionary*, frankly, than anything we have now.'

My mother jumped out of bed and paced up and down, and I noticed how much she sounded like Sven. Or perhaps Sven sounded like her. No wonder they liked to paint together. She even jabbed her finger in the air, just like him.

'One book! That's it, that's enough to piss them off. Now they want to replace me with a third-rate Marxist who thinks Klee and Kandinsky had some sort of eye disease.'

Oma pursed her lips. 'It was all such a long time ago though, wasn't it?'

'What was a long time ago?'

'The avant-garde! You can't blame them for wanting something a bit more... current.'

Mama closed her eyes. 'Mutti...'

'I'm just saying.'

'This is exactly the sort of thing that drives me mad, can't you see that? I'm an art historian in a country that hates art. Yes, hates! My colleagues think the Soviets were right to lock away Malevich's black canvas. Do you agree with that, Mutti?

Do you think it's right to lock away a painting, a mere piece of fabric with black paint on it?'

Oma sighed. 'There's no need to make a big conspiracy theory out of some painting that got lost.'

I knew it was better to stay quiet, but something made me say: 'Why would someone paint a black picture? That's just stupid.'

My mother looked at me with an expression I had never seen before. Surprise, dismay, but most strangely, a kind of fear. As if I were a stranger, an enemy.

'See,' she said to Oma. 'In another generation they won't even have to bother with censorship.'

—

When Papa came home that night, I gathered all my courage and asked him if we could go back to Sven's *Datsche*. The sun was always out these days. The garden would be full of flowers. Mama could set up her easel and paint. It would give her something to look forward to.

My father sighed and put down his briefcase. He squatted down next to me and put his hands on my shoulders, his big hands that smelled of ink and leather. He told me that it was best to forget about the *Datsche*. Sven did not live there any more. He had gone over to the West, but this was something I must keep to myself. If anyone asked me about him, it was best to pretend that I didn't know where he was, and then change the subject to something harmless, like the weather, or what I had for lunch.

Aaron

Berlin 2010

ARON LIKED THE FEEL of shredded paper. Light, almost weightless; and soft, unless you pulled your hand out of the bag too quickly and cut yourself. There was a thin red line on his left hand and two more on his right from that. He wore these with pride: the scholar as warrior. From his desk he could hear the scanners humming next door, the abrupt silence when the paper jammed, then Bernd's curses over yet another reboot.

He had lined up several rather pleasing stamps along the window sill, from the brief and satisfying 'completed' that he used to mark a finished stack, to the one with his employer's enchantingly long name: 'The Federal Office for the Records of the State Security Service of the former German Democratic Republic'. Some shortened this to 'the Office', or 'the Stasi Archive', but to Aaron and his closest colleagues, it was always just the archive.

He was the only foreign intern there, which had initially made him the object of suspicion and scepticism. Occasionally a colleague openly wondered whether his German was good enough to deal with complex historical files. Every now and then, someone interrupted him to correct a case or a pronoun. But the fact that he was working on a PhD helped. Academic titles were currency here, people had a deep respect for them, and even mentioning your vague journey towards one could earn you better treatment. Perhaps more importantly, because his PhD was on archival reconstruction in post-reunification Germany, he had arrived in Berlin with a decent grasp of the Stasi's vernacular, that mix of cryptic abbreviations, clunky compound nouns and euphemisms. His breakthrough in terms of social acceptance occurred when another intern jokingly asked him to come along *zur Klärung eines Sachverhaltes*, 'to clear up a matter', and he correctly identified this as a Stasi pun; it had been their stock phrase for arrests.

His foreignness now gave him a rather privileged position. He often ended up as an arbitrator in discussions between the older and younger archivists, the East and West Germans, the Berliners and provincials: 'You as an *Engländer*, what do you think of...' someone would say, or: 'Aaron, as someone from the island, would you say that...' before going into some argument over wolf-hunting or state-funded childcare or some other subject he would never have imagined being asked to adjudicate on.

Aaron gently fished a tangle of paper ribbons from the bag by his desk and laid them out on the white surface.

`Current state of affairs in ma`

How pleasing. Like the corner piece in a jigsaw, the beginning of a sentence made it much easier to assemble the rest, and there was a good chance that he'd have the whole document by lunchtime. The rest of the phrase would be something like 'state of affairs in main offices', or 'state of affairs in major cities'.

In his early days the tangled paper strips had seemed like an impenetrable jumble of half-destroyed evidence, millions of jigsaw pieces irretrievably scattered across thousands of brown paper sacks, but now he could gradually make out a hidden order. You could scoop out a handful at random and be reasonably sure they came from the same document, a letter to a minister perhaps, a new recruit's handwritten pledge of loyalty, or the transcript of an interrogation.

The archive was housed in the Stasi's former headquarters, a Communist Mordor of brutalist office blocks and vast grey courtyards. The main section had been turned into a museum with all the old decor lovingly preserved, an interior designer's dream of mid-century orange lamps, olive-green armchairs, white plastic telephones, brown glass chandeliers and dark wooden laminate. It all looked rather modest from a twenty-first-century perspective – plain and understated – nothing like the marble and gilded taps of other dictatorships. Even the stained breakfast menu for Stasi chief Mielke, typed up carefully by a busy secretary to remind herself of his preferences, spoke of precision and discipline rather than indulgence: two cups of coffee, one five-minute egg, two buttered bread rolls and a copy of *Neues Deutschland*.

Aaron's own office was in another block, one that had been

stripped of all vintage decor. Except for some old typewriters down in the basement, used to compare Stasi fonts and design the occasional exhibition poster, it was filled with new white furniture. Like a blank page, or, as his colleagues joked in the canteen, like a whitewash. A desk, a bookshelf, two chairs, a filing cabinet and a couple of open bags full of paper strips. Bernd's office was to the right. To the left was the surprisingly humble office of the director of the archive, a heavy, plodding, always slightly harassed-looking man called Herr Dr Licht. It looked much like Aaron's study back in London, small and cluttered, though he'd never actually seen Licht in there. He always seemed to be down in the stacks, or travelling, or at some ministry or other, asking for funding.

From his window he could see another courtyard, a busy road and the bleak tower blocks beyond. Aaron often thought of the Stasi man who had sat here and typed up reports, who had stared out of this window at the tower blocks, had perhaps dreamed of a secondment to Moscow or at least an off-site weekend in Bulgaria. And then, when protesters had stormed the compound and smashed their way into the entrance hall, the man in this office would have barricaded his door with a desk before stuffing file after file into a shredder. Or perhaps he had run down the corridor to ask his boss what to do, shouting over the sound of breaking glass. Or perhaps the shredders had overheated by then, and he had to rip up his pages by hand, pack them into paper bags, ready for the incinerator. Only it was all too late: the protesters were already coming up the stairs, and the man in the office dropped everything and fled down the fire escape, leaving bags full of shredded documents for Aaron to piece together decades later.

Aaron rummaged through the strips until he found the next bit:

`in regional offices.`

'Bingo!' He lined up the two strips at the top of his desk and whistled happily to himself. The humming next door stopped again. Aaron could hear a fresh outburst of curses. They had a little race going on over who could reconstruct more pages in a day, Bernd next door with his scanners and algorithms, or Aaron with his eyes and hands. Things were looking good: here on his desk, the cut-up page was coming together rather quickly. Strip by strip the loose ball of shredded paper unfurled, the broken words and lines eased back into place, a `tow-` was reunited with an `-ards`, and the lower half of `Karl-Marx-Stadt` found its top. People and buildings rose from the pages, the swelling voices of a chanting crowd, the sound of footsteps running down a corridor and shattering glass and smashed-in doors. The clatter of typewriters as the spies documented their own demise:

```
7.12.1989
Current state of affairs in main regional
offices:
Office Suhl: Staff given leave; urgently need
   2-3 senior officers.
```

```
Office  Erfurt:  Demonstration  with  40,000
participants  moving  towards  the  building;
guards  refusing  to  protect  staff.
Office  Karl-Marx-Stadt:  Office's  leader
reported  sick.  No  replacement  available.
Office  Schwerin:  Head  of  office  relieved  of
his  duties  and  placed  under  house  arrest;
no  willing  substitute  available.
Office  Leipzig:  Office  conquered.
```

'Office conquered.' Aaron sighed. There was something pitiful about the reports in which the Stasi had recorded its downfall. They were full of mistakes and skipped lines, and reeked of the frightened resignation of someone who knew it was all over and yet could not stop typing.

Aaron pushed the final pieces into place. Right at the end, the text turned on itself and ordered its own execution:

```
For  the  secrecy  of  specifi--  and  tasks  we
recommend  the  compl--  destruction  of  operative
proc--  and  files.
```

'Finished!' Aaron pushed hard against the desk, rolled to the other end of his office and did a little twirl in his chair. He logged the report in the database. With a personal file, it was always worth checking if anyone had put in a request to see it. It was satisfying when you got a match, when the computer told you that someone was indeed waiting to read the very pages you'd just glued back together. Though he'd be surprised if the former staff of Office Suhl were yearning to read up on their final days.

He went over to Bernd's office, where two large scanners were patiently processing another batch of shredded paper. Bernd was fiddling with the machines with an air of vexed concentration, flitting between the black rubber band that fed bits of paper into the scanner and a screen that showed the final reconstructed page.

'A whole page before noon! Only fifty million to go!' Aaron mimed an explosion. 'Boom. You're so paying for lunch.'

'I bet it's a list,' Bernd said without looking up. 'Lists only count half.'

'Since when?'

'Since fairness.'

'It's a list of offices being ransacked, though.'

'So?'

'So I should get an extra point for historical significance.'

The rubber band stopped. A small amber light by the feeding slot started to flash. Bernd sighed. Aaron looked at the screen. It was an interrogation, and Bernd was right, those were much harder than lists. The beginning was usually pretty formulaic: the rejected request for a lawyer, the tired pleading, the pressure to confess. But after that, each interrogation charted its own course. Evidence was presented, alibis probed, friends and family members dragged into the business. Sometimes you could spend days piecing together what you thought was the opening only to realise that it was the middle section, where the prisoner started to cave in.

'I can give you a hand after lunch,' Aaron offered.

'Yes, please. We've got a request in for this one, and he's been waiting for some time.'

Aaron read on a bit. Poor guy. The interrogators threatened to arrest his son if he remained silent. Yet even after he co-operated, and gave them plenty of names, the final line of the interrogation read:

STATEMENT: We confirm that we will be inviting your son in for questioning.

'Do we have the son's interrogation?' Aaron asked.

Bernd pointed at a tray with a few big, hand-torn pieces, the kind that could be reassembled in no time. 'I think that's the son. It was all in the same bag. Do you want to do his pages, and I'll finish the dad?'

'Sure.' Aaron slid one of the larger sections towards himself and started reading.

'Come on.' Bernd slapped his shoulder. 'Schnitzel time.'

⁓

They took a little detour on their way to the canteen. Bernd wanted to show Aaron a wing that had previously been declared off limits. Aaron took it as a compliment that he was gradually being allowed into the more secretive parts of the building, the stacks where files with ancient military codes were stored, or even just the little room right at the back where Bernd kept an Italian espresso machine.

'See those guys over there?' Bernd pointed at a group of men and women near retirement age who were filling their thermoses with normal filter coffee. 'Those are the elephants,' Bernd continued once they were out of earshot. 'They've been here forever, they're all ex-Stasi in fact, and they know the place inside out. It's very handy.'

'Oh.' Aaron looked back. 'They're not in jail?'

Bernd thought for a moment.

'Well, it's not like they were torturers or anything like that. They just worked here as – I don't know. Stasi archivists, I guess?'

'Aren't you worried they might…'

'… destroy files?' They had reached the canteen, and Bernd picked up a tray and drummed his fingers on it. 'I don't think so. I mean, we'd notice, right? And you do need someone who knows where the bodies are. So to speak.'

'Hm.'

Aaron walked along the counter, considering the merits of schnitzel and chips versus a Greek salad. He put the salad on his tray and immediately regretted it, but it was too late, he'd touched it now and the lady behind the counter was already giving him a warning look.

They sat down by a large window overlooking the courtyard. Aaron never quite grew used to the monumental scale of every-thing, these courtyards that went on forever, the doors that led to corridors that led to more doors that led to more corridors. He sometimes dreamed of these corridors, just like he sometimes dreamed of the Stasi man in his office, hunched over his desk, filing his reports, inspecting the dirt under his fingernails, contemplating how much longer to leave X in solitary confinement.

With a faint pang of guilt he realised that he was treating his internship as a thriller. Which was probably inappropriate given how much suffering these millions of pages documented, but then again, it *was* thrilling; certainly more thrilling than attending post-graduate research seminars at his university back in London.

Bernd had wisely chosen the schnitzel.

'They like to keep to themselves,' he said, and it took Aaron a moment to realise he was still talking about the Stasi elephants. 'It's best not to bother them unless you need help finding a folder, and you've asked every other person in the building, and no one has the faintest idea.'

'You really don't find it weird to have them around?'

Bernd laughed. 'I'm from Bochum, all these East Germans are kind of a mystery to me anyway. But if you think about it, I mean, one of my granddads was in the SS and the other worked in a bomb factory. I'm not going to freak out over someone who helped the Stasi stack some shelves.'

—

On the way back to his office, Aaron passed the reading room where ordinary people could view their own files. An archivist was pushing in a trolley stacked high with folders. Aaron proudly recognised the printed name and number on one of them. K/05.671 had kept him busy for more than a week: he had reconstructed five whole pages in this folder, photocopied them and prepared them for the viewing, carefully blacking out any information on third parties.

The man waiting for these pages in the reading room was about to find out that on a cold January morning in the early 1980s, his clandestine meeting with other peace activists in a small church in Prenzlauer Berg had been spied on by at least three informants. What did he expect, Aaron thought; Prenzlauer Berg was right next to the border. Stupid place for a peace meeting. But still, he felt for the guy. He would read about IM Brücke, IM Schlosser and IM Luchs, and even with some of the information concealed, he would surely realise pretty quickly that they were his mates Oleg, Kalle and Detlef. Plus Pfarrer Hof, the young vicar, who went by the codename IM Sebastian. It must have been getting pretty crowded in that church.

Aaron very rarely came across proper spies in his reports, proper Stasi men with guns and multiple passports. His bread and butter were the Unofficial Collaborators, or IM, for *Inoffizielle Mitarbeiter*. The husband who reported on the wife, the favourite student on the teacher. There was the man who denounced his nineteen-year-old brother-in-law for reading 1984 by George Orwell: three years in jail for 'agitation against the state'. And, of course, people like this vicar, rushing off after choir practice to meet his handler down in the crypt.

He peered through the window in the door. Only one visitor, an old man, sat among the rows of desks and plastic chairs in the reading room. The archivist unloaded the trolley. Her lips were moving, but Aaron could not hear what she was saying. She placed her hand on the different folders, probably explaining in library whispers what was what, and where to start. Then she discreetly withdrew.

The old man opened one of the folders and began to read. He propped up his head with one hand and sat there like a monument, like Fate going through the book of life, perfectly still except for the hand that turned the pages, and the eyes that scanned the pages. His face was gaunt and lined, and his free hand trembled a little. When he was about halfway through his file, he lifted his head. He remained like that for some time. Then without another glance at the open folder, he stood up and left the room. He walked past Aaron, walked down the corridor and disappeared into the courtyard.

—

At his desk, alone with the shreds, Aaron felt that unease again, that sense that something was not quite right. He tried to push the feeling away and focus on the torn-up interrogation. *We will invite your son for questioning.* This was it, the son's transcript. Piece by piece, it emerged from the scraps. The son sounded young and frightened. He did not even ask for a lawyer. Three lines into the transcript, he was already saying that he would do anything, report on anyone, if only they let him go. On the second page, he agreed to report on his father.

It mattered, Aaron told himself. In the end these piles of

paper could explain someone's life to them. Why their brother died in custody; why their daughter, from one day to the next, lost her place at medical school; why their own husband spied on them. If such things could ever be explained.

He reached for his well-used Stasi dictionary, a white hardback entitled *Definitions Regarding Political-Operative Work*. Aaron had spent many hours immersing himself in this book, both because he was fascinated by the Orwellian codewords and because he had few friends in Berlin. He flicked through it.

Hatred. An intense and deep feeling that can fundamentally steer human actions; H. forms a crucial foundation for the passionate and unforgiving fight against the enemy.

Interesting, and not irrelevant to his troubled mood, but not the word he was looking for. The entry he settled on sounded much more mundane, but it had been on his mind for some time. It was about *Gewohnheit*, habit.

Habit. A recurring action that through its repetition becomes mostly unconscious, creating the desire to do it again.

Gewohnheit came from *wohnen*, to dwell, to inhabit. Sometimes an activity could become a home, a shelter. The dictionary entry gave some instructions for making such a habit, such a *Gewohnheit*, out of spying. The handler was to create a pleasant, comforting routine, until his informers came to see their meetings as sanctuaries in the midst of their stressful lives, as restorative breaks where praise and encouragement were doled out. The goal was to get the informer used to the process of reporting on others until it became a natural and even enjoyable activity they no longer questioned. Habit, not the promise of thrills and rewards, was the secret of a successful handler. *See also: 'Trust', on building an informer's trust in their handler; 'Betrayal', on the detection and consequences of betrayal; 'Doppelzüngler', on dealing with unreliable sources.*

Aaron had read this entry many times. There was something about it he could not shake off. *A recurring action that through its repetition becomes mostly unconscious, creating the desire to do it again.* Spying on the intimate lives of strangers was exciting, no doubt about it. He knew that feeling well.

He thought of the old man in the reading room. What had he seen that made it impossible to go on? Aaron tried to remember the details of the report he had put together. Those three friends, and the vicar. Maybe they were still his friends, grey-haired men who met up to play cards once a week. Maybe the vicar was still his vicar, hanging in there long past retirement.

He closed the dictionary and went to see Bernd next door. The machines were humming contentedly now, spitting out image after image on the screen.

'Thirty pages in less than half an hour.' Bernd looked very pleased. 'When they work, they really work.'

'Can I ask you something?'

'If you must.'

'Do you ever remove pages from a file before you send it down to the reading room?'

'Only if they concern third parties.'

'How about things that would just be really upsetting?'

'Like what?'

'Like a son betraying his dad.'

'Ah.' Bernd looked up from the screen. 'You've finished that interrogation already?'

'Just the bits where the son turns against his family.'

Bernd looked confused. 'But that's why people read their files. They want to find out who betrayed them.'

'I don't think the dad wants to find out that his son betrayed him,' Aaron said. 'I think he wants to find out that some guy he never liked anyway betrayed him. Or that nobody betrayed him. If you think about it, he probably just wants to know what the Stasi had on him, and then get on with his life.'

'You've never even met this man.'

'It doesn't matter. I don't want him to read that his son turned against him, and so quickly too, within the first hour of the interrogation basically. I don't want any dad to read that.'

'What are you suggesting?'

'We could leave out the son's interrogation, and just give the dad the rest of the file. He can read all the other reports, there'll be plenty of stuff.'

'But you don't know these people,' Bernd repeated, clearly straining to understand.

'I know more about their lives than they do.'

'I see.' Bernd sat down on the edge of the window sill. 'Why not kill some other pages, while you're at it?'

'That's not what I...'

'Why not take out everything that's potentially upsetting? Why not just hand him an empty file – no, wait – why not just write a less upsetting version and give him that?'

'It was just a question.'

'That man has been waiting to see his file for years. You think you can judge what he should or shouldn't know about his own life?'

'That's not quite how...'

'Look, I know you mean well. But working here is a great, great privilege. It comes with a huge responsibility.' Bernd shook his head. 'If I can give you one piece of advice, try and be a bit more careful about saying things like that. To tell you the truth, we have people here – not that I'm one of them, but I'm just telling you – we have people here who really don't like the idea of having foreign interns at all, and not just because of the, you know, language problems.'

'Actually, my grandparents were German. I don't have any problems with the language.'

Even as he said it, Aaron felt the futility of his defence; insisting you were good at someone else's language was as pointless as insisting that you were funny, or charming, or a good listener.

'You really don't want people here to think – and I'm just saying this as someone who's trying to help – you don't want them to think that you're planning to meddle with the documents.'

That wasn't what I was suggesting, Aaron thought. But there was no point in trying to explain.

'People fought hard to get these files,' Bernd said before he finally returned his attention to his scanner.

'I know.'

Aaron went back to his office. He hated conflict. His idea had not seemed particularly taboo-breaking to him, but maybe it was; maybe this was one of countless archival taboos he was not even aware of, and might violate at any moment. Maybe the next conflict was only one innocent blunder away.

He should have become a medievalist after all. At least five generations back, that would be his own bit of advice to budding historians, at least five generations back, and make sure there are no survivors, because they only complicate things. Imagine if Anne Boleyn went up to an archivist, wanting to read her file. The awkwardness. Though at least she would already know who betrayed her.

The building was quiet. All the other interns had gone home. It was unhealthy, spending so much time with these files; he knew it was unhealthy.

He packed his bag, a beaten brown leather satchel he'd been given by his dad. *What if this guy were my dad* was not a helpful way to approach a job like this. *What if this were me. What if this were my son.* None of these thoughts was helpful, none of them was relevant. Match white paper with white paper, match cream with cream. Match torn edge with torn edge. Match pencil with pencil, match ink with ink. He slung the bag over his shoulder. Match page with page, match line with line, and don't think about the people who will read this, people like that old man in the reading room.

Before he left the office, he took one last look at the son's interrogation. He could just slip it into his bag, drop it into the next canal. Save a stranger some pain. But Bernd would know, of course. And he liked this internship, and did not want to get fired and charged with destroying archival property. These decisions were difficult, and they were also very simple.

Aaron turned around, switched off the light and closed the door behind him.

—

Aaron was renting a room in a flat in Mitte owned by two architects, Petra and Cem. They were in their forties but partied with a stamina and determination that made Aaron feel like a geriatric carer in charge of two grandchildren. Sometimes they came home from an after-party just as he went out to work. Even more confusingly, there were times when they all arrived home together in the evenings, Aaron from work, and Petra and Cem from an after-after-after-party.

They were friendly and often asked him if he wanted to join them, but he had become somewhat cautious after a night out that ended up in a sex club, or perhaps not really a sex club but just a club where many of the people on the dancefloor were naked, and were having sex. In theory Aaron liked the idea of being the kind of person who went to a club, danced a bit, took their clothes off and had spontaneous sex with the person next to them, but he also knew that in reality, he was not that kind of person. That night, he had mostly worried that people would think he was a voyeur. When he'd joked to Cem about it, Cem had laughed and said that was nothing to worry about, because Cem himself was an actual voyeur, which explained why he enjoyed these clubs.

'We left you some dinner,' Petra said when Aaron arrived home from work on Friday night. 'Cem cooked.'

They were sitting on the balcony and smoking, Petra in a red bathrobe, Cem in a pair of grey linen pyjamas. Petra was the less consistent of the two. Night-time Petra was cool and formidable, and often dressed in complicated conceptual clothes with pleats and plastic sleeves. But during the day she liked to curl up in front of the TV in flannel pyjamas, her hair damp and tousled from a bath, her face gently creased, a hot water bottle at her feet. It touched Aaron that Petra made these concessions to comfort. Cem, on the other hand, looked sharp even when he had the flu. He shaved his beard with a cut-throat razor and styled his black hair using an intriguing substance from a tub of 'Gentleman's Grooming Resin'. Once a month Cem took the train down to Stuttgart to see his elderly father, who had come to Germany in the sixties as an Anatolian factory worker. That was the only time he slipped out of the grey shirts and into a red-and-blue jumper knitted for him by his grandmother back in Turkey.

'Mushroom risotto,' Cem said. 'You like mushrooms?'

'That's very kind.' Aaron helped himself to food and a glass of wine and joined them on the balcony.

'We decided to take the day off.' Petra put her foot in Aaron's lap. As often, he wondered how on earth they made a living; how anyone in Berlin made a living. He recalled the conversation between two American expats he'd overheard in the U-Bahn the other day, one of them talking about a woman he was dating: 'She's ambitious and wants to do something with her life, which is a rare thing in this city.'

'What are your plans for the weekend?' The risotto was excellent, like everything Cem cooked.

'We've got a few parties to go to…' Cem let out a dutiful sigh, making it sound like a moral obligation. 'And then, I don't know. How about you?'

'I've got work to do,' Aaron said, and felt like the most boring man in town. Petra took her foot away and straightened her leg in a yoga stretch.

'You have a real sense of purpose, don't you?' There was a note of admiration in Cem's voice, and it touched Aaron. It was true, he did have a sense of purpose, or at least he liked to think that he did. But he was also beginning to wonder whether this was a good thing.

'I don't know. Doesn't everyone? Anyway, I think I really pissed off my boss today.'

'Oh, I do that all the time,' Cem said and smiled at Petra.

She smiled back. 'I'm not your boss, I'm your business partner.'

They cooed back and forth for a bit. Aaron wished he could talk to someone about everything, about the old man in the reading room, about the father and his son, about Bernd exploding over a single page from a decades-old file. He could call a friend back home, but they would just say that Bernd sounded like a psycho.

'So what happened?' Cem asked.

'Did you unmask another vicar?' Petra said and laughed.

Aaron winced. He should not have told them about the vicar. He should not have told them about anything.

'It wasn't a vicar, it was a secretary,' Cem said and turned to Aaron. 'Right?'

Petra interrupted him: 'No, that was a totally different file.

The secretary was the one who spied on the gay publisher, remember? Sorry, Aaron, go on.'

'It was nothing.' Aaron downed the rest of his wine. 'I came back late from my lunch break, and my boss was angry at me for being late. That's all it was, nothing.'

He heard a noise, and looked around. A woman in a cotton kimono emerged from the bathroom. Her hair was dripping wet. She left a trail of little puddles across the white carpet.

'Aaron, this is our friend...' Petra reached for her hand and giggled. 'Sorry, I forgot your name.'

'Oh, we never got round to names,' the woman said, sitting down and lighting a cigarette.

⁓

On Monday, Aaron was asked to re-stack some folders from the reading room. He would work with one of the older archivists, a short, sturdy, earnest woman called Annemarie Schild, who took one look at him, sighed, and said: 'I guess we'll need a ladder for the top shelves.'

They made an efficient team, Aaron climbing up and down the ladder as Frau Schild handed him the folders. She reminded him a little of his grandmother, though she was a couple of decades younger, in her sixties perhaps. There was something about her faint Berliner twang, the bobbed grey hair, the no-nonsense attitude that took him back to those afternoons in Finchley when he'd sat in his grandmother's overstuffed living room, eating *Apfelkuchen* and listening to elderly ladies discuss their health in thick German accents, with Chopin playing in the background. He'd rarely heard his grandmother speak German and yet had learned the language quite easily, as if it had always been there, half hidden in the wings.

'And now a nice, hot coffee,' Frau Schild said when they were done. 'I made *Mokka* today, not that *Blümchenkaffee* you always get at the machine.' Which was another phrase his grandmother used, 'flower coffee', so thin you could see the floral pattern at the bottom of the cup.

Frau Schild poured out two mugs from a thermos. Aaron perched on the ladder. She sat down on a plastic stool. It was cosy there between the high shelves. All that was missing was a piece of *Apfelkuchen*, and someone lamenting the state of their gallbladder.

'Your German is very good,' Frau Schild said.

'I'm doing a PhD in German history. And my grandmother was born in Charlottenburg.'

'Ah. Charlottenburg.' Frau Schild took a sip of coffee. 'She moved to England?'

'Yes, in the thirties. She was Jewish.'

'I see.' Frau Schild nodded. 'Welcome back.'

It was not what Aaron had expected her to say, but he quite liked it.

'You're enjoying your internship?' she continued.

'It's definitely interesting.' He paused. 'Except for, I don't know, sometimes it gets to you a bit, doesn't it? Almost like a sort of archivist's guilt. Maybe that's just because it's all still quite new to me. You must have seen thousands of files.'

'Oh no, I don't work in reconstruction, I only do the shelves.'
Frau Schild finished her coffee, closed the thermos and carefully stored it away on her trolley. 'Thank you for your help. It
was very nice meeting you.'

She disappeared down the corridor, towards the wing with
the elephants, the archivists who had been here since the Stasi
days.

The elephants. Aaron felt a tingling at the back of his neck.
No wonder she had made such a quick exit when he started
straying into more personal territory. He pictured her in the
old days, a young woman in a blouse with shoulder pads, listening to a man in uniform who told her where this and that
file should go. Or maybe she had been the one in uniform,
ordering others to stack the shelves.

He leaned against the long, tall shelves, the shelves Frau
Schild had navigated so expertly, not even needing to check
the labels as she worked. They had walked along them at the
end to make sure everything was correctly ordered, and it had
been, and he had marvelled at how well she knew the place. As
if – well, as if she'd been working there forever.

⁓

Over the next couple of weeks, Aaron spent every day stacking
shelves with Annemarie Schild. Other interns carted brown
paper bags past him on big luggage trolleys, like travellers in
an airport, but he was not once asked to help. He told himself this was a coincidence. It was not possible that his one

comment about gently tampering with someone's file could have permanently condemned him to shelf work. That was one of the problems with working in the Stasi archive, it made you so bloody paranoid. Still, when you found yourself shovelling snow in Siberia, it was only natural to wonder how you'd managed to upset Moscow quite so much.

He kept his interactions with Frau Schild to a friendly minimum, and she seemed to like it that way. They went on separate lunch breaks, and stuck to subjects like ladders versus stools for reaching the upper shelves.

One day, when he was rolling a trolley stacked high with books along the corridor, a woman came out of the reading room, looking rather lost. She was dressed in a threadbare grey jumper, jeans and a yellow jacket; a student perhaps. Aaron stopped.

'*Kann ich Ihnen helfen?*'

'*Oh, das wäre nett.*' She smiled, relieved. 'It's just that I can't quite make sense of this.' She held up a thin grey cardboard file.

'There's usually an archivist in the reading room. She's probably stepped out for lunch.' He glanced at the file, the tight grip of her fingers. There was something odd about her. Of course: she was far too young to be a visitor, to have a file on her past. Curious now, he added: 'If it's about a particular word or something like that, I might be able to help.'

She hesitated. 'I just thought there would be more. There's only one page, and I thought there would be more.'

'Can I take a look?'

They went back into the reading room and sat down at one

of the tables. She was still holding the file. He considered for a moment whether talking to her was normal, or whether he was breaking another taboo. But he could hardly have left her standing there in the foyer. That would be his defence: *I couldn't leave her standing there in the foyer, could I?* (This growing habit of scripting potential future accusations and replies: that was also new.)

'Is this your file?' He reached for it. She moved it away. They spoke at the same time. She said, 'Sorry, you probably see this kind of stuff every day,' and he said: 'If it's too personal...' They stopped and laughed a bit awkwardly.

'Ja, es ist schon persönlich. Die Akte ist von meiner Mutter,' she said. And then, just like that, she switched to English, to a London-tinged accent that shocked him with its familiarity: 'You're British, right?'

He was struck by her complete lack of surprise. She switched from one language to another as if it was normal to meet a Brit here, in this obscure Berliner archive. It was something he had noticed before in East Germans, in the ones who were children when the Berlin wall fell. Nothing surprised them. They seemed to have no expectation of the world being any particular way; they knew that anything could happen, and when it did, they simply adjusted to it. He found it a slightly unsettling but somehow admirable quality, this absence of surprise. It made you realise how naïve you were to take the current state of things for granted, to think you knew what might happen next, to be taken aback when things turned out differently.

'I'm from London,' he said. 'And you?'

'Same, sort of. From Berlin via London.' She pushed the file towards him. 'I came all the way to look at my mum's file, but it's only one page. Is that normal?'

'Let's see.' He opened it.

It was only a fragment, a torn half-page from a transcript.

QUESTION: Why do you think you are here?

ANSWER: I would like to request a lawyer.

QUESTION: Where do you think we are, in America? Let me ask again: why do you think you are here?

ANSWER: I don't know.

QUESTION: Don't know what?

ANSWER: [The accused refuses to answer.]

QUESTION: You think silence is going to help you? Silence is very hard work.

ANSWER: [The accused refuses to answer.]

QUESTION: You'll change your mind. Sooner or later, you'll be begging us to listen to you. You'll be begging us to be allowed to talk. You'll tell us things we never even asked you about. And when we are done, there will be no part of your mind we won't know. We will be completely at home in your mind, we will be there always.

'Your mother was a dissident?' he asked carefully.

She looked distraught, and for a few moments seemed unable to answer. Then she said: 'No, no, she wasn't political at all, not in that way. She was just an art historian.' She laughed quietly, with a sudden air of helplessness that touched him.

'*Kann ich Ihnen helfen?*'

It was one of the staff archivists, who had materialised behind Aaron's shoulder. He wanted to hear this woman's story, find out why she had come here, what she was hoping for. But he was far away from his trolley and his shelves, and the archivist's expression made it clear that he ought to get back there.

'You're in good hands,' he said to the woman, as to a patient about to be wheeled into an operating theatre. 'Good luck.' Then he went back to stacking shelves with Frau Schild.

—

In her lunch break Frau Schild went out into the courtyard. Aaron patted the dust from his hands and contemplated going to the canteen. He might bump into Bernd. In fact, he should go upstairs, find Bernd and suggest lunch. It was not as if they'd had an official falling-out. He had proposed removing a page; Bernd had disagreed. That was all it was. He walked over to the lifts.

'The archivist said it would take at least a year.'

Her again. That yellow jacket, like a flashing light in the dour corridor. Instinctively he waved her into a darker corner by the shelves.

'She said it would take at least a year,' she repeated, 'but that it was impossible to say, really.'

'What would take a year?'

'Finding the rest of the file.' She sounded desperate. 'It's all gone, apparently. They think it might have been destroyed.

It'll be a matter of luck if they even manage to find it at all, that's what she said, a matter of luck. Could be a year, could be ten years, could be never.'

'That's really disappointing,' he said. 'I'm sorry.'

'What guts me most is not knowing. The pages could be right here, somewhere in this building, or they could be dust and ashes. It's really just a total matter of luck.'

She looked shaken, and Aaron felt a little cross with the archivist. This visitor had been in pretty good shape when he left the reading room, and look at her now. This was not how things should be handled. It made him think of Bernd, and the file about the father and his disloyal son. The idea that you just gave people the facts and left them to get on with it: he disagreed with that.

'It's not pure luck,' he said, perhaps a little too forcefully. 'She really should have explained that a bit better. It's not quite as random. We have at least a rough idea where everything is.'

She brightened up: 'So you could help me find it?'

'Someone could,' Aaron said, in what he hoped was a subtle passing of the buck.

'No, I mean, *you* could?'

'I'm just an intern. Your best bet is to go back to the reading room and ask the archivist.'

'She didn't seem all that helpful. And I came all this way.' There was an urgency in her voice, an intensity that was at odds with the blandness of their surroundings, the long shelves, the pale brown and pale green cardboard folders, the beige carpet, the rubber footstools, the office doors with the little printed name tags. This was an environment of ordered calm, of things being done slowly, methodically. A year meant nothing here. Ten years meant nothing here. After all, the beige carpet and the worn footstools had probably been here since Mielke ate his breakfast eggs upstairs. And it occurred to Aaron now that this slowness had nothing to do with inefficiency or bureaucratic inertia. It had to do with caution. The memories they were handling here were delicate, had so much power to damage and disrupt.

Then again, if this woman wanted to see her mother's file – and she clearly did, with an almost violent kind of despair – who were they to tell her to wait? Wasn't this what they were here for, to help people?

'I can ask my boss,' he said. 'If it's a special case, they might prioritise it.'

He heard the lift door open and people walk out, discussing promotions, grants, budget cuts in the way of office workers everywhere.

'This isn't really about my mum, you see,' she said in a low voice. 'It's about my brother. My little brother, Heiko Valentin. He was taken from us. And that would be in her file, wouldn't it? All of that would be in her file.'

She looked at him, anxious and trusting, certain he could fix this. But he could not! He was pretty sure that he could not.

'It's possible,' he said. 'Sometimes files do contain that sort of information.'

Her face relaxed a little. 'What did you say your name was?'

'Aaron.'

'Aaron. Look, Aaron, all I'm asking is... please keep an eye out for me. Maybe something will come up. Maybe there are some inventories or databases you could check. That's all I'm asking.' She wrote down a number, an email and her name: Ella Valentin.

'I've got another appointment here,' she said, handing him the piece of paper. 'In a week or so. With someone called... Licht, I think?'

'Oh, that's our director.' Aaron nodded with relief. 'He's really the best person to talk to about all of this, much better than me. He'll be able to help.'

She gazed at him, deep in thought. 'You think so?'

'I'm sure he will.'

'Hmm. I think he'll tell me not to hold my breath. To join the back of the queue. But we'll see, won't we?' She smiled. 'Anyway, I might see you then.'

'I can't promise anything,' Aaron said and put the piece of paper in his pocket.

'I'm not expecting you to.' She zipped up her jacket. 'Thank you.'

⁓

She left through the visitors' entrance, handed back her pass, thanked the receptionist. Later he realised that he had not once said how sorry he was that her brother had been taken away, that her mother had been arrested, that her family had suffered such a terrible loss. He had been worried about someone spotting them, conspiring in a corner like that, but still, he later thought that he should have shown more sympathy. And this gnawed at him, and made him think that yes, perhaps he could at least go through a few lists and databases, and have a rummage around, even if it did not lead to anything. At least it would show that he'd tried.

He stood by the lift for a long time, heard the ping and whirr of the door opening and closing, the chatter of people walking in and out, and thought about what he should do.

'Aaron!' It was Bernd, who had just stepped out of the lift and seemed genuinely pleased to see him. 'How's it going? Schnitzel time?'

Ella

A Line Is a Dot that Went for a Walk

Berlin 2010

ISMANTLING MY LIFE IN London had been shockingly easy. I'd sublet the boat to an acquaintance from art school. I told the agency to put my shifts on hold for now. It's not that I'd expected people to mourn my departure, gnash their teeth, drive a pair of oxen through Deptford Creek to pacify the Gods for my journey. But still, it was strange to be let go quite so easily. After all my back and forth with Tobi, the actual trip to Berlin was the simplest thing, with a lightness to it, like a sparrow hopping off a window sill.

Through another art-school acquaintance I found a cheap room in Berlin; a Canadian friend of hers was on holiday and happy to let out her place. All the world's artists were in Berlin, of course, to the point where it seemed that places like London and New York must be full of ghost studios, empty easels, abandoned lumps of clay, because everyone had upped sticks and moved to Neukölln. This drift towards Berlin had annoyed me for some time, for no good reason other than that I thought the city was mine alone, mine to feel nostalgic about, mine to revive through memories of Socialist bathtubs. Still, I took it as a good omen that the room was in an artists' residence in Prenzlauer Berg.

The residence was in a former umbrella factory, with studios at the back, an exhibition space downstairs and private rooms upstairs. Above the entrance hung a perspex box with an old black umbrella inside, presumably the old factory's lone survivor.

Two men, curator types in black turtlenecks and horn-rimmed glasses, were standing in the entrance hall and discussing a huge, garish painting in screaming pinks and greens.

'That's a lot of wall power, right there,' one of them said in an American accent.

'The best thing is, it doesn't show anyone shitting or fucking, so you can hang it in the lobby of a bank.'

'Or a hotel.'

'Berlin is so hot right now.'

'Did you know he painted this with a fire hose?'

This was precisely the sort of scene I had been trying to avoid in London, and now it had followed me to Berlin. *Wall power.* Why couldn't I make something with wall power? Why couldn't I make something that would dazzle people in turtlenecks? Then again, I shouldn't care what other people thought. An artist should be like wood, let herself be burnt up in a creative blaze, indifferent to criticism and praise. *I am but a log,* that would be my daily mantra from now on.

My room was small but pleasant, with a bed, a desk and a chair, and a graffito of an umbrella on the wall. There was something distinctly cell-like about it, though the window offered a nice view of roofs and courtyards. I had packed Oma Trude's green gaberdine coat, along with the photo of the blue horses and my mother's journal.

When I came back from the archive, I texted my brother and he called right away.

'How did it go?'

'They showed me her file, or what's left of it. I read a few lines from an interrogation, and that was pretty much it. There wasn't anything about Heiko, not in the bit I saw, but there might be more coming.' I decided to gloss over this part of my visit. Tobi would disapprove of my little arrangement with Archive Aaron. My brother hated secrecy, subterfuge, anything like that. 'Listen, there's so much Mama never told us about her trip to Berlin. She never mentioned this archive, never mentioned her file. I have a feeling she got a lot further than we think.'

'You think she found him?' The excitement in his voice took me by surprise. Always, always Tobi had been the one cautioning us, muttering platitudes about letting bygones be bygones, letting people live their lives. Always he had hinted, or even said outright, that looking for Heiko was about our own need, that it was selfish in a way.

'I don't know. But I'm pretty sure she found something. Otherwise, why leave us that letter from the archive?'

There was a long silence.

'Tobi?'

'Yes.' Another silence. 'Could be.'

'It's not like he just vanished. There are people who know what happened back then, there's a paper trail. I'll try to think who else I could talk to while I'm here.'

'Ella?'

'Yes?'

'That interrogation you read…' He lowered his voice. 'Was it horrible?'

I paused. 'There wasn't anything that would surprise you. It was just weird to see it all written down. They said to her – it was something like, *you'll never forget this*. No – *we'll be in your mind always*. That was it. *We'll be in your mind always, we'll make ourselves at home there.* But we knew that anyway, right?

Tobi said softly in German, and somehow this broke my heart: '*Arme Mama.*' Because when Tobi spoke German, he sounded like a little boy. He didn't know how to speak grown-up German at all.

—

It was the mid-nineties, in London, and Mama and I were sitting on the sofa and watching a documentary together. Friends in Germany had recorded it and sent us the video. There was no internet to speak of in those days, no online forum where parents could meet and swap information. The documentary was about families like ours, East German dissidents who were trying to trace their stolen children. Many of them were told that it was too late, the children had been adopted by nice families.

One of the social workers still had a portrait of Honecker in her office.

A handful of the parents did manage to track down their children, and found that they had grown fond of their adoptive families. If they remembered their birth parents at all, it was as people who had abandoned them. They clung to their adoptive parents, hid their faces, shrank away from the crying, desperate women reaching out for them. There was one mother in particular, who had finally traced her little daughter and arranged a reunion. It went terribly wrong. She argued with the adoptive mother, and at one point slapped her across the face and screamed: 'You red pig! You stole my child, you red pig!' The little girl hugged her adoptive mother's legs and begged her to make the scary woman go away.

My mother stiffened as we watched this scene, but did not say anything. When the credits rolled, she put her hand on my arm and asked in a low, almost inaudible voice – as if half hoping I would not hear the question – 'Do you think Heiko...'

'... misses us?' I offered.

'No, no. I mean... do you think he would be frightened of me?' She sniffed, rubbed her nose, sniffed again.

'I don't know, Mama,' I said, staring straight ahead at the rolling credits. 'I don't know.'

He would be about ten now. A ten-year-old boy playing football. Running home to show his adoptive mother his grazed knee, letting her comfort him, just like this little girl in the documentary. A ten-year-old boy climbing trees. I realised I could only think of Heiko in these generic images, doing generic little-boy things, and that I had no idea what he was actually like now. Perhaps he hated football and was afraid of heights. And the loving adoptive mother? I could not contemplate the alternative. I needed to believe that whatever his circumstances, there was someone who cared for him, who comforted him when he was sad.

My mother shook her head, as if she'd read my thoughts. 'I'm his mother! Would he really be frightened of his own mother?'

'I don't know.'

'Would it be better, do you think, if I let him be? Would it be better if I stopped looking for him?'

She wanted to hear encouragement, she wanted to hear me say that she should not give up, that she must keep going. But I could not bring myself to say what she wanted to hear. I felt very tired, unable to help her, angry with myself for being unable to help her. And so we sank into our habitual silence instead.

After a while, I went into the kitchen and started making dinner. My mother moved over to her desk and buried herself in her manuscripts and books. I warmed up some leftover soup and sliced the end of a loaf of bread, and as I was slicing the bread an image came to me, a moment from the past: Heiko chewing on a slice of bread. He looked at me with his big eyes, reached into his mouth, took out the mushy piece and offered it to me. 'No thank you,' I said, 'I've already eaten.' So he drove the piece around his plate instead: '*Auto!*'

I put down the bread knife. A deep sadness passed through me, an ache I could not have put into words.

⁓

A few nights later I came home, opened the front door and saw Mama's coat and shoes on the floor, as if she had stormed in and flung them off. I looked around the house. She was not in her bedroom, she was not in the bathroom. The bathroom tiles were wet and there was a pile of clothes on the floor. She was not in the kitchen, she was not in the living room. She was not in my room, she was not in Tobi's room. Then I thought I heard a noise from the cellar.

She could not possibly be down there: Mama avoided the cellar. Mama was afraid of the dark. She never went into the cellar, not even to get fizzy water or potatoes; she always sent me or Tobi. Once Tobi had thrown a tantrum and asked why she couldn't just get her own fizzy water, and I had explained it to him, quietly, so she could not hear: *Mama mag den Keller nicht.* Mama doesn't like the cellar.

I heard a noise again, a sob. Not from the kitchen, not from the living room.

I opened the cellar door and shone my torch inside.

There in the dark crouched my mother. She was half-naked, wrapped only in a towel, her wet hair dripping on the earthen floor. She was hugging her knees and crying. Long red scratches ran down her face and arms. Her nails were bloody.

'*Mama, komm.*' I kneeled down next to her, put my arms around her, tried to warm her. '*Bitte, Mama, steh auf. Steh doch auf.*'

But she did not want to stand up.

'Don't punish yourself, please,' I said in English, but it was as if she could not hear me. She was not really there. All I could do was fetch a blanket, cover her with it and hold her.

⌣

My mother's old prison was now a museum. I had looked it up online; it was maybe a couple of hours on foot. The walk through my old neighbourhood would be useful. It might bring back details, fill in the gaps in my memory.

Prenzlauer Berg was looking very cheerful. Gone was the tang of coal fires and cabbage soup. The balconies were firmly attached now, and decorated with spinning pinwheels and anti-nuclear posters. A red sun on yellow ground, clenching its fist in protest: *Atomkraft Nein Danke!* Fathers strapped chocolate-smeared children into buggies. Women swished past on fixed-gear bikes, reflective clips flashing from their ankles. A bearded man in a panama hat sat outside a cafe, carving a clog. There was, in fact, a surprisingly large number of people in wooden clogs about. Another trend I had missed, clearly. Everyone cycled on the broad pavement instead of the road, cheerfully ringing the pedestrians out of the way.

There were mezze platters on the tables outside the cafes, and blackboards that promised *Cold-brew coffee here*, in English. The shops opened at twelve and shut at three. And there were so many children in this neighbourhood: balancing on metal scaffolding, crying over a dropped ice cream, wobbling ahead on their own little bikes, their heads enlarged by duck-yellow helmets. It was all rather fun and uplifting and yet it unsettled me because I could not find myself, or my family, in any of this. It was not just the yoga studios and the restored facades and the ivy winding in and out of the balconies. It was the people. Everyone was so young and healthy-looking. No dimly lit *Kneipen* where men sat and drank schnapps.

I soon got lost. I used to know every dog and lamp post in this neighbourhood. No part of it was alien to me. In my mind I could find our old home within seconds, I was right there. There was Frau Rachmann, holding out my lost woollen glove in her paper hand: 'I think a little goblin must have found it on the stairs,' she said with a smile. 'Shall we go look for it?' And we looked for it, and found a piece of chocolate instead that the goblin had left there for me in a corner of the hallway.

There was Frau Minsky with her mop, there were the bullet holes in the facade. So vivid before my inner eye. But in real life? In real life, they were gone and I was lost.

'A line is a dot that went for a walk,' Paul Klee said. 'Moving freely, without a goal.' That was me, a dot without direction.

I asked a man with a beard: '*Entschuldigung, wo ist die Duncker-straße?*' And he replied in English, with a Liverpudlian lilt: 'Sorry love, I don't speak German.'

I asked another man with a beard: '*Entschuldigung, wo ist die Dunckerstraße?*' And he replied in an American accent: 'Sorry, I don't speak German.'

This was infuriating, and rather embarrassing. How would I ever find Heiko if I could not even find our old street? But I refused to ask them in English. I had spent years assimilating to the English in London, I would not now assimilate to them in Berlin.

'*Entschuldigung...*'

'Sorry sweetheart, I don't speak German.'

Panic rose inside me. It was like one of those nightmares where you come home and no one knows who you are. Your family asks who this stranger is at their table, and your dog growls with suspicion. I walked on fast, sure that this must be the one, here was the Helmholtzplatz after all, here was the bike shop that used to be a grocery with empty shelves, here had been Heiko's nursery.

Oma and I had picked him up from there in the winter, and on the way home he had pointed at all the lit windows in the dark and said, light, light, light, light. So many lights. *Licht, licht, licht.* So if this was the former nursery – another yoga studio – and back there was the Helmholtzplatz – then our street should be over there.

I broke into a half-trot, turned left, turned right, turned left again, and came out not in our street, but at the Bösebrücke.

The smooth broad bridge stretched from Prenzlauer Berg to Wedding. Cars swooshed back and forth. The watch tower, the walls and fences, the tall floodlights: 'All gone!' as Heiko would have said. (Pushing his plate away: *Fertig!* All gone!)

The allotments were still there. From the bridge I could see the tulips and the lilac bushes.

I walked up to a cluster of black-and-white photos at one end of the bridge. They showed cheering crowds smashing through the Berlin wall. I looked at all the faces but did not recognise anyone.

Further on, a memorial stone marked the spot where a young man had been shot while trying to escape. So Sandy hadn't made it up. It was possible now to do this, to find out who had lied and who had told the truth.

I had not spoken to Sandy since that summer. But it should be fairly easy, I thought, to track her down.

FOUR COACHES WERE PARKED in front of the prison of Hohenschönhausen. Lanky teenagers spilled out of the coaches, blocked the street and gaped up at the high concrete walls topped with barbed wire. The large metal gate was shut and we had to file through a smaller side gate, past a ticket vendor. I paid six euros for a guided tour. How odd it was to pay for a tour of my mother's prison. I should at least have asked for a concession!

It was a bleak day, with a sharp wind that seemed to blow in straight from Siberia. I turned up the collar of my jacket and rubbed my arms. The metal gate rumbled open. I jumped; my mother had detested the sound of metal scratching across stone.

When someone drags a heavy saucepan across the hob, that metallic screech.

An entry in her anxiety journal, and this time I could match it to its source. The scraping noise of the gate, the scraping noise of the saucepan. This gate had rumbled shut behind her. Right here, she'd been dragged out of her van. She'd been standing here, in this courtyard, looking up at the grey sky.

'Excuse me?' One of the teenagers tapped me on the shoulder. 'Could you take a photo of us?' He put his arm around his girlfriend and they posed in front of the barbed wire.

In a way I was glad that there were teenagers around, tour guides, pensioners with pens and notepads, because it made the place less threatening. One of the guides, a black-haired woman in jeans and a check shirt, held up her red umbrella to signal the start of her tour.

'Is anyone here claustrophobic?' she asked cheerfully. A couple of people raised their hands. 'You might want to stay out of the rubber cells then. Any asthma?' A couple more. 'Any allergies?'

One of the older men laughed and mumbled something about health and safety gone mad.

The guide frowned. 'Is that a comment or a question?'

'What, we're not allowed to laugh any more?'

'A comment, then? Thank you. Let's start with the basement.' The guide turned her back to the man and herded us down a narrow set of steps, into a maze of underground cells and corridors.

The prison had the usual Berliner history: built under the Nazis, repurposed by the Soviets, expanded and modernised by the GDR, and finally, opened to the general public in the united Germany. The Nazis had used it as an industrial kitchen for one of their welfare organisations; the Soviets had noticed that the kitchen was ideally suited for imprisoning people. Captured Nazis were among the first inmates, followed by Social Democrats, priests, thieves, murderers, suspected spies and anyone else who stood out. I knew, of course, who the subsequent generation of inmates were: the GDR's pacifists, dissidents and failed escapees. What surprised me was the guide's brief aside at the end of her introduction:

'... and after reunification, a few GDR officials were imprisoned here. The head of the Stasi, for example.'

The older man, the one who had laughed at our guide, gave an eager nod. 'You see? Pure revenge! Pure spite!'

The guide sighed. 'Is that a comment or...'

'The people should know the truth!' The man thumped the floor with his cane. The guide did her best to ignore him.

'So this ...' – she gestured at the hot, damp cells – '... this would have been where the prisoners were held when...'

'But under the Soviets!' The man thumped the floor again. 'This part wasn't used by the Stasi at all, this was only used by the Soviets!'

'Would you perhaps like to guide the tour yourself?' The guide offered him her red umbrella. He snatched it from her hands.

'I would, I absolutely would! The people deserve to hear...'

'... the truth.' The guide took back her umbrella. 'Ladies and gentlemen, just to restore some order here, what you're seeing is something we deal with quite regularly, which is that the old guard, the sympathisers...'

'That's defamation!'

'... come here to infiltrate and frankly sabotage our tours.'

'Ah, I'm a saboteur now? Did you all hear what she just said? A saboteur! This one has no idea what she's talking about!'

The guide crossed her arms. 'As it happens, I do know what I'm talking about. I was an inmate in this prison. Seven months and thirteen days.'

The rest of the group watched the row in awestruck silence. We were certainly getting our money's worth. The old man muttered something about free speech and historical truth, but the guide ignored him and went on with the tour as if nothing had happened.

We walked in and out of concrete cells, looked at small objects that inmates had crafted out of wood and mud, took the stairs up to the more modern part of the building where people like my mother had been held. We visited an interrogation room with a desk, a green metal locker and two chairs; a cell with a steel cot; a canteen for the guards.

The more I saw, the less I could relate it to my mother. The reason was, I think, that it felt wrong to be here *without* my mother. If she had taken me here, if she had shown me her cell and told me that this was where they had questioned her and this was what they had said and this was how she had felt, then maybe I would have understood her better and been closer to her. Or maybe not. The fact was that she had chosen not to. My visit was an intrusion, a trespass.

The tour ended, the group dispersed. Our guide leaned against the glass bricks that let in some filtered light. She looked exhausted. I walked up to her.

'I'm sorry...'

She gave a start.

'Yes?'

'My mother was an inmate here. I wonder if you knew her.'

'We weren't allowed any contact with the other inmates.' She wiped her forehead with a tissue.

'Of course. I was thinking, maybe after your release...'

'What's her name?'

'Regine Valentin.'

She shook her head and tossed the tissue into a bin. 'No. But I can ask around. I guess she came to the reunion. I'm Katia, by the way.'

'Reunion?'

'We had a reunion here a couple of years ago, didn't your mother tell you? All the former inmates got together and compared notes, so to speak.'

My mother had mentioned a school reunion around the time of her last trip to Berlin, yes, I remembered that. Only it had not been a school reunion at all. Had she even called it a school reunion? Or had she just said: 'I'm going to a reunion,' and I had not been interested in the details? That's what would have happened. 'I'm going to Berlin, to a reunion,' she said, then waited for Tobi and me to ask her about it. Which we never did, of course.

'Yes, I think she went to that reunion,' I said.

'I don't remember meeting her, but to be honest, I didn't socialise much, I was busy fighting with one of the old guards. I'll ask the others, though.'

'A *guard* came to the reunion?'

'Oh yeah. Not that she was invited, but she somehow found out about it and showed up. Everyone argued with her.'

'You don't happen to remember her name?'

'Yep. Jankowitz. She lives just round the corner from here. Sometimes comes on our tours, thinks we don't recognise her. Like that guy who was here earlier. It's their little game, they still like to keep an eye on us.'

'Can't you throw them out?'

For the first time since we started talking, Katia looked shocked. 'Throw them out?'

'Like, tell them they're not welcome. Ban them from the site.'

She took a step back. 'No, no, that's never occurred to me. You have to understand, it's all very... complicated. It's not like they did anything illegal, right? They just happened to work here. This is their neighbourhood, this is where they've lived all their lives, the guards, the commander, everyone. And if we didn't let them come here and bother us every now and then, they'd harass us in other ways.'

'Like how?'

'Oh, they're creative. Anonymous phone calls, deliveries of things you didn't order, just all sorts of little reminders that they're there and thinking of you.'

I thought of the months after Tobi and I came back from Hungary, and the strange things that happened in our flat that winter.

'Why would they do something like that?' Oma had asked. 'I gave them everything, why would they do this to us?'

Opa had replied: 'To make sure. Just to make sure.'

Katia studied my face. 'You don't live here, do you?'

'We moved to England right after the wall came down.'

'Yes, I thought there was a bit of an accent.'

I wasn't sure how much to tell her. But she was a former inmate, too. Surely she wouldn't judge us too harshly. 'I'm here to look for my brother. He was taken from us when they arrested my mother.'

Katia nodded. 'Sounds familiar.'

⌒

As we continued walking down the corridor, she told me her story.

Back in the GDR, Katia had been a single mother working for a bottle manufacturer. Her five-year-old son had attended a *Wochenkrippe*, an overnight nursery where he lived from Monday to Friday while she did her shifts. Every Sunday they'd both cry over dinner, and he'd beg her to let him stay with her, and she'd explain that it wasn't possible because of work.

Then a friend told her about a West German acquaintance who took people over to the other side by car. All they had to do was hide in a little crawl space between the back seat and the boot.

'I was naive,' she said. 'I was only twenty-three, all I'd ever known was school and then the factory, and this seemed so easy, one short drive and then we'd be over on the other side. I had this idea that in the West everything would be different and we'd have an amazing life together and have dinner together every night. I know, it sounds so stupid. I was such a child, that's all I can say, such a child.'

Katia had inherited some silverware from an aunt, just enough to pay off the smuggler. He suggested they go in turn, the boy first, then the mother.

The crawl space smelled of fuel. Her son cried when she pushed him into it.

'So I told him off.' She took out another tissue and blew her nose. 'I told him off.'

She positioned herself near the border crossing to watch the car. A couple of guards checked the paperwork and the back seat, then the boot. They closed the boot again, she exhaled with relief, but then more guards arrived. They dragged the driver from his seat, reopened the boot, ripped out the concealing partition and pulled her son from the crawl space. She saw her little boy look around him, frantically searching the street with his eyes, as if he hoped she'd come to save him.

'But I didn't.' She lit a cigarette. 'I watched and watched and didn't do anything. Why? That's what I've never stopped asking myself. I knew it was all over anyway, I knew I'd be arrested later, so why didn't I just run over there? Why didn't I show my boy that he wasn't alone? But I didn't. Maybe I thought it would make everything worse, or that they'd start shooting. I don't know. I went back to my flat and sat there and cried and cried until they came and took me away.'

'Did you ever see him again?'

She nodded. 'I tracked him down in 1998. The third of March 1998. He'd just turned sixteen. I tried to hug him and he flinched.'

'And now?' I asked cautiously. 'Are you still in touch?'

'Sort of. He doesn't...' She cast around for the right words. 'He doesn't *like* me very much, if you know what I mean? And I can't blame him. I'm the woman who sent him away every Monday morning and then, one day, I shoved him into a stinking car and told him to shut up and keep his head down. That's what he remembers me for, and there's nothing I can do about it now.'

We stepped out into the rain. In the middle of the courtyard was a flower bed of red roses. They looked tragic against the concrete.

'How old was your brother, then?' she asked without looking at me.

'Younger than your son.'

'Want my advice?'

'Go on.'

'Make sure he actually *wants* to be found.'

'There's no way of knowing that until I actually meet him though, is there?'

'There is, if you're really honest with yourself. I wish I'd thought more about his side of the story, you know? Rather than just wanting to find him for my own sake.'

'It might be different for me. I'm his sister, not his mother,' I said.

'So?'

'So… I'm not responsible for what happened.' I regretted this immediately. Katia looked pained.

'I suppose so,' she said, and tried to smile.

'I'm sorry, I didn't mean that the way it came out.'

'Why? It was my responsibility, you're right. I screwed up.'

'Have you told your son why you wanted to smuggle him across?'

'Oh, many times. "I did it for you, I did it so you could grow up in a free society, I did it so you'd have a better life," over and over.'

I thought about this for a bit.

'I was angry with my parents, too,' I said.

'And now?'

'Less so.'

We stood in the concrete courtyard together, in the light drizzle that first settled on our hair, then slowly trickled down our necks. Katia opened her umbrella and held it over us.

'Interesting,' she eventually said. 'Interesting.'

'That guard you mentioned…' I tried to remember her name.

'Jankowitz.'

'You don't happen to know how I might get in touch with her?'

'She lives in one of those houses over there.' She pointed beyond the prison wall, towards the street with the tour buses. 'That little side street with the green buildings? Her flat is in, hmm, the third or fourth on the right. You'll have to look at the names by the doorbells.'

'It might be better to give her a call first, no?'

'She'll be in the phone book. These people really don't bother to hide.'

A few people were gathering by the roses and waiting for the next tour to start. One or two glanced at Katia's red umbrella. She looked at her watch.

'Sorry, I'd better get started. We can continue talking some other time, if you like.'

We swapped numbers, I thanked her, and she ushered her group towards the basement door.

'Is anyone here claustrophobic?' I heard her ask. 'Asthma? Any allergies?'

It rained harder and I ducked into the bookshop, a bright modern space with a glass front and white walls. There was an extraordinary amount of glass in this remodelled part of the prison, which also housed a research centre and what looked like seminar rooms or classrooms, as if what the architect really wanted to do was to tear down the whole prison and replace it with a terrarium. I assumed the design brief had included words like 'transparency' and 'openness', though the effect was somewhat offset by the rows and rows of books in the shop, which went all the way up to the ceiling and covered much of the glass.

So many books about the Stasi! I leafed through a memoir by a spied-upon pole vaulter, read about informants in the gay and lesbian communities, and found our own little corner of Berlin represented too, in several books in fact, from a large coffee-table volume about secret, private art galleries in Prenzlauer Berg to a densely printed, serious work on academics in the GDR. Several of these books included transcripts from the Stasi archive, which were often reproduced as photographs of dog-eared, machine-typed documents, as if to lend the author added credibility: look, this truly happened, here is material evidence. Already I regretted how I had behaved in the archive. This often happened to me: as soon as a conversation ended I began to rescript it, as if by using a different wording here and there I could have changed its entire direction and achieved a better outcome for myself. Now I saw with some clarity that I had been too eager in my hushed exchange with Aaron, that I should have subtly planted my dilemma in his mind and left it there to grow instead of trying to pressurise him into helping me. He seemed the type who resisted such pressure, who would say *yes, yes*, just to escape the situation, and then quietly hope that by doing nothing, he could make the whole thing go away.

I put back the book about the pole vaulter. There would be plenty of time for regret and self-recrimination later; for now, I had to solve some practical problems. By the till I found what I'd been looking for, a selection of maps of Berlin from different eras, starting with the pre-war period. I had to go through a couple of them before I found one that matched my memory, where each street name was as I had known it. The spot where I was standing right now, this prison and this neighbourhood, appeared as a white shape on the map, a blank space in the upper right corner surrounded by colourful streets, buildings, parks and waterways, though the publishers had tried to mask the blankness a little by printing *Berliner Stadtplan* across it in a chirpy font. The bits to the west of the wall were blank, too, but that was not particularly noticeable because most of West Berlin was off the page, anyway. This was the Berlin of my childhood, with Friedrichshain at the centre, and Mitte and Prenzlauer Berg at the margins.

I could not deny that I found it a great relief to see the city properly recentred and all the streets and landmarks aligned with the pictures in my mind. Only the streets close to the wall looked different. Sandy's street for example had been left out altogether. This puzzled me for a moment, because

I could not imagine that our cartographers would have produced sloppy work, and then I realised this was deliberate, of course, to prevent people from using this map to plot their escape. Everything circled back to the wall, always, and this felt strange because the wall had not been all that important to me as a child. If it hadn't been for Sandy and her stories, perhaps I would not have noticed it much at all, or no more than children in borderlands everywhere notice guards and searchlights. Or at least I would not have been disturbed by it. Yes, that was a more accurate word than 'notice'. I would not have been disturbed by it, no more than the average child is disturbed by burglar alarms, policemen, airport security – all of which are there, after all, to protect us.

In no time at all I found my old home on this map. Here was our closest U-Bahn stop, Dimitroffstraße. Over there was a square named after Felix Dzerzhinsky, and this street right here to the left was named after my grandmother's great idol and role model, the Communist Lena Fabelhaft. I moved my finger to our own street, which had been Dunckerstraße back then and was still Dunckerstraße now. And there, that little box the size of half a fingernail, that was our old house, and if I could have enlarged the map I would have seen a little girl walking up the stairs, backwards and then forwards and then backwards, all the way up to the fifth floor where a little kitchen was waiting for her with a bathtub under the counter.

I bought this map and one from 2005, which said nothing to me, did not stir gentle memories of staircases and the smell of floor polish, but was very useful because it had all the new names, or rather, the restored names from the pre-division days. So Dimitroffstraße was Eberswalder Straße again, Fabel-haftstraße was Schlesische Straße, and so on. My mind easily added these little footnotes to its own map, just as – I thought – my mother might have done, standing here, or in some other bookshop, lining up two maps. For she would have been irri-tated and confused by the different street names, too, and just like me, she would have hated the idea of asking strangers to show her around her own city.

The bookseller told me that Dimitroff had been a Bulgarian Communist, which surprised me, because it was a large and busy road; you would have thought they'd have given it to a Russian.

In the research centre next door I found a recently published encyclopedia of painters in the GDR, with colour plates of farm equipment in oil on canvas, and a couple of surprisingly lovely sketches of women with strong, sturdy, naked legs. In one of them they were fixing nets by the Baltic sea, in another, hanging up laundry in a courtyard. The entry for 'Neo-Expressionists' was very short and included only a handful of names, and there, with one of those electric memory-shocks, I found Sven Hartwig, a neo-Expressionist painter who escaped to the West in 1987, then settled in Dortmund where he lived until his death of lung cancer the following year. (So he did not even see the end of the GDR, I thought. If only he had sat it out. If only we had sat it out! But how could we have known?)

According to the encyclopedia, Sven's most successful paint-ings had been *Worker and Farmer* and *Cat by the Lake*; there was a small picture of the latter, the cat a rich, rusty red, the lake bright blue. Like most paintings by East German artists, they were no longer shown in museums. Too closely associated with the vanished regime. Sven, I learned, had at one point been much favoured by our rulers, and been awarded all sorts of Socialist prizes. As Oma would say: *Today's wine is tomorrow's vinegar.*

I pulled the photo of the blue horses out of my pocket and placed it next to the open page. My father had ridiculed Sven and his fable-like style, but I disagreed with Papa on that one. I liked the horses, I liked the cat by the lake, I had liked the tiger, too. I smiled. Perhaps Mama had also looked up Sven, either in this research centre or in a bookshop or library. The encyclopedia would have pleased her; it was just as she'd hoped: people could see that it hadn't all been tractors, factories and *The Polytechnical Classroom.* We had produced red tigers and blue horses, too.

'Kitsch,' I could hear Papa say, '*kitsch and silliness, a poor man's Franz Marc, and those plasticky blues, aua, they hurt my eye!*' And this made me very happy, to hear him so hilariously cross, so animated. '*But Papa!*' I argued back, '*they're just paintings!*' Which annoyed him even more, until he saw that I was laughing, that I was only saying this to rile him, to wind him up – I looked up, a reader at one of the desks was staring at me. I'd been laughing out loud.

I closed the encyclopedia, put it back on the shelf, quickly stroked the spine. Bit by bit, it was all coming together, and though I could not see yet how this piece fitted with the others, I would store it in my mind until its time came.

My chat with Aaron had not gone that badly, really. He'd seemed friendly; surely he would help. And I had a new ally in Katia, who'd offered to keep her eyes and ears open for me. I left the research centre feeling rather hopeful.

Outside the sky had cleared. Katia was leading a group of tourists into the main building. We waved at each other. There was an open garage in the far corner that I had failed to notice before, or maybe they had only opened it once the rain had stopped. A van was parked inside. I walked closer. The sides were covered with pictures of baked goods, crusty rolls, brown loaves, braided dough rising in the oven, that kind of thing. There was a jaunty slogan, too: 'Always Fresh, Always Good', or something like that; *Immer Frisch; Immer Lecker*, something along those lines. I didn't really look at the loaves and the slogan because my eyes were drawn to the doors at the back of the van, which were open. With a heavy feeling in my stomach I walked around the side of the van and looked into the back, through the open doors, and there, just as I'd expected, were not crates of crusty rolls or boxes of iced buns, but two rows of metal cages.

Berlin 1987: Summer

O MA TRUDE AND MY father disliked each other, and for a long time I thought it was because of history.

I have an old photo album that my parents made when they got married. On one side is my father's family, beginning with portraits of grim ancestors in corsets and high collars. When you flip the album and start on the other side, you see my mother's family history, all two pages of it.

On my father's side are formal black-and-white photographs of women with wide-brimmed hats and parasols, men in military uniforms, children in sailor suits. His family lived in the town of Stolpmünde by the Baltic sea, in a remote eastern region that was then known as Hinterpommern, or Beyond-Pomerania. As progress reaches Hinterpommern, the stiff studio photos give way to snapshots from the promenade: the women hold on to their hats, the children's hair is ruffled by the wind. There is my great-grandfather, who was a Royal Dune Master in charge of the dunes between Stolpmünde and the city of Danzig. As a child I thought this meant he counted all the dunes along that stretch and made sure none was missing; and as strange as it sounds, that really was more or less what he did, because dunes, when not properly anchored by grass and shrubs, are mobile and can suddenly blow into a front garden or market square, covering everything in sand and leaving the townspeople rubbing their sore, red, sand-blinded eyes.

'*Stolpmünde – das Paris Hinterpommerns!*' someone has written across a snapshot of a lady with a particularly daring hat. 'Stolpmünde – the Paris of Beyond-Pomerania!'

In the next photo is my paternal grandfather, a shop owner, strolling through Berlin during the 1936 Olympics, past a row of swastika flags. There is another photograph of that grandfather in his Wehrmacht uniform; his wife will look after the shop while he is away. Then a photo of a chubby baby in a white lace gown – my father! My paternal grandmother, Oma Henriette, wrote across the bottom in old Sütterlin handwriting: '*Dem Führer wurde ein Sohn geboren*', 'A son has been born to the Führer'.

There is Oma Henriette again, posing with a spade. She and other women are digging a trench, the 'Pommernwall', to stop the Russians. A rumour goes around saying the digging work is toxic to their lower bodies and will leave them infertile. This frightens Henriette, who slashes her own leg with her spade, leaving a gash deep enough to be acquitted of any further digging duties. (*Look, Ella dear, that's me. The Russians saw our trench, laughed, put some planks over it and drove their tanks across.*)

Back in Stolpmünde, Oma Henriette spends the last days before the Russians' arrival cycling up and down the dunes with her bandaged leg and crying: 'No surrender! No surrender!' When the booms and bangs of the Russian artillery can be heard, she throws her bike into the dunes, grabs my father and boards the first refugee ship westwards. Her sister misses the ships and has to walk to safety across frozen lakes and rivers, holding her baby daughter to her chest.

It was my mother who told me the story of that walk, not my father, which is odd given that it was not her family. But my father was not that interested in 'family stuff', as he called it – *Familienkram*. So it was my mother who told me about Oma Henriette's sister, who walked across a frozen lake with her baby daughter pressed to her chest under her coat. She made it to the other side and continued along a road, and as she walked on she noticed all the things that people had discarded as they fled – suitcases, clothes, a hatbox, and she thought, *but why are there so many dolls? Why are there so many dolls by the roadside?* And when she looked at one, she saw that it was a baby, a human baby that had died of the cold and been left by the road.

'But her own baby?' I always asked when she told me the story of the walk, even though I knew the ending. 'What happened to her own baby?'

'Her own baby lived, my darling,' my mother said and stroked my hair. 'Her own baby lived.'

Because my mother's side was so much poorer, there are far fewer photographs in her part of the book. A photo of Opa Horst's parents with a pram, then a photo of Opa Horst at some Communist function in the 1950s. Oma Trude's page is even more sparse. I once asked Oma Trude why there were no photos of her family.

'We were poor, child, we were very poor, all the servants at Czarnikau were poor, all servants everywhere are poor.' She stroked my hair. 'We didn't have the money to go to a studio and have our picture taken. The first time someone took a photo of me was when they liberated Buchenwald. There were photographers who came in after the soldiers – photo-reporters, I suppose they were called – and that's the first time someone took a picture of me. But who'd want to keep such a picture?'

The first photo of her in the album is her wedding picture with Opa Horst. He looks a little cold still from his time in the snow at Stalingrad. There is also one of her wearing her green gaberdine coat. She is standing in an allotment, holding a baby in her arms, my mother. Her peace coat and her peace baby.

In the years after the war, Oma Trude was so poor that she sent my mother out to the railway tracks with an empty tin to gather coal splinters that had fallen off the passing freight trains. My mother knelt in the gravel with dozens of other Berliner children, all of them picking black crumbs from the dirt, until her tin was full and she ran home and gave it to Oma, who fed the coal to the always-hungry stove. Once when she was by the railway tracks my mother looked up and a train passed, not a freight train but a train full of American soldiers; they threw oranges to the children and slices of white bread. Where had it come from? Why were there American soldiers in this Soviet-occupied part of Berlin? Had my mother strayed into the American sector? She never found out. She caught an orange and a slice of white bread, which was new to her; she had only ever known grey, brown and black bread. The orange was sour. The bread was a little bland, but sweeter and softer than dark bread. She took two small bites and gave the rest to her parents. All my mother's childhood stories were like that: suffering was being cold and hungry, happiness was being warm and full. And I always wondered when that feeling changed; when exactly she decided that there had to be more to life than bread and coal.

The two sides of my family could not stand each other. Once, when we were sitting on a bus, my father's mother, Oma Henriette, boasted about my father's latest book: 'He has that from me, I've always loved the arts!'

At which point Oma Trude said loud enough for the whole bus to hear: 'Is that why you voted for a failed painter?'

Which everyone later agreed had been in very poor taste.

So this was one of the reasons why Oma and my father did not get along: despite her measly two pages in the photo album, despite her family's poverty, despite her start in life as a servant, despite her history as a former convict, Oma made no secret of the fact that she thought my mother was too good for my father; that my mother deserved someone with a better lineage; that my mother, in short, had married down.

'I'm not going to say a word against them, Ellachen, because they are your family too,' she sometimes muttered when she brushed my hair. 'But it's hard to forget that they're a bunch of old Nazis.'

IN SUMMER 1987 we went on holiday to Hungary, one of our Socialist brother countries. This was a great treat: I'd never been to a foreign country before. Usually we went no further than Oma's *Datsche* or one of the university's holiday homes by the Baltic sea.

On the day we left, Oma Trude hid our suitcases. At first I did not know it was her. We got up even earlier than usual because it would be a long drive. I wish I had more memories of my father that morning, but all I remember is eating breakfast under the weak kitchen light, and my mother running back and forth saying she could swear she had put the two suitcases and the big bag in the kitchen, where else would they be? She wasn't going mad, was she?

'Is this a prank, Ella? Is this a joke? If so, it's a really bad one. Where are the suitcases? Come on now!'

'I swear it wasn't me! I have no idea where they are, I swear!' I looked under our beds just in case someone had put them there. Nothing. When I crawled back out, I had white dust sticking to my hands, flakes of paint and plaster. I called out: 'Heiko!' and he came running. He'd been doing this for some time, running everywhere instead of walking.

'Heiko, what's that under my bed?'

He lay down on his belly with his knees tucked under and his bottom up in the air and peered into the hollow. Heiko had a way of looking with his entire body, every muscle straining to discover what was there. He did this when he looked into bins and buckets too – put his entire head inside, bent so far that he almost fell in. Now he stretched his neck for a better view and gripped the carpet with his little hands:

'Bider.'

'That's not a spider, you silly bean, that's dirt. How on earth did you do that? Were you drawing again?'

'Bider.'

'Look, I don't mind if you draw on the walls.' I lowered my voice so our parents couldn't here. 'I don't mind, OK? You can draw, but don't start scraping the paint off like that, yeah? *Malen, Heiko. Nur malen, nicht kaputtmachen.*'

'*Puttmachen.*'

'Nicht *puttmachen.*'

'Dirty.' He reached out, picked up some paint flakes with his fingers and inspected them. 'Dirty, dirty, dirty,' he repeated crossly and tried to shake off the paint. I wiped it off with my sleeve.

'Ella!' My mother came in, carrying a suitcase. 'Where's your jacket? Where's Tobi? Come on now, time to go.'

'Where did you find the suitcase?'

'Oma hid them.'

'Oma!'

'I know, it was silly of her, wasn't it? Come on now.'

'Was it a prank?' I picked up my doll and my bear.

'You can't take Sabrina,' my mother said quickly. 'I'm sorry, darling, but she'll have to stay at home.'

My parents were always very strict about the doll, and I knew it was because she was West German. I wasn't even allowed to take her to school, though I often did anyway.

'That's fine, I'll just take Nuckabutz, then.'

'No, no, you can't take either of them.' My mother nervously turned towards Papa, who'd just walked in. 'Or what do you think? I hadn't thought about their toys.'

'It'll look weirder if they leave them behind.'

'The doll or the bear, then?'

My father's eyes went from Sabrina to Nuckabutz and back. 'The bear.'

'But then they'll find the doll here…'

'Let's not overthink this. We're just packing for a holiday.' He smiled and clapped his hands. 'Right, all bears on board, all children on board, this train is ready to depart.'

'Choo-choo!' said Heiko and ran out into the corridor. I sat Sabrina up on my pillow, her blue eyes wide open, and apologised for leaving her behind.

'Next time, it'll be your turn,' I said, which was a lie, because I would never travel without Nuckabutz.

⁓

We left much later than planned. When we said goodbye to my grandparents in the downstairs hallway, Oma began to cry.

'Mutti, don't.' My mother looked around in case anyone could see us. 'I wish I hadn't told you.'

'Leave the children with me,' Oma said and pulled me towards her. 'Please.'

What an odd thing to say! It put my mother even more on edge. She pushed us all into Oma's flat and shut the door behind her.

'Are you out of your mind?' she hissed at my grandmother. 'What if someone heard that?'

'You're the one who's lost her mind. Both of you, you're both out of your minds, you don't know what you're doing.'

'We know, Mutti. We've thought this through.'

'But you haven't! It's because of that stupid book, Regine, it's because you're upset, in a sulk, all over nothing. Hasn't our government given you everything you could possibly want? A good education, a steady job, one where you can both sit in nice warm offices all day, looking at picture books...'

'Art books,' my father said through gritted teeth.

'You've never known hunger, you've never known want. Don't you realise how lucky you are?'

'Trude, we're late already,' my father said, and picked up the suitcases.

'Regine, think about the bigger picture. I was a servant and you're a professor. In which other country would that even happen?'

'Lecturer,' my mother reminded her. 'Not a professor, just a lecturer.'

'Lecturer, professor, my point is that you're not a field hand, you're not a maid, and you've never had to wash your face with snow. The things I suffered in Buchenwald...'

'Mutti...'

'And when we were so poor, my darling, don't you remember that? When you had to go and pick coal splinters from the tracks, don't you remember that at all?'

'I do remember.' My mother put her arm around Oma's shoulders. 'Mutti, we're not leaving you. You and Vati can travel, you can come over any time.'

'Don't run away, Reginchen. It was the comrades who helped us survive.'

My mother looked at my grandmother and said in a voice that was quiet but firm:

'Survive? I don't just want to survive, Mutti. I want to live.'

She embraced my grandmother. They stood there for a long time, leaning into each other. I thought of Tobi and Heiko when they hugged, those hugs that ended in a pinch or bite, because the emotions were too fierce, because love and fury were too close together, were perhaps the same. My mother whispered something into my grandmother's ear, and after a while they separated and we left the flat. Outside, my father was already loading the suitcases into the boot.

—

It was our first family holiday outside of East Germany. The plan was to go camping and eat stews and boiled potatoes from jars we had sterilised, filled and sealed before the trip.

Several times we had to stop by the side of the road because I felt sick, or my brothers felt sick. We were not used to such long journeys in our Trabi. I pictured an aerial view of our trip, the route marked by little pools of vomit beside the road.

In Hungary we had dinner at an inn, a special holiday treat. We would open the jars the following day. I had my first and last Hungarian goulash, which they called *pörkölt*. It came with giant soft dumplings. My father cut the dumplings into small pieces for me. I was old enough to do that myself, but he reached over anyway and cut up the dumplings with his knife.

The campsite was in a forest. All night long little flies and midges bit my hands and face. Tobi woke up crying and said he wanted to go home and sleep in his bed. Heiko peed in the tent. In the morning, my father lit a small gas stove and made watery hot chocolate for everyone.

That is really all I remember of the holiday part of the holiday.

⁓

On the second day, my parents had an argument in the car. It was about Oma. I had fallen asleep, and when I woke up, I heard my father say:

'You shouldn't have told her, Regine. You know what she's like. I'm surprised we haven't been stopped yet.'

'How can you say that? She's my mother.'

'I'm just saying.' My father took a few more drags and threw the unfinished cigarette out of the window. They fell silent. My mother bit her nails. Click, click, click.

'What about Sven?' my father asked after a while.

'What about him?'

Papa reached for the cigarettes, then changed his mind.

'Sven.' He drummed his fingers on the steering wheel. 'With his purple tigers.'

'Red.'

'Red tigers.'

'Jochen, we've been through this a thousand times. Why would Sven want to get us into trouble? He's in the West now.' She looked away. 'Besides, he's our friend.'

'*Your* friend.'

'He's your friend, too. He likes you. Otherwise he'd never have helped us.'

'I wonder.' My father reached for the cigarettes again and shook out two, one for himself and one for my mother. She lit them both. We were deep in the countryside. There were no other cars on the road.

'It sounds a bit too good to be true, that's all I'm saying,' he continued. 'If it's really that easy, why hasn't everyone done it?'

'Because no one else knows about this particular spot.'

'Still. It's very nice of Sven, a little too nice if you ask me. He must still be in a transit camp, right? And yet all he's thinking about is how to get you over there…'

'How to get *us* over there.' My mother turned towards my father and ran her fingers through his hair. 'It's going to be OK, darling. I know you're scared, and I'm scared, too. But it's going to be OK.'

'Can you do that again?' he asked, still looking at the road. But there was a smile in his voice. She ran her fingers through his hair, and then she rubbed his neck.

'The trick is not to think about this next bit,' she said. 'It's like when you're in an obstacle race, you have to think about the stretch *after* the obstacle.'

'As if you'd ever run an obstacle race.'

'I have, at school! And anyway, it was only a metaphor. What I mean is – where shall we go first? Quick. The first country you want to visit.'

'Right now? Austria.'

'Come on, humour me. Once we've settled in, once every-thing's normal, what's the first country you want us to visit as a family? Imagine, Jochen! Not as part of a boring delegation, not in the shadow of five colleagues who're there to report on you, but just as a normal man on holiday with his family.'

My mother's voice was heavy with *Fernweh*, the aching desire to be far away, the opposite of *Heimweh*, homesickness. So strong was the longing in her voice that I expected her to open the window and rise out of her seat, to follow her yearning, to rise and rise until she was nothing but a dot in the sky, travel-ling with the wind.

'When I was a little girl,' she said in that yearning voice, '... when I was a girl, I wanted to be an explorer. Have I ever told you that, Jochen? I packed my bag and walked down the street, and I said to myself, I'm going to keep walking until I find a jungle with monkeys.'

'Did you?'

'I made it as far as the park. No jungle, no monkeys. Anyway, our first country. Quick.'

'Italy. The Sistine Chapel, and all the rest of it. Come on, that's not even a question.'

My mother laughed. 'An art historian through and through. You could have just said you wanted to go to a Spanish beach, you know, I wouldn't have held it against you.'

'Well, Spain's on the list, too. The Prado, Goya, Velázquez.' He tapped the steering wheel once for every name. *The Dog* – now there's a beautiful painting. I wouldn't mind seeing that.'

'I want to go to London,' my mother said.

'London? What, because of Turner?'

My mother laughed again. 'To be honest, it's nothing to do with art. I just like their culture, they're so peculiar and eccentric.'

'Yes, I can see why you'd like that.' He focused on the road for a while, and then he said: 'Still, your mother…'

'My mother is secretly glad that I'm doing this. No – more than that – she's *proud* of me for doing this.'

'I must have missed a nuance there…'

'You don't understand.'

'So when she begged us not to leave…'

'You'll never understand it, it's just one of those things – one of those things you'll never understand. She's not blind, Jochen, she can see what's going on, she can see this isn't what she fought for.'

'I think you're giving her far too much credit there.' He sighed. 'Let's hope you're right.'

She leaned over and kissed him.

'Thank you.'

'For what?'

'For letting me persuade you.'

My father glanced up into the rear-view mirror. His eyes met mine. 'Hey mouse, did you wake up just now?'

'Yes,' I said quickly. 'Where are we?'

'Almost there,' my father said, and put on a brave smile.

⁓

We stopped by the road to have lunch from our jars, cold stew and cold rice. My brothers woke up, and my mother gave them some tea from a thermos flask.

I wanted tea, too, but she said it wasn't for me. Later she took me aside and said that the tea was meant to calm down the boys and keep them quiet. She had to tell me something important, she said – I was a big girl now and could be told important things. We were not going to drive around Hungary; we were not going to Lake Balaton. We were going to abandon the car near a field and walk through a forest where there was an unpro-tected stretch of border, Hungary's border with Austria. Once we arrived in Austria, we would contact my father's cousin, the one who had sent me that blonde doll, and he would help us reach West Germany.

A S WITH ANY STREAM of refugees, single young men made up a big part of the East German outflow. But entire families left, too, and it was often the families that made the most spectacular breaks. There was the family of four that paddled to the West in a rubber boat, circumventing the East German navy patrols. Nine hours into the voyage they lost a paddle, and had no choice but to dock at the next island, not knowing if they were in the East or the West until they saw a row of big, shiny Mercedes.

There were the two families, four adults and four children, who escaped in a homemade hot-air balloon, constructed with the aid of a physics textbook and an American magazine for balloonists. To test for the most airtight fabric, one of the fathers developed a device made from a hoover and a glass tube filled with water, whose level rose higher the more airtight the fabric was. Umbrella silk tested well, so did tent nylon, but in the end the families went for taffeta because that was available in the shops.

Then there was the dad who dived into a canal and sawed through four underwater iron grilles to free the way for his wife, daughter and father to swim through.

The unifying characteristic of these families was a certain

amount of technical know-how. It took a rare combination of engineering and dissimulation skills to secretly build a hot-air balloon in the GDR, where even paragliding was banned in case someone figured out how to paraglide to freedom. The families that did these things, I always thought, were the kind of families who also knew how to build a bookshelf, or change the plug on a hairdryer.

Our family, on the other hand, was hopelessly impractical. Two art historians. Between the two, who was more likely to be the grille-sawing, balloon-building mastermind? My mother? Let's just say, if you could unblock a drain by talking about Expressionism, my mother would have been a star plumber. My father? My father could authenticate Baroque furniture from a mile away, but our kitchen table still wobbled.

When the heating failed or a fuse blew out, they would tell me to go and knock on the door of a neighbour, or fetch Oma Trude.

And yet it was their very position as absent-minded, stargazing members of the *Intelligenz* that could have made escaping easy. My mother had been on departmental group trips to Munich and to Paris. My father had visited Stockholm and even New York. No need for my parents to do pull-ups on the kitchen door until their biceps were ready for extensive paddling. No need to dig a hole into the floor of Oma Trude's living room and keep on digging until they emerged into a kitchen with an electric bread-knife, a fruit bowl full of bananas and a copy of *Der Spiegel* on the counter. No need for any of that: with my parents' jobs, escape could have required only the ability to sneak away from the official delegation, put one foot in front of the other and avoid the wrong embassy.

It could have been easy for them – as easy as a Sunday stroll. Leave the Met, leave the lecture theatre at the Sorbonne, and keep walking until you see a building with the West German flag high up on a pole.

But there was Tobi, and there was Heiko and there was me. The ball, the chain and the manacle. The pier, the anchor and the mooring line. No matter how far Mama and Papa went, the three of us always stayed put.

Maybe they did consider just doing a runner. Maybe my mother did once look at the Eiffel Tower and think, to hell with them, I've only got one life and I'm not going back there. Just like Sandy's mother apparently did. Maybe my father did sit in his hotel room on the Upper West Side and think, that's it, they'll forgive me, I wouldn't be the first man in history to dump his loved ones.

They could also have applied for all of us to leave East Germany. Some people did that. But after years of waiting, the application was often rejected, and in the meantime, the whole family was punished, sacked from jobs, barred from studying.

As a family, our most realistic hope was the utterly unrealistic. Our most realistic hope was the fantastical, the outrageous, the never-in-my-dreams. The equivalent of a submarine built from sardine tins, a catapult that would launch us over the wall, a Valentin family space shuttle that soared out into the universe and came back down on the Western side. The world's most powerful trampoline, a people-carrying hydraulic drill, a giant trained mole. Or, failing these options, a holiday in Hungary that ended in a hiking trip to Austria.

M Y MOTHER EXPLAINED THEIR plan to me, and I was horrified. This was a holiday. Heiko and Tobi and I had been having such a nice time. Why did my parents have to spoil it?

I tried to reason with them. I asked them to at least wait until after my *Jugendweihe*. One of my friends' older sisters had just had hers. I could think of nothing else but the *Jugendweihe*, who I would invite, what presents I would get; it occupied my thoughts even though it was years away.

'What about *them*?' I whispered and pointed at my younger brothers, who had fallen asleep. Two Hänsels in a fairy tale.

'I'm going to carry Heiko,' my mother said. 'And your father is going to carry Tobi.'

'It's never going to work.'

'Ella, who taught you to talk to me that way?'

'Please, Mama, let's just have a nice holiday, please.' I interlaced my fingers in a pathetic plea; I would have fallen to my knees if I thought it would help.

'Ella! Of all days, this is not the one to throw a tantrum.'

It was not as if I was unaware of the problems in our world. After all, I knew about Sven and his run-ins with the artists' association. I knew about the man at the Bösebrücke. I knew that my friend Lisa's older brother had got into trouble at school because he refused the *Jugendweihe* ceremony and announced right in the middle of class – to everyone's surprise, especially his family's – that he was a Christian.

At the same time, I loved our flat, our street, Oma Trude, Opa Horst, my friends. I loved art lessons with Frau Obst, who always wore dangling plastic earrings in the shape of triangles or bolts of lightning, and who asked us to decorate the classroom with dried leaves, or imagine the shape of a sound. I loved running through abandoned basements with Sandy.

Who would help us on the other side? Who would be our friend there? Who would tell my mother before she left the house that she still had a pen in her hair? Who would remind my father that it was time to leave for his lecture, when he was lost in a book?

Whenever we ran out of salt or oil, which happened often, I only had to ask Frau Pietsch next door and she gave me a cup of whatever I needed, and always a piece of chocolate, too. Just the other day our building had won a Golden House Number for our exemplary collective cleaning effort. I had chipped in with Frau Minsky's *Subotnik* and she had promised me a reward. Now I would never know what the reward was, let alone receive it!

I absolutely did not see why I should be forced to run away from all these people. It seemed unfathomable to live without them. As for the fact that I could not visit Western Europe or the United States, might never see Spain, might never see Italy: well, my world was quite small anyway. The authority I most chafed against was that of my parents, not the state.

'You know, it's not true that everyone in the West is rich,' I told my mother. 'The children there go barefoot.'

'That's not why we're leaving,' she snapped. 'It's got nothing to do with rich and poor and barefoot. And anyway, what nonsense. Barefoot! The things they tell our children! I'm really disappointed, Ella. I thought you were a big girl.'

'A lot of children in the West take drugs though, that's true, isn't it?'

'Listen, once we're over there, you can ask as many questions as you like. But not now.'

So much for freedom of speech. I was fairly certain that the reports of a drug epidemic in the West were true. Even the West Germans wrote about it. My friends' older siblings were all reading Christiane F.'s memoir in school, with its stories of child prostitutes gathering at Bahnhof Zoo in West Berlin. Our teachers loved that book, they always said it was the imperialists documenting their own disaster. I did not want to live with the imperialists, in a country full of child addicts and American nuclear weapons.

'What if we go home and try it next time instead?' I suggested more carefully. 'Then I can at least say goodbye to Oma and my friends.'

'There might not be a next time. And what do you think will happen if you tell your friends, and they tell their parents, and the parents tell the police?'

'They won't,' I said feebly.

Mama crouched down and looked at me.

'There's no going back now,' she said. 'We've prepared everything. We're ready.'

We got back into the car and drove on for a bit, then turned into a paved road that narrowed to a dirt track and ended by a corn field. My brothers stirred as my parents gently pulled them out of their seats. Outside, they nodded off again. Heiko, I remember, wore a red-and-black T-shirt.

—

We hid in the corn field until my parents decided it was the right time to attempt the crossing. The green stalks stood very tall and straight, full of sap, with long, slender, drooping leaves that brushed against my face. I was a city child, I had never seen a corn plant up close before. The cobs did not grow out of the top, as I had thought, but sat snugly against the stalks, swaddled tightly in their green leaves. It was strange, watching my parents crouch among the corn. They looked completely out of place. Every time they adjusted a leg or stretched an arm, they knocked against one of the plants. This would never work; we were too clumsy and there were too many of us, surely we were making the entire field ripple. It was no good at all.

By the time we edged back to the dirt path, another thought had formed in my mind. If I tore away right now, I could disappear between the plants and make my way back to Berlin. I was small and quick, much quicker than them, it would be easy. And anyway, they wanted to leave, they would not come after me. Then I remembered the man who was shot at the Bösebrücke.

'What if they start shooting at us?' I whispered.

'They don't shoot at people here,' my mother said. 'Look, there isn't even a watch tower, there isn't even a wall.'

Then she said Sven had told her about this crossing. He had sent them a map, hidden in a painting, through an art dealer they all knew. Everything had been carefully planned, everything had been talked about in detail, just not with me. And I realised then that I could not run back through the corn field. I could not change their minds, I could not make them turn around, I could not separate myself from them. I belonged to them, and I had to go with them. In some sense I was already crossing the meadow, I was already fighting my way through the forest and through the invisible wall.

The future had always seemed limitless to me, an empty space to be filled by life. But it was not like that. It had already been filled in for me by others. Others had decided that I would cross this meadow, others had decided that I would walk through this forest, others had decided that I would live in West Germany. Their ideas were my reality. It was like everything else in my life – school, clubs, homework, chores, falling asleep at night, waking up in the morning. It was all arranged by others. I had no power at all – not over the present, not over the future.

The sky was darkening, and my parents said it was time to go. Dark enough to be hidden, but still light enough to see where we were going.

'Come, Ella,' my mother said.

I took her hand and followed her into the meadow.

—

She was carrying Heiko, and my father was carrying Tobi. My parents' legs buckled a little under the weight, it threw them off balance. They made slow progress. The meadow was uneven, treacherous. The vast silence of the countryside at night frightened me. It was as if someone had torn away a protective blanket and left me exposed and alone.

Finally the black cluster ahead of us turned into trees, shrubs, undergrowth. We had reached the edge of the forest. It was dense and forbidding, lined by a barrier of thorny bushes. My parents paused and put down my brothers. My father went to look for a gap in the bushes large enough to slip through. He had taken only a few steps away from us when a beam of light shone on him.

I froze, then ducked between two shrubs. Thorns scratched my face and arms. Cowering under some branches, I watched the light travel from my father to my mother and my brothers. I stayed just outside the bright circle, hidden in the dark. Somewhere in the distance, a man yelled something in a foreign language. I could not see him; it was too dark and he was too far away.

'Take the boys!' my father shouted and handed Tobi to my mother. 'Run!'

My mother grabbed Tobi with one arm and tried to pick up Heiko with the other. She half carried, half dragged my brothers into the forest, trampled on the thorny shrubs, pushed through the undergrowth. I stumbled after her, tripped on roots and fallen branches, stepped into puddles and holes in the ground. Where was my father? I heard him shout again, further away now: 'Run! Don't wait for me, run!'

A shot rang out. My mother froze and turned around.

'Jochen?' she called out, but no one answered.

'Jochen?' she tried again. The boys slipped from her arms. Tobi stirred. We were only steps away from the barbed wire.

My mother paid no attention to the barbed wire, to me, to the boys. She was walking back towards my father, as if in a trance, and then she broke into a run.

—

My father was lying in the meadow. The border guard stood next to him. When he saw us, he switched off the torch. It was darker than before. My mother kneeled down next to my father and touched his head, his face, his chest. The air smelled metallic. The guard was talking to us in his foreign tongue. My mother screamed in German: 'Call for help! Call for help right now! We need a doctor!'

'He fight,' the border guard replied in broken German. 'He fight, what can I do, he fight me.' He switched on the torch again. He was a young man, milk-faced, with a wispy moustache, like one of the teenagers who hung around Prenzlauer Berg on their mopeds. His eyes were wide with fear.

I kneeled down next to my mother and touched my father's chest. It was wet. I withdrew my hand.

Dark shapes were moving across the meadow towards us. My mother held my father in her arms and whispered something in his ear.

The border guard pressed the ball of his hand against his

eyes. He seemed about to cry, he seemed terribly afraid, and I was terribly afraid, and my mother kept whispering words I could not hear.

My brothers must have woken up, because in the darkness of the forest, amid the angry voices of the guards who were now gathering around us, I could hear them crying.

M Y MOTHER, MY BROTHERS and I flew back to Berlin. The plane was full of other detained East Germans, each handcuffed to a handler. We were handcuffed, too. I looked around to see if I could spot my father somewhere. As if she had read my thoughts, my mother leaned over and whispered that Papa was in hospital. Her handler yanked at the handcuffs and told her to shut up.

A woman sat down next to me. She asked me questions that I could not answer because I was suddenly struck with a stutter. I tried very hard to answer properly, fearing she might punish me if I did not. It was impossible. The harder I tried, the stronger the stutter.

When we got off the plane, I reached for my mother's hand, but a uniformed woman picked me up and carried me towards a car. I saw two men taking my mother's arms on either side. They shoved her into the back of a van, not a prison van but an ordinary bakery van with pictures of rolls and loaves on the side. The back door swung open. There were metal cages inside. Our car swerved and I lost sight of the van and my mother.

~

I was taken to a room that was bare but for a desk and a green metal locker. Another uniformed woman brought me juice and a ham sandwich, but I was not hungry. I asked where my parents were and was told to be a good girl and wait.

The linoleum floor was wet. Someone had mopped it in wide circles. The floor was shiny where it had been mopped. It was matte where the mop had missed bits. When I pointed my feet, the tips of my shoes only just touched the floor. I flexed them. Pointed them. The water dried, the shiny bits disappeared. Now the whole floor was matte. First wet, now dry. I wondered what my punishment would be. Sandy's father sometimes beat her with a slipper. It was a secret; she had told me and I had sworn not to tell anyone else. Sometimes our mother slapped us. Grown-ups were stupid, they slapped children and then told them not to hit each other. As soon as my father was well again, we would all be back in our flat. Oma would give us a good telling-off. I would never do anything naughty again, and neither would my parents. If I held my breath for thirty counts, Papa would be well again.

The door opened.

'Oma!'

'Ellachen.'

She opened her arms wide. I ran to her, pressed myself against her big, soft belly, felt her arms close around me. She had put on her best beige skirt suit and a brown blouse. Her arms smelled of perfume, not our special perfume from the West but the usual stuff that smelled like a mopped floor. She loosened her arms just enough to let in another refugee who slipped into the dark fold and pressed himself against me, wet, sniffling, trembling.

It was Tobi.

'Where is Heiko?' I asked, muffled by Oma's suit jacket.

'Not now, Ellachen,' Oma said and squeezed us tight. 'Let's take you home.'

Aaron

Berlin 2010

THE BAR WAS NEAR Rosenthaler Platz and crammed with *Pornobrillenträger*: porn-glasses-wearers, men with large tortoiseshell glasses perched prominently on their noses, like producers of adult movies lounging around a 1970s swimming pool. A female porn-glasses-wearer was mixing cocktails behind the bar. Her black hair was shorn to a stubble on one side, and braided on the other. To Aaron's knowledge there existed no particular Berliner word for a side braid, but there was one for the lower-back tattoo peeking out of the woman's waistband. Two ink-black branches curled up towards her kidneys, like a mighty pair of antlers, and that was precisely what this kind of tattoo was called: *Arschgeweih*, or arse antlers.

Bernd had organised a night out for the interns, a nice gesture. They were sipping cocktails from chipped white teacups with a pattern of pink flowers.

'How's it going?' Bernd sidled up to him, teacup in hand. He looked faintly ridiculous with his big fingers around the dainty handle, but of course they all looked ridiculous, extras from a scene with the Mad Hatter. Aaron raised his own cup.

'Fine, thanks.'

'Not too ground down by the shelves?'

'You know, when Machiavelli was exiled from Florence, he would put on his finest garments every night, sit down at his desk, spread out his philosophy books, and settle down for an evening with the greatest minds of the past.' He took a sip. 'Just like me and Frau Schild.'

'You weren't exiled.'

'What I mean is, there's a way of making the best out of every situation.' The caipirinha must be stronger than he'd thought. It was not in Aaron's nature to challenge and complain. Yet here he was, challenging and complaining, and Bernd seemed not to mind, seemed to find it amusing even.

'We thought it would be good for you to spend some time in the stacks. There are people who spend years there before they ever get to have a go at reconstruction.'

'And indeed people who live there, like Frau Schild.'

'I knew you'd find her interesting.'

'She likes her coffee strong. That's about the only thing I've found out about her. I have a feeling it'll stay that way.'

'She's one of the best. You'll find it extremely useful to have her ear once you're back with us.'

Back with us! Aaron felt giddy at the thought of being up there again in his office with the view over the tower blocks, a promising tray of paper scraps in front of him.

'I've been forgiven?' he asked.

'If that's how you want to put it. Licht really liked your work on those evacuated offices. He might even show your pages in an exhibition he's planning, about the last days of the Stasi.'

'*Stasi: The Endgame.*'

'Something like that.'

They were back to their easy banter and it seemed impossible to imagine that Bernd had once shouted at him, had lost his temper, had banished him to the shelves. Emboldened by this thawing of relations, Aaron asked: 'Out of interest, say if you have an exhibition like that and you want to find files on a specific subject, is there any way of searching the bags without going through them? Like, instead of putting random pieces together and finding out they're about Office Erfurt, could I have had any way of looking specifically for files about Office Erfurt?'

Someone had turned up the music, and a few people started to dance. Aaron feared he had said the wrong thing again, and anyway, it was hard to shout over the noise. He should have just used the opportunity to have a good time with Bernd.

'Not really,' Bernd said. 'Well, yes and no. We do have some inventories, databases, that sort of thing. Hey, I'll just get myself another drink.'

And with that, Bernd disappeared towards the bar. It was only after Aaron had stood there for some time, his almost-empty cup in his hand, that he realised he'd been discreetly shaken off.

It took a few more days for him to be fully rehabilitated. Then he was finally back in the calm white room, with Bernd's machines whirring next door. He tried not to think too much about how Frau Schild must feel, barred forever from this kind of work. Maybe it was just for the outside world, because no matter how much they trusted her, it would look strange to employ a former Stasi worker in reconstruction. Then again, it looked strange to employ one in the shelves, too. He would never understand this place.

The pieces in front of him were an attendance list, some gathering of metal workers. Before meeting Ella Valentin, this would have excited him, just like he'd been extremely excited about the office evacuation reports. But now his mind kept drifting back to their secret conversation by the stacks. He'd photocopied the one page in her mother's file, so he'd have a reference for the kind of font and format he'd be looking for. Only he had no idea where to start. There were indeed some inventories and databases, just like Bernd had said, but searching them had yielded next to nothing. A Regine Valentin was mentioned in a list of inmates transferred from one prison to another. Her name also came up in various reports about authors and publishers. Some of her books were praised, others heavily criticised. He made photocopies of these brief passages, thinking that Ella Valentin might be interested in them. But of the file as such, with its personal surveillance reports and interrogations – there was no sign of that at all.

Ella Valentin would never find her brother this way, Aaron was sure. But it would be nice to be able to help her even just a little – to offer her a few more pages, a tiny bit more clarity. Already he had pictured the rest of the mother's interrogation, as he did with all his fragments. She was an educated and to some extent influential woman, an art historian, an academic. In his mind he tried to reconstruct her voice. How she might have behaved under pressure.

Here it was, the familiar compulsion to fill in the gaps. It was stronger than curiosity even, this urge to reconstruct the missing side. Though of course curiosity was there, too: the desire to know, and to know completely.

In the Stasi dictionary, curiosity – *Neugier* in German, 'new-greed' – was defined as something to avoid:

Curiosity as an emotionally motivated greed for concealed news and novelty can sabotage the process of gathering information. The handler must ensure at all times that surveillance is carried out dispassionately and without any emotional attachment to the outcome of the operation.

Aaron decided that the Stasi knew nothing about what really motivated humans.

Bernd had told him that the dad, the one betrayed by his son, had never shown up to see his file. He'd phoned on the day of the appointment and said he'd changed his mind.

—

By lunchtime he'd barely fiddled together half a page. And he suspected that he'd put the wrong pieces together. The names of the metal workers did not quite match up. He slipped out of the office and down into the courtyard, avoiding the canteen, avoiding Bernd's cheerful requests for updates. It was a chilly day. A woman was sitting on a bench by a flower bed, eating a rye sandwich out of an aluminium foil wrapper. As he walked closer, he realised it was Annemarie Schild.

Aaron sat down next to her and unwrapped his own sandwich.

'Hallo, Frau Schild.' He gave her a friendly nod. 'Can I ask you a question?'

'I'm on my break.' She looked at her watch. 'For another twenty minutes. Come to my office later.'

He did not even know she had an office. He'd just assumed she worked in the stacks. Well, this was awkward. And he could hardly rewrap his sandwich and leave now, either.

'Do you mind if I have my lunch here?'

'You can have your lunch wherever you like. It's a free country.' Her voice was not hostile though, just neutral, and he decided to interpret it as an invitation. He started eating his sandwich.

'Hmmm. Gouda and gherkin. What's on yours?'

She looked surprised. 'Salami.'

'Nice.'

'It's OK.'

He tried to think of a way to keep the chat going. *So, what was it like, working for the Stasi?* Maybe not.

'It's warm today,' he said.

She let out a sigh, wriggled her fingers. 'I'm always cold. Poor circulation.'

'Have you tried those fingerless mittens?'

'I've tried everything. The only thing that works is a scalding bath with rosemary oil, but it has to be really scalding.'

'My grandmother rubs her joints with pine-needle oil.'

'Pine-needle oil.' She took an apple from her bag and polished it with her sleeve. 'That's your Berliner grandmother, yes?'

'That's the one. She also uses sage, but I think that's as a tea.'

And there his knowledge of herbal remedies ended. But even this modest contribution had made a difference. Frau Schild, who'd been sitting with her back ever so slightly turned to him, was now visibly more relaxed. She shifted a little, facing him as they jointly contemplated her health issues.

'You said you had a question?' she eventually asked.

'It's a bit of a personal favour, really.'

'Go on.'

'I'm looking for a person's file. I've tried all the usual lists and things. It would have been from the 1980s.'

'You can put in a special request with Dr Licht, he'll pass it on to us.'

'Thank you, but that would take ages.' He wished he could offer her a discreet but emotionally significant bribe, a handwarmer, a bottle of rosemary oil. All he had was a half-eaten gouda sandwich.

'I'm only here this summer,' he continued. 'It would mean a lot to me to find it.'

'This file, it belongs to a friend of yours?'

'It's about her mother. She really needs to see it. And I'd like to help someone, you know, not just sit here and glue lists back together and then leave.'

'You want to do things properly,' she said.

'Exactly.'

'You want to finish what you started.'

'That's right.'

'That's a good attitude. We should all finish what we started.' She dropped the apple core into the bin next to them and wiped her hands on a paper towel. 'Give me the name. I'll see what I can do.'

'That's really kind of you. If I can ask one thing – do you mind not telling Dr Licht?'

'I'll see what I can do,' she repeated. She looked at him. 'And maybe one day, when the time comes, you'll remember that I helped you.'

She was asking him to make a commitment of some sort – a pledge, a promise. A promise to do what? He had no idea, and he wasn't sure that he wanted to promise anything. But he said:

'I will, Frau Schild. I will remember.'

⁓

A week went by. No word from Frau Schild. At the weekend, he went to a party with Cem and Petra, and drank enough to feel worry-free for the first time in ages. He texted Ella about the bits and pieces he'd found – the book reports, the list of prisoners. It's not much, he wrote, but it might be all I can find for you.

On Monday, he returned to his desk. The metal workers were still far from complete. The abandoned shreds stared at him accusingly. He sat down, and his feet pushed against something soft. He looked: under his desk, a brown paper bag. About half full.

He got up, carefully closed his office door and moved a chair in front of it.

Then he got down on his knees, crawled close to the bag under his desk, and with the gentlest of movements, scooped out a tangle of paper.

⁓

All the scraps were typewritten.

```
INFORMATION
The following has come to our knowledge
through IM Erna:


allow me, dear Comrade Minister, to thank
you and t


ANSWER: I don't know why you're asking me all
   these questions when you know everything
   already.
```

Aaron looked at the pieces, white and off-white, tried to find differences and sort them according to the differences.

Someone had scribbled in the margins of that first scrap, right next to the codename IM Erna: 'IM Erna – Doppelzüngler?'

He'd seen that before somewhere. A 'double-tonguer', a liar, was that it? There it was again, on another scrap of paper, just a couple of lines:

```
This information may have to be treated with
some caution due to separate claims that IM
Erna has shown herself to be a Doppelzüngler.
```

He reached for his Stasi dictionary, worn and well-thumbed by now.

Double-tonguer. Dishonest persons who convey different opinions on one and the same subject towards two or more other persons. D.s present a special danger as they can disorient the operative work and bring other citizens into disrepute through invented or false accusations.

It was not for Aaron to judge these documents, to evaluate them, to form hypotheses and conclusions. But already he was looking at IM Erna's account with some scepticism, was in fact looking at the whole scattered lot in front of him with some scepticism, because if IM Erna was a liar, and all these shreds were lies, then what was the point of putting them together?

He glanced at the door. This was foolish. Bernd could come in any minute and kick him right back to Siberia. He carefully lifted the tangle, like moving a bird's nest, and placed it at the back of the desk. Then, working as quickly and lightly as he could, he freed strand after strand, smoothed them out a little and placed them in his satchel. It was roomy, with sturdy walls; he could safely carry them home in there without damaging them. But what about the rest? He could hardly smuggle the whole bag past the receptionist!

Aaron stayed late that night and used the quiet evening hours to free a few more strands. It might take a few days to get the contents of the whole bag home. He would do it in batches, hoping no one checked his satchel on the way out. Yes, that could work. He picked up his bag and made his way downstairs. The receptionist had already left. A night porter wished him a safe journey home. This was not theft, he told himself. He'd make photocopies, work on them quietly at home, restore the shreds to the bag. Nothing would change, nothing at all.

—

Cem and Petra lived in an elegant turn-of-the-century building. On the way up to the flat, Aaron stopped in front of one of the wide double front doors. The frame was painted white, with two barely detectable indentions at eye height, about a finger-width apart. Aaron ran his hand across them. Filled-in nail holes, from two nails that had been driven into the wood at a slight diagonal. There was only one object that left these kinds of holes in this kind of position: a mezuzah – the short, slender wooden or metal case containing a scroll with a blessing for the house. Aaron did not consider himself religious – he ate prawns and bacon butties, but it pleased him that he recognised these faint traces, already covered by layers of paint, invisible to most of the people who passed. A few more years, and they would disappear entirely.

As a boy, Aaron had spent enough time in Sunday school to remember the ancient debate over the ideal position for a mezuzah. One Talmudic sage argued that it should be vertical, another that it should be horizontal, and in a compromise, everyone agreed on diagonal. Equally important was the scroll. Every so often you were supposed to take it to an expert, have it checked for smudges or other damage, to ensure that the blessing for your house was still beautiful and intact. If it was beyond repair, you had to find a scribe to replace the scroll or buy a new mezuzah in a specialist shop. An entire mini-economy would have existed around these barely visible nail holes, and it had vanished just as the mezuzah had vanished.

Aaron's grandmother had asked him to go to the Berlin Zoo for her, because as a child she had lived near the zoo. Every weekend her parents had taken her to see the monkeys and feed them peanuts. Aaron had done as he was told, visited the zoo several times in fact, took pictures and sent them to his grandmother. Now when they spoke on the phone they always spoke about the zoo. She did not ask any other questions about Berlin, not about her old neighbourhood, not about her old school, only about the zoo; she wanted to know, for example, if it was still permitted to feed the monkeys there. In the end, the unsaid was as important as the said.

Aaron knew he would not tell his grandmother about the holes from the mezuzah, because there was nothing to say about it other than what she knew already – that something had been here and was now no longer here.

—

The kitchen smelled of wine and fish. There was a black pot of mussels in broth on the hob.

'Help yourself!' Petra called from the bedroom. 'We've already eaten.'

'Thank you, but I'm allergic to shellfish.'

She came out of the bedroom, wearing what looked like a brown monk's habit and a necklace made from a slashed bicycle tyre.

'There's bread and cheese, as well.'

'Thanks. That's really kind. I'll cook tomorrow.' He was impatient to get to his own room and look at the scraps, but Petra was clearly feeling chatty.

'We've got a super-difficult client right now.' She picked a mussel from the bowl and cracked it open. 'Super-difficult. Cem is in such a mood.'

'I'm sorry to hear that.'

'What are you going to cook?'

'I'll have to think about it.' He cut himself a slice of bread and put it on a plate.

'That all you going to have?' She fished out another mussel.

'I'm not hungry.' He hated being rude. 'I'm sorry, but I think I'll have to eat at my desk, as it were. So much work.'

'Jesus, they're really beasting you, aren't they? And I bet you're not even paid.'

'Hmm.' He gave her a little wave. 'Catch up later, OK?'

He was good at this by now. You had to start with the corners and fill in the rest, just like with a jigsaw puzzle. And he knew a bit about Regine Valentin; he knew her general circumstances. That made it easier. He considered calling Ella and asking her if she wanted to be part of this. But no, that would only slow him down. And also, if he was honest, he wanted to do this. He wanted to do it properly, as Frau Schild had said; he wanted to finish the job.

The more he came to know the Valentins, the faster he was able to work. Batch by batch the shreds left the archive. The little piles on the desk in his bedroom grew. He spread them out on the wooden floor, tiptoeing between the little islands of text.

A family emerged. Jochen, Regine and their three children. A grandmother was mentioned, and a grandfather. A cousin. Some family friends, a painter. A bohemian crowd, that was how he pictured them, drifting around Prenzlauer Berg. Gallery openings, public readings, grant applications, book reviews. There were plenty of scraps in the bag from this aspect of Regine Valentin's life – newspaper clippings, seminar programmes. He set them aside for later, because this was not really what Ella was after.

Then there were the reports. He placed these apart, too. They formed the backbone of the file. He had the bottom of a preliminary report explaining why the family should be placed under surveillance, but could not find the rest. There was IM Erna, the potential *Doppelzüngler*, and various other informants. It would take him a while to fight his way through this thicket, because reports were not as standardised as lists or even interrogations. You had to work a bit more subtly, tease out the stylistic quirks of the individual informants and guess their relationship to the family, decide who'd written the one about the faculty meeting where Regine Valentin appeared to have made some unwise remarks, and who'd been standing at the corner, watching who went in and out of her home. Another job for later.

There were photographs in the bag, photographs of three children, each pinned to a form. He read their names, Ella, Tobias and Heiko, and another name scribbled in the margins. All this would be very significant to Ella, he was certain of that, and so he fixed the forms first, the forms for the three Valentin children.

Again he thought of texting Ella. But now he was deep in the file, and wouldn't it make more sense to show her the forms along with the rest? Who would want to read about their past in serialised form, gagging for the next instalment? Nobody.

Next, another easy triumph. A letter, printed on heavy, embossed paper, that had been carelessly ripped in two. It was signed by Mielke, and he paused for a moment. Had some Stasi underling deliberately failed to destroy this one properly, hoping to sling a bit of mud at his boss? Impossible to tell. Maybe it had just not seemed particularly damaging. Just another Mielke document, like that menu with the rolls and the boiled egg.

Dear Comrade Minister!

Please allow me, dear Comrade Minister, to thank you and the relevant branches of your ministry for the valuable support you offered the Ministry of State Security following our request for measures concerning the GDR citizens VALENTIN, Regine and Jochen.

It was only through your effective co-operation that the first suspect and her three children were apprehended and extradited from Hungary to the GDR.

Allow me also to express my condolences, dear Comrade Minister, for the attack on your border guard. I commend his brave and decisive response and wish him a swift recovery.

With socialist greetings

Mielke

Huh. Interesting. He could roughly see what had happened, how the bohemian Valentins had walked into disaster. What surprised him, though, was the high-level treatment of the case, the formal letter between two countries. This one he'd need to think about. He placed the letter in a far corner, next to the yucca plant, thus designating it the Corner of International Affairs.

After the letter and the forms, he moved on to the interrogations. Here he had a key: the one page from the reading room that had already been fished out of some pile and repaired.

He used that page to prime his eyes for the visual aspects of the text. The shape of the letters, the way the words were arranged on the page. From there it was not hard to go through all the scraps and separate the ones that looked about right.

Night after night he worked until his eyes ached, a dry, itchy soreness. In the mornings he dragged himself back to the archive, did his best there, counted the hours until he could be back home with the Valentins. When he finished the bulk of the interrogations, he felt a rush of pride.

QUESTION: You seem more co-operative now.

ANSWER: I didn't do anything wrong. All I did was go on holiday to Hungary.

QUESTION: Are you saying our state harasses innocent people? Agitation against the state, that's punishable by up to five years. Frankly, we are very tired of your lies and stubbornness. An official was attacked in a Socialist brother country, that's a serious offence.

ANSWER: I don't know why you're asking me all these questions when you know everything already.

QUESTION: We found a map in one of your bags. Who gave you that map?

Gradually the scattered paper islands on his floor merged into small continents. From a thousand tiny glimpses of the Valentins, he'd created a meaningful overview. Here by the door was their life before Hungary, the book reviews, the admittedly still somewhat incomplete reports. Then the forms and proto-cols from the arrest. Over by the yucca plant, the international angle. Then the interrogation, and the other documents that went with that.

In the centre were the scraps that remained a mystery to

him. A handwritten note in Hungarian, which unfortunately he could not read. A list of artworks, with a scathing assessment of their artistic merit. And a torn piece of paper:

`The child Ella Valentin, b. 4.2.1979`

It did not belong to one of the forms, that was the strange thing. It was written in the same type as IM Erna's reports, the surveillance reports, and he was pretty sure that it was part of that dossier. But this confused him because it was rare to see children mentioned in surveillance reports. Not unheard-of, but rare. What could you really say about a child? She went to school, she came back, she picked her nose. Maybe he would ask Ella about it; then again, he did not want to alarm her.

That night, Aaron fell asleep with black ink on his fingers.

QUESTION: Whose idea was it to flee the Republic, yours or your husband's?
ANSWER: I can't remember.
QUESTION: We have evidence that it was your idea, and that you were helped by a former GDR citizen who is now resident in West Berlin. How did he contact you?
ANSWER: Who told you that? Did you spy on us? Who told you all these things?
STATEMENT: Answer the question.
ANSWER: I don't know, I can't remember, I don't know.
QUESTION: We will come back to this later. Your neighbours describe you as a very loving mother. Do you agree with that?

ANSWER: Of course I love my children.

QUESTION: And you want nothing but the best for them?

ANSWER: Is that a threat?

QUESTION: Are you accusing us of threatening you?

ANSWER: Whatever you do, please don't punish my children. Please.

QUESTION: You punished them yourself when you decided to break the law of the Republic. It's up to you how soon you will see them again. We always reward those who co-operate, and there are many ways of co-operating with us. Are you ready to co-operate?

II

Wall Power

She gave us everything
Sun and wind and she never deprived us.
And where she was, was life,
And what we are, we are because of her.

She never abandoned us,
When the world froze to death, we were warm.
We were led by the mother of the masses,
Carried by her powerful arm.

The Party, the Party is always right!
Comrades, that's how it is;
Because whoever fights for our rights
Is always right,
Against exploitation and lies.

'The Song of the Party'; party song of the Socialist Unity Party
of Germany. Composer: Louis Fürnberg, 1949

Ella

An Open Door

Berlin 2010

I WAS SITTING IN my room at the artists' residence. From the kitchen came the sound of laughter and chatter, mostly in Spanish. Someone was playing the guitar and singing:

Solo le pido a Dios
Que el dolor no me sea indiferente...

There was a knock on my door.
'Yes?'
The door opened a crack and a woman peeked in, holding a bowl of stew in her hands. Her hair was wrapped in a yellow scarf printed with red boats. 'Would you like some dinner?'
'Oh. Thank you.'
'It's vegan. With chickpeas and chard.'

I took the bowl from her, touched. 'I should really have it in the kitchen with you guys. It's just…'

'No, no, we respect the need for solitude.' She held up her flat hand, as if to cast a spell against the demons of social pressure. I liked her already, with her chickpeas and her kindness. We chatted for a bit. She came from Argentina and was working on a topography of concrete in Berlin.

'And you?' She looked around my room.

'Me?' *Oh, I'm just in Berlin to look for my lost brother and consult my mother's Stasi file. Yes, there's a whole file on her; I was surprised, too.* 'I'm working on a topography of…' I tried to think of something. 'Of memory. I'm working on a topography of memory.' It wasn't even a lie, and it seemed to satisfy her. We talked a bit more before she went back to her party.

⌣

The next day I took the S-Bahn back to Frankfurter Allee, then walked to the Stasi archive in the eastern neighbourhood of Lichtenberg. The archive was in a vast, grey compound, large enough to house thousands of Stasi employees, surrounded by equally vast, grey tower blocks. I remembered Katia's comment about the former guards who still lived close to the prison. Presumably the Stasi spies had also stayed in their flats, and were sitting on the balconies above me, or walking past me with their shopping bags.

There was a small exhibition in the foyer about daily life in the GDR. I walked past display cases full of beige housecoats, magazines with travel tips for the Soviet Union, vats for home-made Russian kvass, a lawnmower made from old car parts, a rocking horse made from a chair. Physical, durable proof of our inventiveness and improvisation skills, and of the fact that we and our world were now a mere curiosity. In the last display case they had reconstructed an old GDR kitchen, complete with a bathtub under the counter. I felt tempted to pull it out and lie down in it.

I asked the receptionist for Dr Licht. She scratched her chin.

'He's been changing offices a lot recently. Let me check.' She tapped away at her computer. 'He's a bit like those migrating salmon, you know, every now and then he becomes restless. OK, got him.'

She gave me directions to an annexe a couple of courtyards away. I left the building, crossed the courtyards, looked for the entrance to Licht's unit, and must then have taken a wrong turn. I found myself in a deserted part of the compound that seemed to go on forever, a city within a city. This whole place seemed designed to baffle and disorient. How had the Stasi officers ever found their way back from the bathroom? Through the windows I could see office interiors that looked like they had been left untouched since the 1990s, and long empty corridors where the teenagers of Berlin had been practising their graffiti skills. A group of squatters in torn T-shirts and military boots occupied one of the floors. They told me that the archive was at the other end of the compound, no one ever came here.

'Only the ghosts,' one said in a broad Berliner drawl, picking at his teeth with his fingernail. 'And us.'

'I'm looking for Dr Licht,' I said, because anything seemed possible at that point, and maybe he liked the solitude and had chosen to perch up here with the squatters and the ghosts.

'The only doctor I know is the one who sells me my pills,' the squatter said. He had dyed his hair black and shaved one side off completely, and I hadn't seen that particular hairstyle in such a long time that it made me nostalgic. This was how I pictured my old friend Sandy, I realised that now. I always imagined that she'd grown up to be a hardcore, alternative activist of some sort.

'Just randomly, do you know someone called Sandy?' I asked my new friend with the asymmetrical hairstyle. He laughed, and the others joined in.

'What am I, the phone book?' But he said it in a friendly way, and in any case, the phone book reference was so quaint and curiously old-fashioned, like the haircut, that I realised we must be about the same age. I was quite sure that they were East Berliners, certainly the one I was talking to, with his broad accent. I wanted to reach out to them somehow, to express this feeling that we were from the same batch, that we'd all read about Soldier Heinz at school, and added up tanks on one page and apples on another, and maybe even all had that one teacher who was a bit different and asked us to do things like close our eyes and paint while she played a piece of music.

The one with the haircut, I was sure of it, would have had a horrible time at school. Our country had been no country for people with funny hair.

Because I did not know how to say these things, and because

I had an appointment with Dr Licht, I just thanked them for their time, gave them some beer money and walked away feeling vaguely regretful.

—

I had to walk all the way back to the receptionist, listen more carefully this time and cross the two courtyards again. It ended up taking me ten, fifteen minutes, which made me anxious because lateness was never a good thing here, and when I finally arrived at Licht's office, his office door was open. I took this as a silent form of reproach and, instead of taking a seat in the waiting area, went right in.

'Frau Valentin?' A large man with a beard and round glasses stood up behind his desk and came towards me. 'How good to see you. I'd offer you a coffee but the machine is broken.'

I was about to close the door behind me, but he reached past me and gently steadied it so it remained slightly ajar.

'You've seen your mother's file?' he asked. 'Britta told me you came to the reading room.'

'Only what's left of it. She said it might take – well, it might take forever to find it.'

'Oh, she was being too cautious there. I've taken a look at one of the old inventories and I think we should be able to locate it within a reasonable amount of time. It was in a part of the building that wasn't too aggressively ransacked, and while I obviously can't give any guarantees, I'd say your chances are pretty good.'

'Can we look at it now?' I asked, and only then remembered Aaron. What if he'd already found the shreds?

'I'm afraid that would be against our protocol,' said Licht.

I was beginning to understand the frustration my mother must have felt during her search. It was all very nice and clean in here, all these orderly files and long white shelves, all these brisk researchers walking up and down the corridor in their corduroys and cardigans; the visitors politely waiting their turn to enter the reading room. How well behaved we all were; but one mistake, one carelessly redacted file, and we'd all be at each other's throats.

'I'm not really interested in the file as such,' I continued. 'I just need to see if there's anything about my brother. I don't know if my mother mentioned him...'

He nodded. 'That's why she came here. It's terrible what happened to your family, it's absolutely terrible.'

Then why won't you help us? I wanted to ask, and my face must have shown my impatience. Licht turned up his palms in a gesture of helplessness.

'We talked for a long time, your mother and I. We even ended up going for lunch together, which is not what I usually do, but we came from a similar sort of background, I suppose. She was very frank with me, strikingly frank.' He took off his glasses and rubbed his eyes. 'I'm not sure how to explain this, Frau Valentin. When you work in a place like this, you have to be very disciplined with yourself. You can't allow yourself to speculate, if you know what I'm saying, because otherwise you'd quickly lose your hold on reality. But that's what your mother wanted me to do, she wanted me to help her look into all sorts of speculative scenarios, and that was… that was difficult for me.'

'What sort of scenarios?'

'Oh, she had the same concerns as everyone else who comes here – not just about your brother, but the more usual fare, as it were. Whether someone had betrayed her to the Stasi, and if so, who, and when, and why. Apparently, her interrogator brought up certain details about the trip, about her life – details she hadn't told him. She said your flat must have been bugged.'

'Why?' I tried to smile. 'To find out the latest news on Cubism?'

'Well, there would have been an incident of some sort, a report by someone perhaps, or an observation of some suspicious activity, and that would have triggered an official surveillance operation.'

'Did she suspect anyone in particular?'

He shook his head. 'It was sort of the other way round. She kept asking me what *I* had seen in our records, or what remained of them. Had there been any names, any codenames, any reports, any agreements to co-operate… She was very insistent.'

'You could check, couldn't you?' I asked. 'Even if the file was destroyed, you could check if there are any Stasi wires behind the walls of our old flat.'

He laughed, then quickly turned serious when he saw my face. 'You're right, in all probability the wires are still there, behind some new wallpaper perhaps. That is, if there were any wires in the first place. But we're an archive, we don't walk into people's flats and start chiselling off plasterwork.'

Plasterwork. They would have installed the wires while we were out. In the morning, when our neighbours were at work and the students still asleep. Behind the skirting board, possibly: that would have been easy enough, take it off and screw it back on. Inside the curtain rails. Behind the wallpaper, somehow. A few discreet holes drilled into the wall.

'I found some white dust under my bed once,' I said slowly. 'Before we went to Hungary, I happened to crawl under my bed one day and I saw someone had done something to the wall there, scratched it or something like that.'

Now it was his turn to look doubtful. 'It *could* have been from someone installing a surveillance system, yes, that's a theoretical possibility. They were very careful though, they always made sure no one was in, and they cleaned up after themselves.'

'It *could* have been them, though.'

'Frau Valentin...'

'Yes, yes, I know, there's no use speculating.' Again I felt my frustration take over. 'If you were in my situation, you'd understand.'

'I have been in your situation,' he said softly, looking at his hands. 'And I do understand.'

'Oh.' I sat back. 'I'm sorry.'

'I was in the shower, the door rang, and there they were. And I'll never know who told them. No one's ever found a trace of my file, and believe me, we've looked. One of our older staff members said it was part of a batch that was shipped off and burnt. See, you're in a better situation than many of us. Eventually, you'll get your answers. Whereas in my case...' He raised his hands. 'That's it.'

How ignorant I was. Meeting Katia should have prepared me; I should have known that the world I was entering was full of people like us. All these years I had avoided going back to Berlin, thinking our stigma would be all the more obvious here, when actually the opposite was the case. I felt far less of a freak here than in London. Give me another week, I thought, and I'll be surprised if someone *isn't* a former prisoner.

I stood up and thanked Licht for his time. He accompanied me out into the corridor.

'Your mother and I had quite a few things in common.' He looked back through the open office door. 'I don't feel all that comfortable in closed rooms, you see, so I always keep my door open. She appreciated that.'

⁓

On my way out, I stopped to text Tobi.

Met archive director. Might be able to help us. Talk later. x

I wasn't sure how much to tell him. Tobi was always so protective. If I mentioned Licht's comments about the bugging and all that, he would only start worrying. The big courtyard was empty now, the last tourists had moved on. I shivered, drew my jacket around me and walked towards the main road.

'Ella?' A hand tapped my shoulder. Startled, I turned around.

'Aaron!' I was surprised by how happy I was to see him, to find a familiar face and voice here, a steady force amid the chaos.

'Do you mind if we go somewhere else?' He looked much more nervous than the last time we had talked.

'Sure.'

'Would Mitte be OK? I don't trust any of the places in this neighbourhood.'

'Right. Of course. The entire neighbourhood...' I made a cutting gesture with my hand. 'Totally contaminated. Toxic, Stasified for good.'

He laughed. 'OK, maybe it's not quite like that, but I live in Mitte and know a *Kneipe* there that's always empty. Sorry if I sound paranoid.'

'Nothing wrong with being paranoid – it reminds me of home.'

He smiled. 'Mitte, then?'

'Whatever you say.' I was tired of making decisions.

'And then I can give you your file.'

I jumped. 'You have it?'

'Can we go, please? My boss could show up here any minute.'

'You took it from the archive?'

'I made a photocopy.' He was walking very fast, and I did my best to keep up. 'I didn't mean to steal it or anything, I just started making copies because I wanted to work on it from home.'

'That's very noble of you.'

'I hope you don't mind.'

'Not at all.'

I did mind, a bit. It would have been nice if he'd asked me.

Still, he was risking his job for this, and I didn't want to seem ungrateful.

He glanced at me. 'How was it with Licht?'

'More helpful than I'd expected. Maybe because he'd been in prison as well.'

'Licht was in prison?' Aaron stopped. 'How do you know all these things?'

'I keep my ears open, don't I?' I tapped my ear, my open ear.

Aaron hesitated. 'I just wanted to say, I'm really sorry about what happened to your dad.'

'Oh.' I was a little taken aback. 'So you know everything that happened? It's all in the file?'

'Not everything,' he said. 'You'll see.'

—

We did not talk on the train to Mitte. I could not help looking at Aaron's bag, a cracked leather satchel that could have done with a bit of love. That cardboard edge peeking out, was that the file? What if someone stole the bag now? Aaron seemed to sense my nervousness. He put the bag on his lap and closed his arms around it, almost with a kind of tenderness.

In Mitte he took me to a dark, old-fashioned, wood-panelled boozer that had resisted the tide of hipster bars. The men at the bar looked like they had been there since Honecker kissed Brezhnev. Grey moustaches, beer bellies, shot glasses next to their beers. The place reminded me of Sven somehow, poor Sven who had not lived long enough to enjoy life in the West.

I could see him here, with his beer and his fag, getting into arguments about art and politics.

We ordered two beers and carried them to a table in a quiet corner. Aaron glanced over his shoulder again. He was dressed in jeans and a hoodie and looked rather like a hacker, partly because of the combination of sportswear and glasses, partly because of his secretive tics.

'If you keep doing that, people will think you have something to hide,' I said.

'I can't help it, it's become a habit.'

'Because of your work?'

'Possibly.' A smile, an apologetic shrug. 'It does make you feel a bit watched. I guess it's like reading about lice and starting to feel itchy.'

'Thank you for doing this.' I smiled. 'How come you're interning at that archive, anyway?'

'I thought it would be fun to spend a summer in Berlin.' He grimaced. 'Did that sound flippant? It's obviously a great privilege...'

'Summer in Berlin sounds great. Better than having a Stasi fetish.'

'That actually exists, you know.'

'What, Stasi fetishists? Two people call each other and a third listens in?'

'No, seriously, we get tons of requests from people who want to have a party in Mielke's office.'

He placed his satchel on the chair between us. We both stared at it for a moment.

'I hope I'm not getting you into trouble,' I said, and knew it was a bit late for that. We were very contagious, we Valentins; we came up with half-baked plans and dragged the rest of the world into them. I should not have asked him for help at all, really, and yet I also knew that I would do it again, of course I would.

'It's fine.' He shifted a little in his chair. 'This does have to stay between us though, OK?'

'Of course.'

'Great. So...' He pulled three thick cardboard folders out of his bag, each wrapped with a thick yellow rubber band. 'This is it. Some pages are still missing, but this is most of it. I made a note where I wasn't exactly sure if I'd put them together in the right order.'

'You actually glued all of these pages together yourself?'

'It gets faster over time, once you're familiar with the material. And the pieces were pretty big.'

'Still – I didn't realise – I thought, you know, you'd just found the file.'

'I told you, that's why I had to take them home, to work on them.'

'I just thought...' I'd thought nothing at all. I'd spent not a single thought on how exactly Aaron was going to retrieve the file, what he would do with the pieces, which rules he might be breaking. I felt ashamed of my selfishness, my mad focus.

'It's incredibly kind of you to do this,' was the best I could offer.

'I did have my doubts. But, I don't know, I felt that if I didn't help you…' He cleared his throat. 'I felt it would be one of those things I'd regret all my life.'

I did not know what to say, and so said nothing. It moved me that this stranger had spent his time puzzling together our story.

'Look.' Another glance over his shoulder, then he opened the top folder. 'I've made it as accessible as possible. The interrogations are under the blue tabs, red is for the prison records, and the surveillance reports are under…' He looked up. 'This isn't too weird for you?'

'No, it's fine.'

And it was. Talking to Katia and Licht had felt like a mutual confession, intimate and slightly shameful, but this was completely different, easier somehow and almost weightless, detached from any emotional anchors.

It must be because we're talking in English, I thought. The words 'interrogation', 'prison' and 'surveillance' were just tabs in a folder; they referred to objects and experiences without actually evoking them. They had no power over me, they were lifeless. Whereas the German equivalents, especially the terms that would have been used in East Germany – *Vernehmung*, *Haft*, *Überwachung* – grabbed me by the throat. I heard them, or even thought them, and was in a damp cellar, barbed wire hanging over my head, an unseen thing crouching in the corner. Darkness, rustling leaves, the sound of my own breath, and then a sudden light.

I turned the pages. 'And the green section?'

'That's about your brother.'

I looked up. 'So you know what happened to him.'

'It only says that he was adopted.'

'What? Where?' I frantically flicked through the dense transcripts until I saw the photo.

Heiko Valentin.

Our Heiko, our baby. Registered, photographed, catalogued. Our pouty, chubby-cheeked darling. For years, for decades we had searched for him, and here he was. That little face, alone on a cold piece of paper. Big eyes, such big, big eyes.

Oh, I could not look at it, I could not look at the photo at all. I pushed it away and the whole folder would have fallen off the table had Aaron not caught it. I wanted to scream. Heiko lying in a cold bed in some children's home, face red with tears, 'Mama! Papa! Mama! Papa!' No, it was too much. It broke me, it was physically unbearable, just like it had been all those years ago. It had been unbearable back then, and I had found a solution to make it bearable, but here – that photo!

Heikolein, Liebling, kleiner Süßer, Bärchen. Mein frecher Affe, mein kleiner Schatz.

They had taken him away, and we had let them. We had let them! That was the truth of it, we had let them, we had let them, we had let them. Our fat little boy, throwing porridge at the wall. Smearing carrot mush into my hair. Running towards me when I walked into the room, arms outstretched, face shining:

Eyya! Eyya!

Say Ella.

Eyya.

I started to cry. My body gave way, I slumped against Aaron. Sobbing, I told him about our return from Hungary. *And Heiko? Where is Heiko?* The empty cot, his little spoons in the kitchen drawer, a pair of socks still drying on the radiator. He had always lost his socks. His little brown Heiko-socks.

'But you know all that.' I took a deep breath. 'You read it all in the file.'

'No, I didn't know that.' Aaron gently rubbed my back. 'The file just says he was adopted. It doesn't say anything about... spoons. And socks.'

'Sorry, of course not. I mean, they're not important.' I blew my nose.

'On the contrary, socks are really important,' he said, and I thought how strange and lovely it was that he understood.

THERE WAS A BIG party at the residence, with people dancing in the kitchen and stumbling in and out of the studios. I slipped into my room and spread the folders out on my desk.

I felt calmer now, more in control. Aaron and I had agreed that I would read everything at my own pace, then call him if I had any questions. The trick was to distance myself from the transcripts and reports, to read them as if they concerned another family, otherwise I would never get through it all. And I had to get through it, because I had to find Heiko. It was that simple. No more of this: *oh, but what if he doesn't want to be found, oh, but privacy, oh, but the passage of time.* Fuck the passage of time. That photo! He was our boy, our little boy. It did not matter how old he was now. It did not matter if he was a drug dealer now or a skinhead, a happy family man or an equally happy brainwashed Stasi apologist – inside he would always be our little boy, that little boy in the picture. That had happened. That little boy had been kidnapped. And it was no use crumpling in my chair or refusing to look at the file or weeping over my loss. I was his older sister. I had to bring him back.

My phone beeped. Three missed calls from Tobi, and a message:

You there???

I started composing a reply, but it was too difficult. I did not want to tell Tobi about the file until I knew what was in it. The phone rang again, and I stuffed it under my pillow.

—

My grandmother's favourite writer, Christa Wolf, described in her final book how she consulted her Stasi files after the fall of the wall. She had been a literary star in East Germany; the archivist carted out more than forty-two big folders on her, plus phone transcripts, all stored in a large green wooden box that Wolf came to call the 'seaman's crate'. Day after day a friendly assistant fished the files from the seaman's crate and laid them out for Wolf, who immersed herself in them and learned exactly which of her editors, mentors and friends had betrayed her over the decades. She thought what a relief it would be to make a big bonfire and burn all this paper. Reading her file destroyed the past and poisoned the present. It was the Stasi's language that did this. It distorted reality as she remembered it and covered it in dirt until she herself felt dirtied. Then came the last day in the Stasi archive. She had worked her way through it all, she had discovered the names of the traitors and forced herself to forget them again. It was finally over. The friendly assistant hesitated a little and said without looking at Wolf:

'There is something else.'

'What?'

'There's your perpetrator's file.'

The assistant fetched a separate file of reports for the Stasi and said quietly: 'That's your handwriting, isn't it?'

And it *was* her handwriting. It was Christa Wolf who had written these reports about her colleagues for the Stasi many decades previously. She had been spied on, and she had spied on others.

'I had completely forgotten about that,' she said. The assistant replied: 'We hear that a lot here.'

I believed Christa Wolf. I believed that she had forgotten her brief affair with the Stasi as a young woman, because a human life is very long and many memories vanish along the way, especially the more inconvenient ones.

What had my mother really hoped to find in the archive? A trace of my brother? Information about the traitor? Or the opposite: reassurance that no evidence remained at all, that no one could ever accuse her of anything, that the past would remain forever silent? My mother had been a victim, of course she had been a victim. But there had to be a reason why she had not told us about the file. She had felt ambivalent about it, maybe even frightened. Perhaps her own conscience had not been free of guilt.

Ah, this was what Licht had warned me about, the danger of speculating. But it was impossible not to speculate.

—

I forced myself to look at the photos. My own scowling face, poor scared Tobi, Heiko with his big, startled eyes. He was looking right at me. There was a scribbled name in the margins: Peter Bauer, or Peer Bauer, or Petra Baner. The name of some official, probably, but I looked up all the versions online just in case.

Millions of results popped up, images of men and women that looked not even remotely familiar. Not surprising; no one would scribble a boy's adoptive name in the margin of a form, especially not an East German official. There would have been a procedure, a certificate, a separate piece of paper marking the passage from Heiko Valentin to – to whoever he was now. How had we Germans ever survived without paper? I pictured the first medieval scribe sitting in a damp castle in Nuremberg and clutching a sheet of woven hemp: *On this flat and surprisingly sturdy piece of material we will write down everything – music, religion, philosophy, poetry, as well as the names of all the people we have tortured and burnt at the stake, and future generations will read it and admire us.*

A tiredness came over me. I had spoken more about my family in the past twenty-four hours than in the previous twenty-four years, and yet I was as confused as ever. I put Heiko's form to one side and looked at the section with the transcripts.

The layout was like that of a play for two actors. Reading the lines, I soon recognised my mother's voice: stubborn and defiant at first, later pleading and frightened. The second voice, the interrogator's voice, changed from page to page. It was friendly, it was threatening, it was brutal, it was reassuring, it was relentless, it was full of empathy, it was so cold as to be almost inhuman. *Question. Answer. Question. Answer. Question. Question. Question.*

When we are done, there will be no part of your mind we won't know. We will be completely at home in your mind, we will be there always.

I tried to picture my mother's interrogator. Was he one person, or many? Did he, or they, have a name? I turned to her notebook and scanned the long rambling lists for a description, a clue to an identity. I found a scribbled aside:

In some way I looked forward to my interrogations. I had been in solitary for so long, and at least he was another human being.

And, a few pages later:

Years ago I was in the supermarket with Ellachen and saw a man who looked like my interrogator. I turned around and walked out and only when I reached the corner of the street did I realise that Ellachen was still in the shop. I had just left her there.

I remembered the incident, remembered running from aisle to aisle and asking strangers if they had seen my mother, remembered the manager's office, the kindness on the manager's face when she leaned close to the microphone and asked the mother of little Ella to come to the office next to till number five, please.

I remembered waiting and getting more and more anxious and then seeing Mama in the door, pale-faced, sweaty, tearful.

What I don't remember is a man who looked like an East German interrogator. What did East German interrogators look like, anyway?

Page by page I went through the entire file. My progress was slow, my German clearly worse than I had thought. I opened one online dictionary, then another. I looked up abbreviations, bureaucratic jargon, jailhouse euphemisms. Towards the back of the file I found a photocopy of a heavily damaged document. The page was criss-crossed by thin black lines where it had been taped together. It was a list of dates and names: guards on night duty, guards on day duty, guards who escorted the prisoner to her interrogation, guards who escorted her back to her cell. And then:

```
17.9.1987 Interrogation conducted by: Hptm.
Kuboweit
```

Hptm. I racked my brain, frustrated again by the limits of my German. One of the dictionaries helped me out. *Hptm.* stood for *Hauptmann*, a military rank, about the same as captain.

I found Hauptmann Kuboweit on four or five other pages. He had meticulously signed off each transcript after correcting it. Small errors were circled or struck out. Each change was carefully initialled. It was risky to construct a phantom image from a voice on a page and a few handwritten lines, but I could not help it. I pictured him as a small, pedantic, ferret-like man; quick, sharp and sarcastic; smelling of aftershave, of Privileg. Perhaps he had even been charming, at times.

In some way I looked forward to my interrogations.

I typed 'Stasi Kuboweit' into a search engine, expecting nothing much, but found a few forums for former GDR prisoners that mentioned him. His name was on photocopied lists of Stasi employees that had been distributed illegally by protesters in the years after reunification, and later scanned and uploaded. People had apparently stolen these lists from archives and handed them out on public squares, in universities, at factory gates, like flyers for a concert. It made me uneasy, this form of virtual mob justice, yet here I was, benefiting from it. What surprised me more was how active these forums still were. It was not just former prisoners who commented; former Stasi officers weighed in as well.

Görlitz62: Stasi pigs: we're coming for you.
FähnrichP: CRY BABIES. When will you ever get over it?!!

An entire thread was devoted to Kuboweit, chronicling his seesawing career. He'd quickly found a new job after reunification, first as a private security consultant, then in real estate. Now he ran an executive coaching service.

The people in that thread who'd met Kuboweit, who'd been his prisoners, did not say much about what he'd actually been like, or what he'd done. In fact, not a single person in the thread talked about their own experience in any detail. And this made it all feel so genuine to me, because I could see my mother at her computer, carefully considering each sentence before she typed it, keen to avoid giving too much away, or indeed giving anything away. It was all about Kuboweit, his whereabouts over the past few decades, his estimated pension, and how outrageous it was that he was walking about, a free man.

At the bottom of one of the threads, someone had posted a link to Kuboweit's new coaching business. I clicked, and a bland, plain website came up, with some text about strength and strategy, and a contact form. Not even a photo; I wondered if the business was just a front. I went back to the thread, to the post with the link, which also included an address.

Mob justice was wrong. Outing people online was wrong. Spying on spies was wrong. I knew this was not the right way of going about things, but I wrote down the address anyway, and wondered what I would ask Hauptmann Kuboweit, and how he might respond.

—

I returned to the transcripts. In the reading room I had struggled to picture the scene of the interrogation, but after my visit to Hohenschönhausen, the images came easily. A small room, no windows except for a few glass bricks. My mother on one of the two chairs, handcuffed, drugged by tiredness. A metal filing cabinet in the corner, an empty desk, another chair. He was standing by the desk, looming over her. Every now and then she tilted to one side, and a guard appeared from behind and straightened her up.

I read page after page. First slowly, carefully, and then I began to flick through them, skipping ahead, thinking that I could always go back to this and that bit. I needed to know now, right now, what this file could tell me about Heiko, because that was what mattered most.

It was long past midnight by the time I'd looked through everything. In any case, sleep would be impossible. I picked up my phone.

Just finished, I texted Aaron. He replied almost immediately.
The whole file?
Yes.
That was fast. You OK?
I could do with a drink.
Sure. Same place?
God no. Prenzl Berg? Pub at the top of Lychener Str.? "Rosalind".
I added a second text: *I don't know why it's called Rosalind.*
He replied: *I'm on my way.*

I flicked back to one of the transcripts and very carefully took it out of the folder. Then I pinned Heiko's photo to it. I thought, if I ever waver during this search, if I ever think it's taking too long, or taking over my life, or just not worth it, I will come back to this transcript, I will read it again, and I will keep going.

Transcript of the Interrogation of the Accused
Dr VALENTIN, Regine
born 6.1.1947 in Berlin
2/3

ANSWER: There is no reason to put my children in a home!
My mother promised to take care of them.
QUESTION: Your mother knew about your plan?
ANSWER: No, no, we only agreed that she would take them
if anything happened to us. I'm very tired, I don't think I
can continue answering these questions.
QUESTION: She was going to take them if you were arrested,
you mean?

ANSWER: She was going to take care of them if we ever had an accident or if we fell sick. Those are normal arrangements that all families make, no? I don't know, I'm so tired, I'm finding it very hard to concentrate.

QUESTION: Your attempted escape from the Republic, was that part of your normal family arrangements, too?

ANSWER: I've told you, my mother knew nothing of our plans. If she had known, she would have tried to prevent us from leaving. My mother is completely loyal to this country and the party, but I don't need to tell you that, you know that already. Do we need to go through this again? I'm so tired.

QUESTION: And you, you're not loyal to this country?

ANSWER: Of course I'm loyal to this country, I just don't like what it's been turned into.

STATEMENT: That's agitation against the state.

ANSWER: I apologise. I'm tired, I don't know what I'm saying.

STATEMENT: We've spoken to your mother. She has long been ashamed of your hostile attitude towards the state and said you often neglected your children to attend illegal gatherings in your neighbourhood. Her exact words were, and I quote, 'What can I say, she made her bed and will now have to lie in it. I cannot take the children and I believe they are better off in a children's home where they will receive a solid Socialist upbringing.'

ANSWER: I don't believe those are my mother's words.

QUESTION: Are you accusing us of fabricating your mother's statement?

ANSWER: I'm sorry, of course not, it's just that it doesn't sound like her, surely you understand that to me at least, it doesn't sound like... I don't know. Yes, maybe she said that, I don't know. If you say so. It must be right. Yes? Is that a good answer? I'm very tired. Please, I can't think straight. I'm really very tired.

QUESTION: Who gave you the sedative you administered to your children?

ANSWER: I've already told you, I made it myself, I grew valerian in my window box and then I made a tea with it and gave it to them. No one helped me.

QUESTION: A few more sips and you would be sitting here as a child murderer.

ANSWER: It was only a homemade tea, I don't think it was that strong.

STATEMENT: If we charge you with attempted murder, you will never see the sun again. You will spend the rest of your life in prison. And believe me, child murderers don't have it easy in prison. Why don't you co-operate? You could be out of here in no time at all, you could be back with your children. Don't you care about them? Ella, Tobias and Heiko. Heiko is only two, isn't he? I hear that he has stopped eating, surely that cannot be what you want.

INTERJECTION: He has stopped eating?

STATEMENT: His carers have no choice but to force-feed him.

INTERJECTION: Why carers? Why isn't he with my mother? You can't force-feed my little boy, please don't, he will eat if you're patient with him, please be gentle with him.

STATEMENT: You can be back with your little boy by tomorrow if you co-operate. All you have to do is tell us whose idea it was, who else knew and who helped you. We can see that you want to tell us. You want to unburden yourself, yes, that's what you want, isn't it? To let it all go, to let go of all that weight, and then go back to your bed and sleep. Come now, let's start at the beginning.

Berlin 1987: Autumn

H OW CAN I DESCRIBE our return home, to Oma, to our
little flat with the bathtub in the kitchen? For the first few
days I was down with a raging flu, sweating through pyjamas
and bed sheets, shivering until my bones rattled, groaning
from the deep ache in my arms and legs. Tobi fell ill too, so
ill that Oma called a doctor. He recommended cold-soaked
linen wraps around the legs and a hot potato wrap around
the throat.

I lay in bed and thought of Heiko. Where was he? Was he
with Mama and Papa? And where were they? Maybe they'd
been taken away to prison. And Heiko, to a prison for children. Maybe he was lying on a bed all by himself. Clutching
his pillow and whispering, '*Auto.*' The thought was unbearable. The thought of Heiko being alone was unbearable. He
had never been away from us, not a single night. All he knew
was our home, and Oma's flat, and his nursery. He would be
terrified among strangers. And because it was unbearable,
I told myself that it could not be. It could simply not be. He
had to be with Mama, at least. Papa was in hospital, slowly
getting better. Heiko was with Mama. He missed us, he was
confused, he wanted to go home, but at least he was with

Mama. She held him tight, and let him wipe his nose on her shoulder.

Opa dismantled the empty cot and stored it away.

At night, in the darkness, no little boy sang garbled songs to himself. No little voice said 'Auto', 'Bussss', 'wheel', as if to remind himself of everything that was beautiful in the world.

Sometimes I felt an icy little hand on my face or my arm, tugging me out of my sleep. It was Tobi, asking to come into my bed so that when the burglars came, they would find his own bed empty.

—

The flat felt like a waiting room. No one tore about, shrieking and yelling. We waited and waited for someone to call us in and tell us that a mistake had been made, and here was our family, and everything would go back to how it used to be.

Oma made pancakes and milk rice, heart-shaped waffles topped with icing sugar and cream, meatballs with onion gravy, golden fried schnitzels, potato salad dripping with mayonnaise and chives, goulash stew with dumplings, sweet baked apples in pools of vanilla sauce.

'Eat, Tobi! Ellachen, eat!'

'I'm not hungry,' I said.

Tobi pushed away his plate. 'Where is Mama?'

One morning I asked Oma how much longer Papa would be in hospital. She flinched.

'Is he getting better?' I asked. 'Can we go and visit?'

'No,' she said slowly, 'no, we cannot go and visit.'

She took a loaf from the bread tin, cut off two slices and spread them with margarine.

'Ellachen.' She waved one of the slices in front of my face. 'Ellachen, please, you have to eat.'

'When is Papa coming back?'

'I don't know.'

'And Mama?'

'I don't know. Don't you like bread any more? Would you like some cheese instead?'

'And Heiko? Where is Heiko?'

'Heiko is being looked after.'

'Where? Who's looking after him?'

'Don't ask me these questions, Ellachen. I can't answer them. I know less than you do, I wasn't even there.' She avoided looking at me, picked up a rag and began to wipe down the kitchen surfaces. 'What's your mother going to say if she hears that you're refusing to eat?'

'Where is she?'

'Ella, I said I don't know. I don't know for sure. But I think the police are asking her questions about what happened, that's what I think.'

It was the most honest conversation I would have with Oma during that time. Later someone must have spoken to her and convinced her to adopt a different script, because in the weeks that followed she told me that Heiko was being looked after by friends of my parents who lived in the countryside, too far away to visit. It was no use phoning, either, because he was too small to understand and would only be upset at hearing my voice. My mother, she said, was in a place where she would have some time to think about her actions. No, she could not come to see us, not for a while.

'You mean she's in prison?' I asked.

'Shush!'

But a few days later, she said I could write my mother a letter, it would cheer her up.

'So she *is* in prison?'

'I didn't say that.'

'What do people eat in prison?' I asked. 'Nothing but bread and water?'

'It's not really a prison, at least not compared to the prisons in my day,' she said. 'If anyone asks, tell them your parents are away for work.'

Another time she said: 'Not another word about this. You're putting us all in danger. Is that what you want?'

It took me a week to write the letter, and when I gave it to Oma she put her arms around me and kissed my hair.

'We can't post all that, my darling.'

'Why not?'

'That's not a letter, that's a book.'

'Please, please send it to Mama.'

I had drawn everything for her – our street, our building, our flat. I had tried so hard to get every detail right – the chicken in the oven, Heiko in his cot, his socks on the radiator, the picture of the blue horses on the wall. My father standing in the kitchen with the wooden spoon in his hand.

Mama would stick it on the walls of her cell, and it would be as if she was here with us.

'Ellachen, you have to be very brave now.' Oma squeezed me tight. 'Papa isn't in hospital.'

'Where is he?'

'He's dead, child.'

'But where is he?'

'He's in a cemetery.'

'But where *is* he?'

That was all I could think about for a long, long time. Where was my father? If he wasn't here, and he wasn't in hospital, then where *was* he?

Oma took me to a cemetery and showed me a stone with my father's name on it, but even then I didn't believe her.

Papa has slipped through the barbed wire, I thought; he's over on the other side, and soon he'll write to us and ask us to join him.

⌐

'Oma, can we go and visit Mama?'

'We can't, my love, but she'll be back very soon.'

'How soon is very soon?'

'I don't know.'

'Is it next month?'

Next month seemed unbearably far. I had only said it as a provocation, to make her say: *Of course not as late as that!*

But she looked at me sadly and shook her head and said no, certainly not next month.

There is one memory that stands out from that time. We were reading a story at school, a modern retelling of the tale of the fisherman who catches a fish that begs him to save its life. In return, the fisherman is granted a wish. The fisherman's wife forces him to go back to the fish with more and more wishes, for a bigger house, nice clothes, and so on, until the fish in a burst of anger at their greed takes it all away, and they're as poor as before. I remember getting more and more heated as we discussed the story. The teacher encouraged us to take sides with the generous fish and blame the materialistic, unreasonable wife for not understanding when enough was enough.

Right there, I had a strong feeling that I had nothing to lose. I said the fisherman was not to blame, the wife was not to blame. No, the fish was to blame for taking it all away. The wife had only done what anyone would do: reach up, want more, ask for more. How nasty to argue that this woman had asked for too much, that she had brought her misfortune on herself.

The room was silent after I finished. You could hear the mucous breathing of the boy in the very last row, who always had a cold.

'That's a curious interpretation,' our teacher said finally, 'because if you think about it, in real life, asking for too much does get you into trouble. Whereas the happiest people are the ones who are grateful for what they have.'

On my way out, a boy sidled up to me and said: 'You know what they're saying about you behind your back?'

'No,' I snapped, feeling clever. 'I can't know if it's behind my back, can I?'

'They're saying that if your grandmother hadn't struck a deal high up, you'd all be in a children's home now, all of you, not just your brother.'

I slapped him hard on the cheek. He looked at me with stunned surprise. His hand flitted to the reddening skin. Then he turned on his heel and ran away.

Walking home, I tried not to feel too bothered by it. Who was this boy anyway? His family came from the middle of nowhere, some godforsaken place near the Polish border. We called that part of the country the Valley of the Clueless, because they couldn't get West German TV there, not even with an antenna the size of a tree.

—

I was very lonely during that time. My friends at school avoided me. The worst was Sandy, my best friend. From her I had expected unquestioning solidarity. She never cared what others thought, after all. But Sandy did not want me any more when I came back from Hungary. She had moved to sit with another girl, and the chair next to mine stayed empty. In the breaks I could not find her. After school I watched her disappear down the street in a gaggle of girls. Pigtails, braids, bowl cuts, bobs. Heads tucked close together, whispered secrets passed from ear to ear. They played hopscotch in the breaks, and that jumping game with a giant rubber band. Their hands tied together in cat's cradles, their ankles joined in three-legged races. I sat alone on a concrete bench by the rubbish bins and ate my sandwich. The janitor walked past and picked up discarded salami slices and chocolate wrappers with long metal tongs. I watched small birds dive in and out of the bins. I tried to look immersed in their fluttering business. I had better things to do than to play hopscotch.

Even Frau Obst, my beloved art teacher, sided with the rest. She had always praised my talent, and given me little extra tasks, which was usually frowned upon at school, because we were all equal. Now she avoided talking to me, and when I asked her one day if I could borrow some watercolours to paint on my own after school, she simply did not reply. It was as if I did not exist.

The neighbours in the *Vorderhaus* avoided us, too. Whenever I spotted *die Minsky* in her open doorway, leaning on her mop and yawning with boredom, she stepped back and closed the door. Frau Pietsch still occasionally gave us chalky slabs of Süßtafel chocolate but she no longer asked Oma to come along to party meetings. Our only true friend in the building was old Frau Rachmann. Sometimes we went to see her in her musty flat where a nurse or helper fed her cold cabbage soup because she could not be trusted to say when it was too hot. When we passed her in the hallway she smiled and stretched out her thin hand. The skin was loose and dry. She stretched out her hand whenever someone passed – it was no sign of special affection, but I was still glad that she did not turn her back on us.

Oma moved up to the fifth floor so that we would not have to give up the flat. Opa Horst stayed behind on the ground floor. Oma slept in my parents' bed, and I could see it made her uncomfortable, but there was no other way. One day I came home from school to see that she had sorted my parents' clothes into big boxes. Some of my mother's dresses were still on the hangers. Oma was sitting on the bed, clutching my mother's black party dress, the one she had worn to the exhibition where she had met the painter. It was the first time I saw my grandmother cry.

I N THE WORLD OUTSIDE, two years passed. In our flat, time took on a different shape. Sometimes it seemed to move backwards. I would wake up in the morning feeling happy, convinced that Papa and Mama were sitting in the kitchen and drinking coffee.

At other times, I could almost see them from the corner of my eye. When I was pouring a glass of water from the kitchen tap, I could feel Papa behind me, sitting at the table with an open book in front of him. He was propping up his forehead with his forefinger and thumb. With a pencil he made light, quick marks in his notebook, with such a gentle touch, as if he was afraid of hurting the page. Sometimes he let out a funny little hiccupping sound, a little half-laugh, out of amusement or surprise. That was how he was sitting behind me, exactly like that, but when I turned around, there was no one. It was as if he had only just vanished, had only just stood up and left.

Next to his books and manuscripts, my father kept a collection of miniature old farming tools mounted on a board: a tiny plough, a hoe, a sieve to separate the chaff. Reminders of the rural origins of some of his ancestors, Pomeranian and Silesian farmers with hands like pitchforks. My grandmother had mothballed my parents' clothes, but she had not yet touched the books and trinkets. The miniature farming tools were still there, my parents' wedding photo, my mother's marked-up manuscript, even a stack of old messages that had once been pinned to our door, with shopping lists that rhymed.

I looked after these things with the greatest care. Everything had to be in place for when my parents came back, so that they would know we had been thinking about them, and had made sure they would feel comfortable when they returned. It did not matter how many times I was told that Papa was not going to come home. I still kept his notes in order, and his books lined up just as he had left them.

Once a week I dusted the plough, the hoe, the sieve, the scythe with its delicate metal blade. When Oma remarked that we might pack up some of the books, I protested. My father had been working on a book about the Bauhaus: an entire shelf was lined up with books for that project, weighty hardcovers with pencilled notes in them, comments, cross-references, question marks. If he came back, he would need those books. And not only that: he would feel deeply hurt if he saw that we had chucked them out as if they no longer mattered.

He had pinned index cards to the wall with quotes for his book. I unpinned one by Klee and put it up over my own bed.

You can't even catch me in this world. For I dwell just as much with the dead as with the unborn. A little closer to the heart of creation than is usual. And not nearly close enough.

It sounded comforting, strong, larger than my daily worries: the concrete bench, the empty kitchen table, the times when I would sit on the edge of a playing field and wait for someone to pick me for their team. That was where I wanted to dwell, with the dead and with the unborn. Close to the heart of creation.

I tried to read my father's Bauhaus books, but they were too difficult. The only one that spoke to me was the story of Friedl Dicker-Brandeis, who taught the basic course of the Bauhaus to children in Theresienstadt ghetto. The children drew pictures of their families and the pets they had left behind, they painted open landscapes and the cramped rooms of the ghetto. And it seemed to me that if art had helped these children, who had been caught in far crueller circumstances than myself, then it would also help me. After that, I began to draw pencil sketches and paint with watercolours every evening. I had an idea that painting had somehow saved Friedl and the children, that they had painted their way out of the ghetto and into gentle water-colour landscapes and brightly crayoned homes, although the truth was of course that all of them were later deported and murdered at Auschwitz, and art had not saved them at all.

One morning I was sitting in the kitchen eating rye bread and jam. Tobi was sitting next to me, his own slice of bread untouched. He was not eating well in those days. At night he cried under his duvet, thinking I could not hear him. He got into fights with the teachers at school. Both of us were behind in every class, but while my own bad performance did not bother me much, I was worried for Tobi. He had always been popular, bright and happy, with a large group of friends. Yet in those days he was as friendless and withdrawn as myself. He lost weight, and looked pale and bloodless.

I pointed my piece of bread at the painting of the blue horses that now hung on the kitchen wall. 'Mama told me a secret about that painting,' I began. 'She said I should tell you when you were old enough to understand.'

He looked up, a rare flash of interest in his eyes.

'Look,' I continued. 'The blue horses, that's meant to be us, you, me and Heiko. It's like a code.'

And then I told him the story of the three children who lived in a flat with a bathtub, just like ours, until one day the evil sorcerer came and turned them into three blue horses. He kept them in a dungeon and fed them nothing but bread and water. All is lost, they thought, we will be here forever. But then! The clouds opened, a great thundering noise cracked the sky, and their grandmother swooped down from above like an eagle, her arms spread like wings. She fought the sorcerer and killed him; she waved her magic wand and turned the horses back into three children. And just like in the story, *we* would be freed, too. Oma would get Heiko back. All of us would be back together. It would be just like it was before, or at least almost like it was before.

'But I asked Oma,' Tobi said. 'And she said she can't bring Heiko back.'

'Then *I'll* bring him back.'

225

'Promise?'

'Promise,' I said.

—

I often looked at the painting, and each time I noticed something new. The blue horses were standing on a meadow dotted with wildflowers. To the right was a corn field, tall stalks swaying in the breeze. At the back, towards the horizon, loomed a dense forest.

It was *the* meadow, and *the* forest. It was the place where we had tried to cross.

Sven must have discovered the meadow during one of his painting trips to Hungary. A quiet area without a watch tower in sight, without a border guard. He had painted it, and months later he had gone back, crossed the meadow and climbed through the barbed wire.

Sven crossed the border here, my mother had said to me. *It's all right, it's safe.*

I wanted to tell someone about this painting, which surely showed that it had all been Sven's idea. My parents were blameless; he must have talked them into it.

'Oma,' I said, 'Oma, can't you see? That's the meadow, that's the forest, that's where the guard shot Papa.'

'Ellachen, the things you come up with!'

'But Oma, Sven must have sent Mama a map, or maybe he just sent her a secret letter and said, go to that village in Hungary, look for the meadow, it's just like in the painting…'

'No more, Ella! No more!' She put her hands over her ears.

The next day the painting was gone. In its place hung a painting of a dozen red-cheeked boys and girls harvesting golden wheat. And when I asked Oma where the painting of the blue horses was, she said she had no idea what I was talking about, there had never been such a painting.

S TRANGE THINGS HAPPENED DURING that year.

There was the winter of the pets. On a few weekends in January, our doorbell rang until the neighbours complained. Outside were clusters of men and women holding baskets full of kittens, dogs on leashes, cardboard boxes rumbling with guinea pigs and rabbits. They all told us we had answered their ads, placed shortly after Christmas to get rid of unwanted gift pets. Oma stood her ground: she had not answered any ads, nor had her husband. There must be a misunderstanding. Some of the people grew angry: they had come from afar; they demanded we at least pay for their fuel. Opa Horst turned tetchy and short-tempered. One day he shouted at the whole crowd to get lost, for goodness' sake, this was worse than Stalingrad. My solid, un-shakeable grandmother developed a slight tremor in her hands.

The pet visits stopped. Other curious events followed, sudden spells and jinxes. One day all our yellow towels were gone. A week later, they were back. The same thing happened with our duvet covers. The striped ones remained in place. The flower-patterned ones vanished, and returned a while later.

I overheard Oma and Opa talking about the strange things late at night, when they were sitting in the kitchen and thought I was asleep.

'What do you expect?' my grandfather said. 'It's one way to make sure we don't make a fuss about what happened to Jochen. They show us they can walk in and out of our lives as they please, and on top of it, it makes everyone else think we're crazy. Two birds with one stone.'

Oma sounded weak and brittle, not like herself at all: 'But why would they do something like that? I've never made a fuss, I've never wavered. I've given them my entire life. Horst, *I went to Buchenwald for them*. Why would they harass me like this?'

'To make sure.' His voice was infinitely gentle and sad. 'Just to make sure.'

I slipped out of my bed and spied on them through a crack in the door. Oma was pouring herself a schnapps.

'I'm not going to let them intimidate me.' She downed the drink, and her voice strengthened a little. 'Let me tell you, my friends in the party would be furious if they knew about this. It's just some grubby low-lifes stepping over the line. I'm going to make a complaint, Horst, I'm not going to put up with this, I'm going to have them called to order.'

'You think the party doesn't know? This is the party, Trude.'

'It can't be! You'll see, you'll see how they'll take my side.'

'They'll take away the other two, that's what they'll do. One complaint, one wrong word, one question about Regine and Jochen, and they'll take the others, you know they will.'

'They wouldn't do that.'

'Oh, but they would. They've taken one already, haven't they? And we don't even know where he is.'

And with that, my stoical grandfather turned to the window

and hid his face, and now it was my grandmother who tried to console him, with low, deep murmurs and a helpless hand on his back.

AFTER A YEAR I received my first letter from Mama. She was very well, she said. She missed us and hoped we were well, too. My mother, who for years had filled hundreds of pages with beautiful words and sentences, seemed to have run out of things to say. Her letters arrived irregularly; we would not hear from her for weeks, and then two came at once. She encouraged us to be good and work hard on our homework, to do what Oma told us, to make sure we ate well and kept ourselves healthy. She mentioned neither Heiko nor my father, but on one of the letters she drew a picture of three little blue horses.

I wrote back to her, and drew a little picture of three blue horses on my letter, too, but I was never sure if it reached her.

In summer 1989, two years after our holiday in Hungary, we received a yellow parcel. I could not imagine who it was from. Our friends in West Germany had long stopped sending presents, possibly to avoid creating even more problems for us.

Oma put the parcel on the kitchen table and said she had to tell us something.

'It's good news, really,' she said slowly. 'Well, it's good and not-so-good. The good news is that your mother is no longer in prison.'

I gripped the table to prevent myself from sliding off my seat. 'She's coming here?' I frantically thought of things we could do to make the flat more welcoming: put up paper chains, tidy our room, bake a cake. I could not help picturing both of them bursting through the door, Mama and Papa, laughing at us because we had thought Papa was never coming back.

'No.' My grandmother smoothed the table cloth. 'No. She's been bought out by the West.'

'The West *bought* her?' Tobi asked.

'Well, yes. They paid money to our government and flew her over to West Berlin.'

This was a shock. I had heard of spies being exchanged on the bridges between East and West Berlin, but I could not imagine my mother being that important.

'Is she going to spy for them?' I whispered.

'No, it's nothing like that. It's just what they do sometimes – they pay our government for prisoners that our government does not want.' And she looked at the table as she said that. It hurt me to hear my mother spoken of in such a way, as a person who was not wanted. I wanted her. Tobi wanted her. Why had no one asked us?

'And so this parcel here,' my grandmother continued, 'this parcel, I think, is from Regine.'

'But if she's over there, we'll never see her again!'

'Can she at least come and visit us?' Tobi asked anxiously.

Oma took a deep breath. 'I don't think so. I don't think they'd let her in. So that's the not-so-good news. But she – she can ask our government to let you two go and join her over there.'

Another deep breath. 'It'll take a while, but I suppose that's what'll eventually happen.'

My head was spinning. Ever since that day in Hungary, the only certainty I had had was that Tobi and I were still here, in our flat, in our neighbourhood. This was the kitchen table where my father had read his books, and where, in my imagination, he was still reading his books. Stuck to the fridge was a rhyming shopping list in my father's handwriting that no one dared remove. Sour cream was on it, chicken and potatoes: the ingredients for his extra-special Painter's Potatoes. Here was the table where my mother used to paint her face for her evenings out. There in the living room, they had received friends, put on music and knocked back shots. In the bedroom, Papa used to whistle as he ironed his shirts, and joke that he was good at ironing because he had been a bachelor for so long before he married my mother. In my drawer was a brush that smelled of my father's hair; he had used it for his beard. And anyway, what about Heiko? Was my mother asking the government to let him go, too?

'Don't think about it too much, my darling,' my grandmother said and stroked my hair. 'As I said, it'll take a while anyway. The important thing is that she's not in prison anymore. Now shall we open the parcel?'

Inside were children's clothes: a yellow T-shirt and a pair of jeans for me, and a red T-shirt and a pair of jeans for Tobi. They were fantastic clothes. The jeans in particular looked very fashionable and West German. But they were too small for me. My mother had miscalculated my size. I tried them on and could barely get the jeans over my knees. The T-shirt stretched tightly over my belly, exposing a hand-width of flesh. Tobi's clothes were too small as well. I gave him my set. His clothes, I thought, would fit Heiko.

There was a letter in the parcel. My mother wrote that she was in West Berlin. She was still finding her feet, but as soon as she had a job, she wanted to rent a flat in Wedding. Wedding was right next to Prenzlauer Berg, on the other side of the Bösebrücke. She would look for a flat on the top floor, with a window facing east, and every night she would flash a torch three times in the dark. That would be our sign. We might not see the light as such, since there was a wide strip of train tracks and no-man's-land between Prenzlauer Berg and Wedding, and anyway, we would not know which window to look at. But she would do it anyway, and hoped that we liked the idea and found it comforting.

—

From then on, I often looked out of the window at night, hoping to see three flashes of light. I knew that my mother was right, I would never be able to see them; our street wasn't close enough to the wall. But she had also been right in thinking that I would find the idea itself comforting. Three flashes in the dark, one for each of us children.

Aaron

Berlin 2010

IN THE BARE, WHITE room, on the bare, white desk, a dozen or so photocopied pages lay in a row. Taped tears and creases ran through them like scars. Aaron was done. Not that Regine Valentin's file was complete. Some pages were still missing and would probably always be missing. But he had finished piecing together what scraps were available.

This, he thought, made sense. But it left him with a rather big problem. He should never have agreed to help Ella. He felt like those people in movies who accidentally kill someone and hide the body, but the neighbour finds the body, so they have to kill the neighbour, and then the postman finds the neighbour's body and the first body, so they have to kill the postman. Twenty minutes into the movie, they are serial killers and they don't even know what happened.

Aaron got up to wander down to the secret coffee machine. He took the stairs, walked slowly, made his espresso with care. This was a tricky situation, a very tricky situation. His phone rang.

'Ella!'

'Is this a good time?'

'Yeah, no worries. I'm on my lunch break. Well, coffee break.'

'What are you working on?'

'The metal workers' meeting, still.'

'I told you, I think that's going to turn out to be really interesting. You'll be surprised. They'll be plotting an illegal strike or something.'

'Three cheers for your natural optimism.' He smiled. 'Hey, they're going to display one of my reports in an exhibition; well, not my report, the one about the offices.'

'See? Interesting!'

He could hear the attempt at cheerfulness in her voice, at normalcy. As if this was something people did, call each other to pass the time of day and chat about the surveillance state. Even after reading her mother's file she'd been like that. They'd met for drinks and he'd expected her to be in pieces, as she had been when she first saw her brother's photo, but she'd walked into the bar looking completely unshaken. He wanted to tell her that she did not have to do this, that she could put her misery on full show if she wanted to, but maybe that would be patronising. Or maybe she simply did not know how to be any other way.

'I got in touch with one of my old friends the other day, you know,' she said. 'A girl called Sandy. I had high hopes for her, really high hopes. She was one of those kids who was kind of everywhere and heard everything.'

'And?'

'And, nothing. She lives in an ashram in India. We Skyped.

She said she remembered me, of course she remembered me, but that she wasn't actually at our school for very long.'

'Was she the one who lived by the wall?'

'That's her! She was my best friend. She mattered so, so much to me. But when we spoke, the way she told it, it was like we'd maybe passed each other in the playground once. At which point I obviously started to doubt myself, so I checked. I did check. I asked her about specific things that happened, like that stupid thing we did where we stuck out our tongues – anyway, I ran it all past her, and she said, yes, it was all true, all of that had happened. And then she said something like, yes, we were really close that summer. Something like that. *Yeah, we were thick as thieves that summer.* But it all sounded so – as if that's something children do, they're thick as thieves, and then time passes, and they forget, and it's not important. But to me it was so important! It's still so important!'

'She probably just felt bad about what happened to your family.'

'That, too. You're right. I think she felt bad about it.' Ella sounded quite calm, quite matter-of-fact. 'She blanked me after we came back from Hungary, I remember that pretty well; she just ignored me. But I wouldn't still hold that against her, after so many years.'

Ah, but you would, Aaron thought. And she knows that you would. And she holds it against herself, too. He felt a bit sorry for this Sandy in her ashram, who would be sitting there right now, cross-legged probably, trying hard not to think about the summer of 1987.

'I told her that I knew she had her own stuff to deal with. Her mum went over to the West, you know. But she didn't want to go into any of that.' She paused. 'Hey, I thought she'd at least offer me a discount on her next meditation workshop. Or a free yoga mat.'

'I bet she's posting that mat right now.'

'She shouldn't feel guilty. I didn't call her for an apology, I called her because I thought she might be able to help, or even just to reconnect in some way. Oh well. She's meditated it all out of her mind. Anyway, I just wanted to check how you were, and I've ended up talking about myself again.'

'I'm fine. Nothing new here. Just matching white with white.'

'Things OK with your boss?'

'I think so. He hasn't shouted at me recently.' Aaron glanced towards the door. 'Listen, I'd better go. But let's meet up – I don't know – this weekend?'

When he hung up, he realised that he was looking forward to seeing her. He whistled to himself as he walked back to his office. There on his desk was the problematic page. He placed it on a high shelf, and tried to focus on sheet metal production targets.

'Lunch?' Bernd was standing in the doorway.

'Sure.' God, was he knackered.

'Everything OK?' Bernd in caring mode was somehow even worse than Bernd in bullying mode. Then again, he was good at his job, Aaron had to grant him that; he was a conscientious researcher and very sharp. If only there was a way of asking for his advice without the risk of detonating him again.

'I was just thinking,' Aaron started cautiously. 'Were the Stasi always right? Not in the sense of being morally right, obviously. I mean, in the sense of being factually right. Were they always factually accurate? Like, if someone read those transcripts and took them to be an actual record of things, just as an example, would that be accurate, or would it be better to doubt it? But then again, some of them seem to be verbatim transcripts and actual descriptions of events, so...'

'Excellent question.' Bernd peered at Aaron's desk, at the sheet metal reports. 'Anything specific you're wondering about?'

'Not really.' Aaron tried to look innocent. 'Just as a general thing.'

'It really depends. Spies are just people, and people are unreliable. The Stasi had a word for them...'

'*Doppelzüngler,*' Aaron said.

'Very good!' Bernd smiled. 'It's amazing how much your German has come along.'

My German is FINE, Aaron wanted to yell, *IT IS FINE,* but he needed Bernd now and so he just said: 'Thanks.'

'But then again, if you think about it, it would have been very risky to make things up. You'd have been accused of being a double agent, probably.' He moved dangerously close to the high shelf. 'So, within reason, yes, we can assume that these people here really were discussing how much sheet metal they could roll out despite the coal shortage. That probably happened.'

'OK, that's useful. Thanks.'

'It would help if you told me what this is all about.'

'It's about my eternal quest to be a better intern.' Aaron picked up his bag. 'What do you say, time for another race? My pages are really picking up speed.'

They walked down the corridor. Aaron could tell he hadn't fooled Bernd, of course not. Bernd spent his life cross-examining Stasi records; he knew when something was fishy. Still, Bernd did not question him any further, not over their lunch of spinach dumplings with cheese, not over their clandestine coffee after.

They carried their little cups and saucers up to their offices, past the reading room.

'When I started here, I thought I was going to help people. I thought I was going to do all these amazing things and everyone would be grateful,' Aaron said.

'We do help people.'

'And yet that dad never wanted to see his file in the end.'

'But we gave him the choice.'

'Maybe he guessed that his son was somehow implicated.' They were in Bernd's office now. It was always very warm in here, because of the heat the softly humming machines gave off. Suddenly Aaron thought, sod it, so what if I offend him? So what if he sends me back to the stacks? There was only so long you could tiptoe around someone.

'If I had a surveillance file, I wouldn't want it to be in an archive,' Aaron said. 'It's a private document, if you think about it. It's about one person, and maybe their family, and it's nobody else's business.'

'It's also everybody's business, unfortunately.' Bernd moved a mouse, and a black screen sprang back to life. 'But I know what you mean.'

—

The zoo was almost empty, not surprising on a weekday afternoon. It had become one of Aaron's favourite places in Berlin, despite being tinged with guilt because of the animal rights aspect. He tried to ignore the signs of distress through captivity, the weaving from leg to leg, the repetitive head-shaking and paw-gnawing, the low, hopeless moaning and grunting. Still, despite that occasional pang of fellow-feeling, it was a good place to go for some quiet time. Green and tranquil, with various oriental-looking pleasure domes that housed giraffes and elephants. Aaron especially liked watching the penguins. How human they looked, whizzing down their plastic slide and splashing into the water.

He put his hand into his pocket and felt the folded paper in there.

He knew now who had betrayed the Valentins, and he wished he didn't. That old man in the reading room, the one who read through half his file, abruptly stood up and left without even looking at the rest: Aaron finally understood him.

The penguins queued for the slide, flapping their wings with great self-importance. Aaron watched them for a while longer, then moved on to the polar bears.

Ella

The Laundry Woman

Berlin 2010

'WHAT I DON'T LIKE is the phrase "psychological torture",' said Frau Jankowitz, pouring me another coffee. 'For me, torture means pulling someone's nails out.'

I had indeed found Frau Jankowitz in the phone book. We were sitting in her living room, which was decorated with dozens of dangling succulents in macramé baskets. Photos of children and grandchildren lined the walls, of colleagues at some Socialist event, of Frau Jankowitz in uniform. She had worked at Hohenschönhausen from 1985 until 1989. In fact, she had been one of my mother's jailers. Not an interrogator like the perfumed Hauptmann Kuboweit, just the kind of person who locked and unlocked steel doors, who nudged the prisoners towards the interrogation room and dragged them back to their cells afterwards. I did not know the etiquette for this kind of meeting.

On the phone Frau Jankowitz had sounded cautious, but now, in person, in her own home, she was growing more confident. She had dressed up for this: a blue skirt, a lilac blouse, an amber necklace. Her face was carefully made up with pink lipstick and blue eye shadow. A scent of sugary violets hung in the air. She had laid the low table very carefully with blue-and-white cups, saucers, plates and a matching tall coffee pot, little tea spoons and cake forks, and a large white porcelain platter with homemade jam biscuits. They were very classic German biscuits, quite fiddly to make, with the red cherry jam shining through a heart-shaped hole in the top layer.

'Pulling someone's nails out is not the only form of torture,' I said carefully.

'However you define it, we never tortured any prisoners. The very idea is ridiculous.' She straightened the table cloth and brushed some crumbs into a palm. 'But I suppose people can say anything they like about us these days. As long as it's nasty enough, the public will believe it.'

I took my mother's notebook from my bag and opened it.

'What about this?' I turned it over so Frau Jankowitz could see the passage I had highlighted.

The guards handcuffed me to a shower and turned on the water. It was winter and the water was very cold. They left me there for many hours and afterwards they asked me again to sign the form to release my son for adoption. I refused. They took me into a stone cell in the basement and shut the door. I was still wondering how long they would leave me there when I heard a hissing sound. I looked down and saw that there were little holes in the walls just above the floor, and there was water rushing in. Slowly it filled the bottom of the cell, and then it rose.

I thought they were going to drown me. But when the water reached about knee height, or maybe it was a little lower than that, it stopped.

Later, they took me outside and again asked me to sign.

Frau Jankowitz read the passage slowly and carefully, then handed the notebook back to me.

'That would have been at another institution, not at ours. Your mother would have only been with us until she confessed, you see.' She looked satisfied, pleased to be able to correct my error.

'But I saw it for myself,' I said. 'At Hohenschönhausen, I saw a black rubber cell without any windows.'

'That was, as you say, a *rubber* cell. We sometimes used that to protect prisoners from harming themselves. What your mother describes here is something quite different, it's what was known as a *water* cell, but we didn't have any water cells at Hohenschönhausen.'

I was glad we were not in a court room; this was what it must feel like to watch a trial fall apart.

'Why did you go to the prisoners' reunion?' I asked, to change the subject.

'I wanted to be heard.' She adjusted the doily on the table. 'Yes, I wanted to be heard. Why do you think I agreed to speak to you? For the same reason, to be heard. You should see the rumours they're spreading about us these days, when it wasn't half as bad as they say. You were doing it yourself just now, jumping to conclusions about that water cell.'

'Maybe it wasn't bad for you because you weren't a prisoner.'

'And why wasn't I a prisoner? Because I respected the law! That's what no one dares to say these days, and whoever does gets slammed. Fleeing the Republic was a crime, people knew that, they knew the consequences. It's just that some people always think they're better than the rest. Listen, how much did the West pay for your mother? Probably more than my annual salary. If you think about it, she got what she wanted in the end: a ticket to the other side, first class probably.'

I refused to snap at the bait. There was no use arguing with Frau Jankowitz, it would only end with her throwing me out.

'So what happened at the reunion?'

'Well, they all got very upset with me.'

'Including my mother?'

'No, your mother treated me very politely, very respectfully.'

My mother, polite and respectful! Jankowitz was clearly making this up.

'Did she remember you?' I asked.

She avoided my eyes. 'At Hohenschönhausen, one wasn't allowed to talk to the inmates at all.'

Man durfte ja gar nicht mit den Insassen sprechen. My German had been sharpened by the past few conversations. I was beginning to catch nuances that had eluded me before, like Jankowitz's slippery shift to the neutral, objective, general and absolute. As if all this was not really about her or my mother or the prison, but about a remote and untouchable rule, the not-talking-to-prisoners rule. Had we shaped the German language to create these moral loopholes, or had they always been there? Hannah Arendt had made a similar point about Eichmann's love of stock phrases, but I knew that bringing up Eichmann would swiftly end this meeting.

'In any case one would have been too busy to chat,' Frau Jankowitz continued. 'But she was a little bit famous, your mother. The others were only referred to by their cell numbers, but her we called *die Waschfrau*, the laundry woman.'

'Why?'

'For some reason your mother was familiar with the rules of the prison. I don't know how she managed that. She knew that prisoners had the right to wear their own clothes if they wished. So she insisted on keeping her own clothes, but our prison laundry only accepted prison clothes. Which meant she had to wash her clothes in the sink in her cell.'

It pleased me, this tiny act of individuality. I recognised my mother in it, her stubbornness, her insistence on being different, and yes, her belief perhaps that she was better than the rest.

Without thinking, I reached out and ate one of the jam biscuits, which earned me a sharp little smile from Frau Jankowitz, as if she had known all along that I would eat her biscuits in the end.

'What else did she do in her cell?' I asked.

'What they all did, I suppose. During the day they had to sit on a chair and place their hands on the table like this, and at night they had to lie on their backs with their hands on top of the blanket, like this. That's why we had to switch the light on and off at night, to check that they were complying. Now people call it sleep deprivation, but we needed the light to ensure that they were in the correct position, that was all.'

'My mother sometimes still slept like that when she was at home.'

'How peculiar.' Frau Jankowitz looked intrigued. 'I thought they would revert to something more comfortable when they were back home.'

'I don't think she dared to.' It was impossible to move this woman; she seemed to have no sense of contrition. I took a sip of cold coffee. 'And during the day? What did they do during the day?'

'Nothing, really. They would just sit there until it was time for the next interrogation.'

'Right.' I shifted in my seat. My shoulder brushed against one of the succulents, a plump and spiky little plant that left a few needles in my jumper. The room was too warm, and oppressively cluttered with its dangling plants and trinkets. The scent of sweet violets felt overpowering, cloying, like air freshener in a hot car. Beads of sweat glistened in the fine hairs that lined Frau Jankowitz's thin upper lip. She dabbed her face with a white handkerchief. I resisted the urge to open the window, or to pull down all that macramé.

'My brother was taken away from us after my mother was arrested,' I said. 'My mother was looking for him. Did she say anything at the reunion you attended?'

'Not to me, no.' She bunched the handkerchief in her fingers and crossed her arms. New beads gathered on her lip.

'That happened quite often, did it?' I asked, feeling a little bolder. 'That political prisoners had their children taken away?'

'No, Fräulein Valentin, that didn't happen at all, because we didn't have any political prisoners in the GDR. People went to prison for breaking the law, just like in any other country, and when they did, the state made sure their children were taken care of.'

I noted her use of 'Fräulein', as if she wanted to emphasise my relative youth, my inexperience. And I wondered if Heiko had been adopted by someone like Frau Jankowitz, an ordinary East German following the rules and tending to her house plants. An image came to my mind of him in his high chair. He liked to eat with both hands at once, like a little gorilla, stuffing food into his mouth at double speed. When he did not like something, he dropped it on the floor, as if that were the only way to get rid of it. With infinite patience, Oma showed him what to do instead. *Put it nicely by your plate, put it right there on the table if you don't want it, look, like that.* And one day, just as he was about to throw a piece of carrot on the floor, he stopped himself, and he put it by his plate.

Surely he remembered me too, even if it was just my voice, or my smell. *Eyya! Eyya!*

'Fräulein Valentin?'

'Yes. Yes, sorry.'

'Have more.' She pushed the platter towards me. 'I can't eat them. My doctor said, no more sugar.'

I dutifully ate another biscuit.

'History is written by adults, isn't it?' I said.

She smiled pleasantly. 'Well, yes, obviously. Though there are some very young authors.'

'What I mean is, adults always tell it from their perspective, and then they say things like, oh, children forget, or, oh, children live in the moment anyway; children get over it. Even the word "tantrum", if you think about it, that's a very mean word. My brother sometimes got very upset over things that mattered deeply to him, but so do all of us, no? And he was so little, he didn't yet know how to put on a mask for the world. He was very honest.'

I expected Frau Jankowitz now to extol the virtues of some ancient Prussian parenting style, and recommend rewarding honesty with a good hiding. But she nodded, and for the first time in this conversation we found some common ground.

'Children have no power in this world. That's a fact, a terrible fact.' And she added, almost in an aside: 'I do hope they found a good home for your brother.'

The trial was over, and no verdict had been reached. Frau Jankowitz might have been a particularly severe guard or a relatively gentle one, she might have mistreated my mother or behaved better than the rest; I would never know. She talked about the building site along the main road, and how it blocked the traffic. Then she told me the recipe for the biscuits, and then we ran out of things to say.

After a while, I gathered my jacket and bag. I thanked her for her openness. She responded with a relieved nod. Her shoulders relaxed, her fingers stopped fussing with the platter. In the end she was not that different from me. She had been frightened and now she was relieved because it had not been that bad.

'At Hohenschönhausen, did you ever meet a certain Haupt-mann Kuboweit?' I tried to make the question sound casual. 'He was one of the interrogators.'

'No,' she said a little too quickly. 'No, I never spoke to any of the interrogators, that was a completely different world from ours.'

'You would have known their names, though? You would have known if...'

'I'm sorry, I really can't help you with that.' She placed an unexpectedly firm hand on my back, guided me out into the hallway and opened the door. Cold, fresh air streamed in from the linoleum-covered staircase.

'Why did you do it?' I asked.

'Do what?'

'Why did you work as a guard in a prison like that?'

'I had to make a living somehow, didn't I?' She played with her amber necklace. 'We can't all be glamorous young artists in London.'

There was a long silence.

'I didn't tell you I was an artist,' I said. 'Or that I lived in London.'

She smiled. 'You did, you mentioned it right at the beginning.'

I knew I hadn't.

I wanted to ask her if she went to the pub every Tuesday night for a little catch-up, as Katia had suggested; if it felt good to still know things about other people, and to surprise them with that knowledge. But Frau Jankowitz had already closed the door behind me.

I WAS ON THE tram back to Prenzlauer Berg when Katia rang. She had found someone who knew my mother from her second prison, Hoheneck. That prison had been in the mountains, or at least near them: the Erzgebirge mountains, well away from Berlin. The woman's name was Frau Benedikt, and Katia said she was willing to meet me.

'And another thing.' Her voice was even raspier than usual. 'I saw my son the other day.'

'That's wonderful.' I hesitated. 'I mean, was it?'

'It was nice. I'm not going to say that he flung his arms around me and said, all is forgiven, Mutti. But he didn't launch into his usual thing of saying I'd ruined his life, either.'

'I'm so glad to hear that.'

'Though I *did* ruin his life, I don't deny that. Anyway, I said it would be nice to see him more often. You can't force these things. We'll see.'

'Maybe we can all meet up one day.'

'Hm. There's an idea.' She coughed, and then I heard her light another cigarette. 'Good luck with Frau Benedikt, huh?'

Back in my room, I texted Tobi about the various developments. He replied immediately, sounding rather annoyed. I should not have gone to Hohenschönhausen without telling him, he wrote; that had not been part of our agreement. Was I in Berlin to find our brother or to dig up our mother's secrets? I texted back explaining that it wasn't like that. I was no longer directing the search; the search was directing me.

My phone rang.

'You met with her *prison guard*?' I could hear the steam blow out of Tobi's nostrils.

'Tobi, listen…'

'Without even telling me? Have you gone completely mad?'

'It happened so quickly. I called her and she was free the next day.'

'You didn't even bother to call.'

'I wanted to get some proper results first.'

'From Mama's torturer?'

'I'm sorry. I know I should have asked you first. I wish you were here.'

'I can't. Some of us have to work.'

'If I only stick to nice people, my pool's going to be pretty small,' I said.

'What about the guy at the archive?'

I hesitated. 'He turned out to be very, very helpful.'

'You mean he's found the file? And you didn't tell me?'

'I wanted to read it myself first. Tobi, there are some really terrible things in there. I don't think… I can just tell you what it says, if you want.'

There was a long pause.

'I should read it though, shouldn't I?'

'You don't have to.'

'No, I want to.' His voice wavered a bit. 'It's just, and this is not an excuse, it's more like an admission. I don't know if I'd understand everything.'

'We can go through it together at some point. How about that? One day when I'm back in London. There's nothing in there you don't already know, Tobi.'

'What about Heiko? Does it say anything about Heiko?'

'Yes and no.' Again I was reluctant to give him the whole truth. 'There's a picture of him, and of us. But, oh Tobi, it broke my heart. I can take a photo of it and send it to you, but it would break yours, too.'

Another long pause.

'Maybe we can look at it together some time,' he said, and I had a feeling this meant, never. *I never, ever want to see this awful file; please, Ella, don't ever show it to me. Tell me what I need to know, and keep the rest well away from me.*

Hadn't that always been our unspoken agreement? Hadn't I always been his shield, his filter? To my friends in London, Tobi had always been my younger-elder brother, the sensible one, the one with the job and the money, the one who bailed me out, the one I called when I was in trouble. They never saw how it really was. This was how it really was. Of course, Tobi would never see the file. I would share with him what he needed to know, and protect him from the rest, so that he could continue to walk through life unharmed.

—

I spoke to Ute, the acquaintance who managed my lodgings, and she agreed to cut the rent if I cleaned the common areas and the cafe and checked in new guests. Gradually the rush of London life eased inside me and I adapted to the ambling pace of Berlin.

Frau Benedikt, the former inmate, proved hard to pin down. She cancelled two meetings, then left a long voicemail complaining that I had stood her up. I initially suggested several central, public places, one of the museums on the Museumsinsel for example. After the cancellations, I offered to meet her at a cafe in Heiligensee. It was her own neighbourhood, a West Berlin suburb right by where the wall used to be, the more remote part of it that went around the city. The shorter her journey, I reasoned, the greater the likelihood of her showing up.

Even then, she remained elusive. I took the S-Bahn all the way to Heiligensee, only to receive a text twenty minutes after our appointment saying she was not going to make it. I told myself to be patient. She was clearly reluctant to talk about her experiences, and would open up when she was ready.

Every morning I served the freelancers in the cafe their lattes and herbal teas, which they sipped all day over their laptops. The most shameless ones brought their own vegetable soup in thermos flasks, despite the big sign that said NO FOOD FROM THE OUTSIDE PLEASE, WE NEED TO MAKE A LIVING TOO!

In the evenings, I stalked Hauptmann Kuboweit online. I read everything about his coaching business, I knew all the forums that discussed his past as an interrogator. I could not decide whether I should contact him. Yes, he might have information about my brother. But I hated the idea of giving him the feeling that he still had power over us, that his silence or co-operation could shape the fate of our family. I did not want my search to depend on his goodwill.

⁓

One Saturday I took a bus out to the countryside, to a small village. It was a warm day and the slow old bus smelled of rubber warming in the sun. We passed lakes, a few abandoned factories, the odd Prussian manor house. In one hamlet a handful of people got on, all of them elderly. Then they got off at the next one and I was alone with the driver. When we arrived at the village, I wished him a nice day, and he looked surprised and thanked me.

From the village it was a good thirty-minute walk to the lake. I had last seen Sven's studio in the summer. I hoped this would help me, that even if the human traces had been blurred by time, the trees and shrubs would help me orient myself.

The lake was much smaller than I remembered, not the vast, wild expanse of my memory, but a rather tame pond with a few weeping willows. I walked around it until I found the pier, or in any case, a pier. Instead of Sven's *Datsche*, there was now a small hotel. A sign promised wellness and Kneipp baths. There was a woman at the reception desk who turned out to be the owner. She'd moved here from Munich, had bought the hotel a few years ago, and was unaware that a painter had once had his ramshackle studio here. But she beckoned over one of the cleaners, a woman about my age who was from the village. After some reflection she said that yes, she remembered there'd been a painter here; he used to come into the village occasionally and swap his paintings for eggs and milk and such. That's all she could tell me. Her own parents had no interest in art and never took part in those swaps.

In the village itself most houses were boarded up. The only shop was boarded up, too. I found a little train station, but the rail tracks had been removed, for scrap presumably, and tall yellow grasses and wildflowers grew between the two platforms. On the side of the empty station building were an old election poster and a sign advertising the wellness hotel. I waited for the bus back to Berlin, one of two a day. The air smelled of dry grass, and of streets baking in the heat. In my bag were some simple, cheap crayons and a blank sketchbook. I sat down on the warm pavement and drew a sketch of a painter and a farmer trading canvases for eggs. Then I drew another sketch, of three blue horses. Then another, of a *Datsche* by a lake, and one of three raucous children tearing through a studio. They were fast and fun and cartoonish, and before I knew it, I'd filled the whole sketchbook. Three children splashing in a ridiculous pull-out bathtub. A little boy toddling about with a paint bucket on his head.

In the distance I could hear the bus. I tore out the sketch of the painter and the farmer, and slipped it under the door of the boarded-up shop behind me.

⌒

I did not want to harbour suspicions about the long-dead painter. Perhaps the border guard's sudden appearance in that meadow had been pure bad luck. Or perhaps not. He had approached us just as we had been about to enter the forest, and his reinforcements had arrived pretty quickly. It was almost as if they had been waiting for us. Just because you swapped your paintings for eggs did not mean you'd swap your friends for freedom. Sitting on that bus, watching the sun go down behind the abandoned factories, I felt unexpectedly warmed inside, and grateful to Sven for letting us run about in his lakeside kingdom. If I ever found Heiko, I had to offer him more than bitter memories. I had to tell him about all the good things – the wild days in the countryside, the mishaps and laughter at home. Maybe I could show him the sketchbook, maybe he'd like that. It would be a start.

⌒

When I got home, I found an email from my old friend Sandy in my inbox. It was short and carefully formatted, the kind of email you rewrite several times before pressing 'send'. It said:

Dear Ella,
For as long as I can remember, people have been suspicious of me. First because my mother left for the West. Then, after the fall of the wall, because people accused my father, and by

extension myself, of some unsavoury dealings with certain people.

You contacted me in the hope that I might know what happened to your brother. I do not know what happened to your brother. I do, however, remember the summer you asked me about. I remember the pain I felt when I heard that you had tried to leave, without even telling me, or saying goodbye. In light of our conversation, I now realise that you were similarly disappointed by my behaviour after your return, though it is easy to explain. I could not be associated with the daughter of another escapee. This, I always thought, would have been obvious to you.

In my own experience, travel, mindfulness and the discipline of a spiritual routine can all be very helpful in coming to terms with the past. I have no desire at all to return to Germany, and was surprised to hear that you are in Berlin. But we all have to find our own paths in life.

I am sorry I was not a better friend to you.

With much love

I noticed that she had not signed it, perhaps because she had not wanted to sign as Sandy, but could not bring herself to use her ashram name with me. At first I bristled at the tone, at that somewhat sedated voice of retreats and meditation centres everywhere. It saddened me that my wild, rebellious friend had been pacified. Then I thought, it's very sweet that she did this. She did not have to do this. She went all the way to India, and here I am, chasing her online. I wrote a reply thanking her, and promising not to disturb her peace again.

—

The artists were in the kitchen, talking about the rising rents in Berlin. Was it time to look for an alternative? But where else offered the same combination of vast post-industrial studio spaces and cheap living costs? Detroit? Minsk? Chernobyl? (A bitter laugh at that one.)

One woman had constructed a wheelie suitcase with a screen that picked up random broadcast signals: security videos from shops, and even grainy pictures of sleeping babies and toddlers from the baby monitors in the flats around us. The images of the babies and toddlers cut right through me. The very monitors that were keeping them safe were broadcasting their signals out into the city, dissolving all barriers, exposing them to the public.

I was a little cagey with the artists at the residence. I did not tell them about my search, for example. I did not want my life to flash up on their screens and be made into art. I told them I'd come to Berlin because I was creatively stuck and hoped for renewal, which at least was not that far from the truth. When they asked what I was working on, I mumbled something about the topography of memory.

The only one I confided in, and even then just a little, was the Argentinian, because her own family had been trade unionists and had suffered under the old dictatorship there. We spent some time talking about parents and politics and at one point she said that in Chile and Argentina many dissidents' children had been forcibly adopted. She did not look at me when she said that. There in South America it was the grandmothers who were driving the search for the lost grandchildren.

'And when they find them,' I said, my heart beating faster, 'are the grandchildren glad, or would they rather have been left in peace?'

'Some are glad.' She touched my arm. 'Those who are glad, are really glad.'

—

On Sunday, Aaron and I met up in the Mauerpark. We dodged footballs and out-of-control tricycles, then took a narrow, overgrown path along the rail tracks. I told him about my meeting with Frau Jankowitz, and he listened carefully without interrupting.

We walked at the same speed, quite briskly, without hurrying. For so long I had not done anything in a pair, and it struck me what a pleasure it was to go on a walk with someone, and how different it was from walking by yourself. Aaron pointed out things I would never have noticed, like a tiny plastic Eiffel Tower that lay half hidden by the grass, or a crumpled piece of paper with a crossed-out poem on it. He collected these scraps in a small metal tin that he carried in his back pocket.

'When you work in an archive, you can't help but start to see the whole world as an archive.' He drew a wide circle with his hands. 'If you think about it, *everything* could be archived. And then you get to the point where it seems unfair *not* to archive something.'

'Because it would be like saying, no one is going to care about this plastic Eiffel Tower, ever.'

'Exactly. And who are we to make that decision?'

'I saw a bathtub just like ours in an exhibition at your archive.'

'That's what I mean! One day someone might put this poem in a display case. And the tower.'

'And us.'

'And this whole city.'

I nudged him. 'And then you'll be there with your metal tin full of treasures.'

'Fifty years from now, this Eiffel Tower could be worth millions.'

'That's what hoarders say.'

'Archivists are basically hoarders.' He picked up a stone, turned it over in his hand, put it back.

'What was wrong with it?' I asked.

'Nothing.'

'But you didn't add it to your collection!'

'Of course not. It's just a stone.'

'Poor stone.' I picked it up and put it in my pocket. 'I'm going to create an alternative collection of everything you reject.' I was about to say something else when I looked up and saw the Bösebrücke.

'That's where that man was shot,' I said and pointed at the bridge. 'The one who tried to escape through the allotments.'

We walked up to the photo display of protesters breaching the wall. It all seemed so fantastical now. One day the only reminder of the wall would be signs saying 'Mauerweg', and people would pay them no more attention than they did to medieval city walls and gates. I showed Aaron the little memorial for the man who'd been shot.

'Is there one for your dad?' Aaron asked.

'A memorial stone? In Hungary? I don't think so. I mean, that was… a different situation.' I could feel the familiar tension in my neck and jaw, the physical strain of trying to find the right words. 'I think what happened was… he wrestled with the guard, and a shot was fired. It was an accident. I don't know, I don't know.' I massaged my temples. 'I don't know what happened. I was in the forest, I didn't see anything. I think it was an accident.'

The tension had spread to my chest. Minutes ago I had felt so light, so contented. Now the old heaviness was back.

'He was such a lovely dad,' I said. It sounded trite. I would never find the words to do him justice. Aaron said nothing, just listened, which was nice.

We sat down on a bench under a white lilac bush.

'When you gave me that file, I really thought it had all the answers,' I continued. 'But it doesn't, or maybe I'm just not seeing it.'

'That other prisoner could be helpful. Frau Benn?'

'Frau Benedikt. I'm not so sure. She seems to be avoiding me.' I sighed. 'There's someone else though. I don't know if you noticed, but the file mentions the name of her interrogator. It took me about two seconds to find him online.'

'Her *interrogator?*' He stared at me. 'You sure that's a good idea?'

'He must know everything, right?'

'Do you want me to come along?'

I hadn't expected that. 'You would do that?'

'If you think it would help.'

'That's really generous.'

I leaned back and closed my eyes.

'I'm so glad you decided to get in touch with me,' I said.

'Are you?' He sounded uneasy.

I opened my eyes. 'Of course! Why wouldn't I be?'

'Oh, I don't know.'

'Let me show you something.' I took the photo of the blue horses from my pocket. It was a little creased from all that handling and carrying around. He took his time with it, studied it with slow concentration.

'That's beautiful,' he said eventually. 'Early twentieth-century?'

'Ha, no, it's from the eighties. Neo-Expressionism, or pseudo-Expressionism, if one wants to be unkind.'

'Did your mother paint it?'

'A friend. But my mother used to draw those three horses in her letters to me. And then I found this photo between the pages of some art books that she left me. That can't be a coincidence, right?'

'Who knows.' He looked at me, concerned. 'Sometimes people do just leave photos in books.'

'You think I'm reading too much into all of this?'

'I'm the wrong person to ask.' He shook his head. 'I probably read too much into *everything*.'

'Here.' I held out the photo. 'Take it, for your tin.'

'Are you sure?'

'It hasn't brought me much luck, has it?'

He hesitated, then carefully stored it away in his satchel. I felt an unexpected sense of relief.

ONE MORNING, FRAU BENEDIKT called me and asked if I could come to Heiligensee right away. She would meet me at the cafe by the station.

I arrived at the cafe wondering if she was actually going to show up. A couple in their twenties were sitting at the window table, dipping two long spoons into a tall glass of ice cream and chocolate sauce and feeding each other. Outside, a group of lunching mothers were pushing their prams back and forth with one hand.

I ordered a black coffee and watched the door. A homeless woman shuffled towards the mothers. A few awkwardly fumbled for their purses and dug out a few coins, eyes averted. The woman was perhaps in her sixties, though it was hard to tell; the deep lines, bloated face and leathery skin could have been from booze rather than age. I had already noticed her outside the station; she had sat on the kerb, smoking, her elbows on her knees. Her hair hung over her shoulders in dirty blond spirals, her tracksuit was stained and threadbare.

Such women always seemed like spectral warnings to me, ghosts from one of my possible futures, and I half pitied, half feared them. In a crowd of people it was always me they approached, as if recognising a kindred spirit, or an apprentice of sorts. So I was not surprised when this homeless woman walked towards my table. I opened my wallet for change, hoping to get rid of her before Frau Benedikt showed up.

She waved away my change, dumped her torn plastic bag on the chair next to me, opened her mouth and lisped through a row of grey and crooked front teeth: 'Sorry I'm late. Got held up.'

Blood rushed to my face. I was still holding the coins, which I now placed on my saucer, as if I had only been counting out a tip.

'Thank you for making the time,' I stammered. 'Can I get you anything?'

'A beer and a schnapps, darling, that would be nice. And a packet of fags, if you don't mind.'

I fetched the cigarettes from the shop next door. When I came back, she was already on to her second schnapps.

'Schnapps glasses were bigger in the GDR,' she said, tapping her glass. 'That was the only good thing about it, really. We drank more than the Hungarians, we drank more than the Poles!'

She downed her schnapps and ordered another one. The fag breaks and the shot glasses dictated the rhythm of the next hour. I asked her about my mother and their time in prison, she fed me a few precious details, and then she drifted off into general complaints about the state of Germany then and now, about her string of ex-husbands, about the foreigners who were ruining the country. The next schnapps refreshed her focus and allowed me to ask more questions, until she drifted off again. Yet she never seemed drunk. I felt no guilt at all for feeding her addiction, only greed for everything she knew about my mother.

'I met her in the work brigade at Hoheneck,' she said, and wiped her mouth with the back of her hand. '*Castle* Hoheneck, in fact; it was a real castle, you know. The water in the bathrooms came straight from the mountains, those Erzgebirge mountains with the tin and silver mines, and I swear it tasted of metal. And so cold! Like putting your head in a freezer. There were ghosts in that place as well, prisoners from a hundred years ago mostly, because it used to be a jail under the Kaiser and then a jail under the Nazis and then our guys took over and guess what they did, put their own prisoners in there, of course. It was convenient, I suppose; all the dungeons were still there, and the cells. Oops.' She coughed. 'Dry throat, do you mind...'

I ordered her a glass of water, but she coughed again and said she preferred beer.

'So, the ghosts, some believed in them but I didn't. To be honest we didn't need any dead people wandering around to be scared, the living ones were bad enough. A dozen to a cell or more, the child murderers with the politicals, the thieves with the arsonists. There was one who'd drowned her toddler in a bathtub, another who'd stuffed her baby into the washing machine and turned it on. One who'd locked her children in her flat and gone to stay at her lover's house for a month, and when she came back they'd died of hunger. So they were all charming company, really. Thanks, love.'

She drank her beer.

'But the creepiest thing was, all the child murderers were completely obsessed with children. You should have seen them – whenever we got out pictures of our kids, they were all over them. *Look at that one, isn't she cute, isn't she adorable?* Like that. Still sends shivers down my spine.'

'There wasn't a special wing for political prisoners?'

'What special wing? Everyone was lumped together. We even had two old concentration camp guards in there with us: the Blonde Angel of Ravensbrück and the Beast of Ravensbrück. Not that the Angel was blonde any more, she'd gone grey and white; she'd been in there for decades. She really loathed the politicals. Whenever a bunch of them were bought by the West, she'd hiss: "Into the urn with you lot, into the soup!" and that sort of thing. But the Beast was nice enough, if you ask me. She was in our sewing unit, that was the unit your mother was in as well. I got along fine with the Beast. She worked all the time, even though she was half blind, and when we asked her what she wanted to do if she ever got released, she said, move to a place with a forest and water, where I can work. That was all she wanted to do, work, work, work. I wonder if she's still alive. Probably not, she'd be over a hundred now. Where was I? Your mother. That's right, your mother was in my sewing unit. Which was an OK unit, not like some of the other ones where everyone was at each other's throats all the time. What we did have was quite a few people who tried to swallow needles or who, I don't know, pushed the needles under their skin, like this, to get a few days in the sick station or because they

wanted to kill themselves, or maybe they just wanted attention. And lots of people tried to swallow forks and knives, that
happened pretty much all the time. But most of the time we
just sat there embroidering cushions and it was OK, no worse
than the other units.'

I sat up. 'Cushions? What kind of cushions?'

'Nothing fancy, just those little blue flowers, forget-me-nots,'
Frau Benedikt said.

*Cushion covers embroidered with little flowers. Not as bad as the rest;
slightly unpleasant.*

'She hated embroidered cushions.'

'Yeah, I'm not surprised; I can't stand the sight of them
either. Another beer, darling, do you mind? My throat's dry as
dust from all this talking.' She raised her empty glass, and the
waitress gave her a wary nod.

'Did she ever talk about herself? Or about her family?'

'All the time; she talked about her family all the time.' Frau
Benedikt wiped her mouth. 'We really worked hard in there,
you know. These days you see everyone having a good time
on benefits, but back then…'

'What did she say about us?'

'I honestly can't remember, it was all such a long time ago.
Thanks, darling. And another schnapps, if you don't mind.'

'When she was at Hoheneck, my mother gave up my brother
for adoption,' I said. 'Were you aware of that?'

Frau Benedikt chewed her wet lower lip. She seemed to be
weighing her options. After a while she said: 'Yeah, well, that
was a bit complicated. I kind of had a hand in that. See, because

we were working side by side we got to know each other quite
well. So I told her about how I grew up in care. I said, look, here
you're the dirt of the dirt, right? In a children's home, it's the
same, but worse, I said. Children's homes are really just like
Hoheneck, but for smaller people, and there are even more
beatings, and in the evenings the older boys corner you in the
bathroom and pull down your pants and so on, that's what I
said, cause it was true. And your mother said, that's terrible,
my boy's in care. And I said, good luck to him then, cause it's
even worse when you're the child of an enemy of the state.
Other children get a birthday cake, you get nothing. Other
children get taken to the zoo, you're told to stay behind. You
look forward to a group hike in the forest, can't sleep because
you're so excited, guess what, you're not allowed to come along.
Why? Because Mama's a traitor, because Mama's an enemy of
the state. And you're the one paying for it, until you hate Mama
more than you hate the people who took you away.'
   'You told my mother all that?'
   'It was true, and anyway I didn't have a choice.'
   'Why not?'
   'Look, I'm not going to lie, it's all in the past anyway. Maybe I
got a few perks for helping convince her to let your brother go.
What's wrong with that? It was all true; everything I said about
growing up in care was true. Your brother should thank me.
If it hadn't been for me he'd have spent his entire childhood
in hell.'
   'Or my mother could have got him out after she was bought
free by the West.' My voice cracked.

'Have a schnapps,' said Frau Benedikt, then called out to the waitress: 'Two more, love.'

I drank the schnapps, and wouldn't have minded another.

'Were you bought free as well?' I asked.

'What do you mean?' She gazed at me with her watery, red-rimmed eyes, and then she laughed with boozy glee. 'Wait, you thought I was a political, too? I wasn't, darling. I wasn't anything special, I was your ordinary, run-of-the-mill jailbird. No one turned over their precious West Mark for me. I was just a dumb bitch who got framed, all I did was – I didn't even do anything, always picked the wrong men though, always the wrong men. What was I saying?'

Up until then she had seemed sober, but now she was slurring her words.

'The truth is, we despised people like your mother,' she continued. '*Intelligenz*, they were called back then. *Intelligenz!* Too stupid to crawl through some barbed wire, too stupid to just stay fucking put, but still they thought they were better than us.'

'I thought you were her friend.'

'Her *friend*? Outside, someone like your mother would never even have looked at me. I said to her, I said, if I'd been in your shoes, I wouldn't have risked it. Look at you, I said, you had everything – job, husband, kids, flat – and now look what you've got, which is nothing, and it's your own bloody fault, that's what I said. No one to blame but yourself.'

'Shut up!' I jumped to my feet. 'Shut up! It wasn't her fault! How dare you say it was?'

Everyone else in the cafe had fallen silent and was staring at me. The waitress pursed her lips in disapproval. I sat back down.

'No need to shout...' Frau Benedikt's voice petered out. She looked frightened and confused. She started again: 'No need to shout. I was only...' But again her mind deserted her. Eventually, she asked me for money to buy more cigarettes. I gave her a ten-euro note and watched her leave the cafe, plastic bag in hand. The shop was on the left. She turned right. I waited for twenty minutes, half an hour, but was not surprised when she did not return.

TOBI CALLED THAT EVENING, as usual. 'How's it going?'
'It's not going anywhere. I've run out of people to meet.'
I stood up and walked to the window. On a rooftop across the
courtyard, people were drinking beer and dancing. 'You were
right. Mama never left a trail for us to follow. She just bounced
around Berlin in her usual erratic way.'

'Don't say that. You've done well.'

'I so desperately want to find him, Heiko – sorry, Tobi. Tobi,
I want to find him, I really do. But that's not enough, is it? This
whole trip has been a failure. I've been told that Mama had a
terrible time in prison, that it totally broke her, that she felt
guilty about everything. What's new about that? We've known
that since we were kids.'

'You've found out loads of stuff we didn't know – loads. And
I was thinking, I could come to Berlin this weekend,' Tobi said.
'I've just finished a project, and I'm free until Tuesday. It's not
fair that you're doing this all by yourself.'

'It would be a wasted trip, I think.'

'There must be someone else you could contact.'

'Not really, no.' I stopped myself. 'Well. There is someone.'

'I knew it!' And he sounded so optimistic and trusting that
I did not have the heart to tell him that this someone was our

mother's former interrogator, who lived in a pleasant home in a Berlin suburb, a home I had been looking at from many angles on various online maps and real-estate sites. He had a bird bath in his front garden and a cat-shaped mat outside his door. One of his windows was decorated with sticky foils that looked as if they had been painted by children; his grand-children, perhaps.

Berlin 1989: Winter

A FEW MONTHS AFTER we received our mother's yellow parcel from West Berlin, our quiet street filled up with protesters. It was November, cold and dark. We were sitting in the living room of Oma Trude's ground-floor flat. Dozens, maybe hundreds of people streamed past the window. My grandparents seemed to have forgotten about bedtime; it was almost midnight. A man peered into our room, banged on the window and shouted: 'Come out! The wall's gone! The wall's gone!'

The crowd picked up speed, people tossed aside their banners and sprinted down the road.

'How can it be *gone*?' I asked Oma.

'Of course it's not gone,' said Opa Horst, slowly and pedantically. 'He just means that they've opened the crossing.'

Opa was a quiet man and usually let Oma do the talking. But Oma was unable to reply. She let herself fall on the sofa. The one-woman *antifaschistischer Schutzwall*, the Anti-Fascist Rampart that was Oma Trude, finally gave way. It was over. She put her head into her hands and cried.

Opa Horst sat down next to her, this stoical man who drank buttermilk mixed with chopped onion and linseed oil every evening and said it would help him live to a hundred. He said: 'Yes, well. So.' And then he too hung his head.

If the wall was gone – or going – that meant we would see my mother. We might even see her the very next day. If the wall was gone, we might all live together again, and Heiko would come back to us. No, we would never live together again. My father was not coming back, not ever, not even if a hundred walls were torn down.

There was anger, too. All my parents had to do was wait a little! What had they always told us? Not now, wait a little, don't rush, have a little patience. No, you can't have your pudding now, you can have it after dinner. No, you can't open your present now, you can open it later when the others are here. But they, they had been unable to wait – they had rushed straight into that barbed wire, straight into that border guard.

⌒

My grandmother could not stop crying. She gathered us in her arms, as if wanting to comfort us. She held back the tears for a few breaths, then she burst into violent sobs again. 'It wasn't all bad,' she said. 'You know that, don't you, Ella? You're old enough. You know it wasn't all bad.'

'There, there.' Opa rubbed her back. 'We don't even know what will happen. Let them all go to West Berlin and take a look around. They'll see it's not all chocolates and roses over there, and they'll come back soon enough. There'll be a few reforms, that's not a bad thing, is it, Trude? You've said so yourself.'

'A few reforms!' She blew her nose. 'Don't you understand? This is it. There's no stopping now. This country's gone, it's over; they're going to swallow us up in one big gulp.'

'Ach, Trudi,' Opa smiled. 'I can't see that happening. There are enough people who love our country and who want to hang on to it. We'll be seeing some changes, but that's fine, we've pulled ourselves up by the bootstraps before.'

Oma shook her head. 'It's over, Horst. All those years of fighting, it's all been for nothing; and I shouldn't even be surprised. Think I don't know what people said behind my back? Didn't I see them gloating after what happened to Jochen and Regine? That it was *my* daughter who tried to do a runner, that it was *my* son-in-law who attacked a border guard – that red old Trude lost her grandson – oh, I could almost see them rubbing their hands with glee.'

'I'm sorry you're sad, Oma,' I said. Tobi teared up, but I think he did not really know why, and was only crying for Oma.

'I'm not really sad, Ellachen,' she said, drying her eyes. 'To have been here from the start, to have built a Socialist country out of the rubble – no, I'm not sad about that. That was a wonderful thing.'

'Then again, some things weren't wonderful at all,' my grandfather said quietly. 'Good riddance to that part of our lives, no? Good riddance to the bad parts.'

Oma stared at him.

'Horst, the party makes mistakes, the party corrects itself.

You *know* that. The Soviets don't send half of Moscow to the Gulag any more, do they? The party learns, that's what dialectics is all about. You have to have some faith.'

And then my grandmother began to sing, first quietly, then more loudly:

She never abandoned us,
When the world froze to death, we were warm.
We were led by the mother of the masses,
Carried by her powerful arm...

'Will we see Mama soon?' I asked. 'Now that everything's going to be different, is she going to come back to us?'

'Of course, my darling,' Oma said. She ruffled my hair and pulled me close. 'You must be bored of my songs, but what can I say, it's been a long life.'

⁓

Oma and Opa did not want to join the crowds who were rushing to the wall. They made beds for Tobi and me on their sofas, then went to sleep in their own bedroom. My grandparents seemed very dignified to me in their stubbornness, more dignified than the chanting and crying masses outside. It would have been disappointing to see them suddenly run over to West Berlin after years of hearing them preach that we had everything we needed here. But as I lay on the sofa and listened to my snoring brother and the voices outside, I began to feel very restless.

My mother must be just on the other side of the Bösebrücke. She lived in Wedding – she had written in her letter – right across the tracks from Prenzlauer Berg. I pictured her leaning out of her window as she did every evening, flashing her torch three times, and suddenly hearing the noise of thousands of people from the direction of the border post. Surely she would drop everything and run down into the street, towards the bridge, and then she would see that the bridge was open and that East Germans were rushing across. And then? Well, she would not be able to cross over to our side. The rush of people towards her would be too strong. She would be frightened of the guards. The more I thought about it, the more convinced I became that my mother was standing there right now, staring at the celebrating crowds. It could be no other way. She would not be sound asleep in her bed, expecting the crossing to stay open a few more days, or even forever. No, she was not one to sleep through an opportunity. She was there in the dark, stretching her neck to see better, calling our names. Hoping perhaps that Oma or Opa would take us across to see her that very night.

I did not believe the border would stay open. If this stream of people continued for days or even weeks, our country would be empty. There would be no one to drive the buses, no one to sweep the streets, no one to teach us in school, no one to sell us green oranges and scrawny chickens. I tried to picture our neighbourhood without any people in it, wholly deserted, the coal buckets left carelessly in the gutter, the milk curdling in the shops, the parcels undelivered, the buildings cold and silent. It was impossible. Much more likely was that they would let this first rush of people through, then they would shut the border again and have a sensible discussion with the rest.

In school we had listened to a speech by Walter Ulbricht, who was head of state when the wall was built. That was exactly what he had said back then. He had thanked the workers who built the wall, and then he had predicted that after some grumbling and moaning in the West, things would return to normal: 'Das Leben geht seinen ruhigen Gang.' Life goes on in its tranquil way.

Yes, after this strange and noisy night, life would revert to its usual, calmer pace. It could not be any other way. But before that happened, before they closed the border again, I had to see my mother.

I slid off the sofa as quietly as I could, pulled a jumper over my pyjamas, put on socks and shoes and a thick coat and hat for good measure, picked up a bunch of keys and slipped out of the door, pulling it softly into the lock.

'I CAN'T BELIEVE SOMEONE brought their kid,' said a man with long hair and a moustache, who was swinging a fringed woollen bag with a deer on it. He stared at me. 'Aren't you a bit young for the revolution?'

'Pssst.' His friend looked over his shoulder. 'You never know who's listening.'

'What? Don't you get it? The wall's down! We can say whatever we want!' The long-haired man ran ahead, and his worried friend had trouble keeping up. They looked vaguely familiar to me, perhaps because many of the students in Prenzlauer Berg had long hair and walked around with those fringed deer bags. I followed them.

It was frightening, being stuck among so many adults. Everyone around me was singing and shouting and whooping. People stepped on my feet, hit me in the face with their handbags, pushed me aside without even noticing. I fought my way through the crowd until I saw the two students again. We were on Bornholmer Straße, where the tram usually swerved to avoid the bridge. Ahead of us were the border post and the watch tower. The more cautious of the two men stood still and stared at the border post, at the people pushing through. A Trabi honked and honked. People waved flags and banners.

The lights from the border post brushed over my face and blinded me, and for a moment I was far away in a meadow in Hungary. I reached out, grabbed the handle of the deer bag and clung to it.

'Hey!' The long-haired man, bolder than his friend, had been moving confidently towards the open crossing. He tugged at his bag. 'It's you again! Where's your Mami?'

'On the other side.' I started to cry. 'She's on the other side, she's in West Berlin.'

'Shit. Shouldn't you be at home? Look, go home, and I'm sure someone will find her tomorrow.'

'No! She's there *now*. I want to see her now.'

'Oh, man. Honestly, I can't really...' He looked around for his cautious friend. But the friend had disappeared. The people behind us were pushing against us and sweeping us up in the rush.

'Fine then.' He took my hand and pulled me with him, through the open border post, onto the bridge. Here was where they had shot that man who had escaped from the allotments. Here was where the guards used to stand with their guns. Where were they? All I could see was ordinary people – laughing, crying, hollering ordinary people. The bridge was wider than I thought, with people all around us – a wide river flowing west. I was no longer afraid. I held the hand of my reluctant friend. He was strong and tall, like my father. And then it seemed to me that it really was my father taking me across, that his kind warm hand was guiding me, that there was nothing to fear.

When we reached the other side, the crowd grew denser. Some stopped to feel the ground beneath their feet, to take in the moment. A man accidentally elbowed me in the face, and I gasped for air, pressed and squashed by all those slow big bodies. I was pushed one way and my friend the other, and our hands came apart. A woman's thick coat covered my face. I struggled to breathe, fought through the crowd, emerged in a pocket of air just by a lamp post. A window opened above me and I felt a pair of hands lift me up and prop me up on the window sill.

'Watch out, girl! You almost got crushed in there!' A woman of about Oma's age was holding me in place on the window sill and smiling at me. A West Berliner. 'Now, why don't you sit here and wave so your family can see you?'

'I need to find my mother,' I said.

'Can you see her? What does she look like?' The West German Oma scanned the crowd.

'She's got long brown hair...' I realised she might have cut her hair. She might even have bleached it. 'And glasses.'

'Right. Let's look sharp. And wave, remember to wave.'

I waved. In my confusion, I looked at the faces coming in from the bridge. Then I realised my mistake and turned the other way, westwards.

'She won't be coming from there, love,' the woman said gently. She had curly grey hair and was wearing a nightgown.

'No, that's definitely where she'll be coming from. She's already in West Berlin,' I said. And at that moment, I saw her. My mother was standing in a doorway on the other side of the road. She was not looking at the people walking past her. She was simply standing there, staring straight ahead, as if she couldn't quite believe what she was seeing.

'Mama!' I screamed at the top of my voice. My mother flinched and looked around her, panicked and frightened, and then she saw me. She pushed her way across the street, right through the mass of people, was shoved back and forth, and when she reached my side, I jumped into her arms.

—

The nice Wessi-Oma let us sit in her living room. It did not seem all that different from our own living room. There was a big TV and an expensive-looking telephone, but apart from that, the furniture could have been my own Oma's: broad sofas printed with roses, a rocking chair, a basket of wool and half-knitted socks.

Mama held me on her lap, her arms around me. She kissed my face, ran her fingers through my hair, kissed my face again, and we both cried, and the Wessi-Oma cried as well. I curled up like a baby and Mama rocked me.

'I'm sorry, doll,' she said eventually, put me down and shook out her arms. 'I'm so weak. Where's Oma? And Tobi?'

'At home.' I told her what I had done, how I had snuck across the border, how I had followed the man with the deer bag. As I talked, Mama became very pale. She pulled me onto her lap again and I noticed how thin she was. Her face was gaunt, her hair streaked with grey. She had a nervous tic, a twitch of the chin. Her hands were rough and thick-skinned, with calluses on her fingers.

'You came over *by yourself*?' She shuddered.

'The guards are gone.'

'What if the Russians had sent in their tanks? You must never do that again, Ella, do you hear me? Never!'

And then we looked at each other and laughed, because the idea that there would ever be another night like this was ridiculous.

The Wessi-Oma went into her little kitchen and came back with a bottle of wine, a glass of juice and a tray of sandwiches.

'I thought we'd have a little celebration. Out there, they're certainly going wild.' She raised her glass. 'Call me Lilo.'

'Regine,' my mother said and raised her glass, too.

'Call me Ella,' I said and raised my glass, and the others smiled as if I had said something funny.

We looked outside. West Germans were mingling with the new arrivals. TV crews with big cameras invaded the crowd. People were handing out chocolate and beer. My mother began to cry again. Lilo said she had lived in this flat for twenty years and never thought the day would come. Her Berlin, finally united.

My mother wiped away her tears. 'You don't know our government. They're not going to give in that easily. They've got something up their sleeves.'

'Can I live with you now?' I asked her.

'Yes. No.' She rubbed her forehead. 'I don't know. I think it's better to wait and see, Ellachen.'

'Why?'

'Because – because – because we don't want them to do any-thing bad to Oma and Opa, do we? And… to Tobi.'

She fell quiet and I knew she was thinking of Heiko.

Lilo suggested we call home to let everyone know I was safe. Mama shook her head. 'My mother doesn't have a telephone anymore. They cut her off after I was arrested.'

The noise outside was swelling. There was music now, the sound of breaking bottles; people were dancing and hugging each other. Mama combed my hair with her fingers again. She never used to do that when we all lived together. It was a little strange, like having a slightly different mother, but it was also nice.

'I'll have to take you back,' she said. 'We'll stay here a little bit longer, and then I'll have to take you back.'

Lilo drew her nightgown around her. 'I can come with you, if you like. I'm not afraid of them. If they arrest us, there'll be an international incident.'

'I think this is an international incident,' my mother said, and nodded at the crowds outside. She finished her wine. 'Really, it's extremely kind of you, but we'll manage.'

'One second.' Lilo disappeared into the kitchen again and came back with a plastic bag stuffed with gifts: chocolate bars, a box of cornflakes, packets of sugar and coffee, a jar of rasp-berry jam, and, rather strangely, a doily.

'I made the doily myself!' She handed me the plastic bag with an expectant smile. I thanked her but felt a bit embarrassed. We had food at home. We did not need to be fed by others. Still, I thought, Tobi would be pleased with the chocolate.

My mother looked like a warrior as she moved towards the bridge, hard and heroic, unstoppable. I had never seen her like that and would never see her like that again.

When we approached the border post she slowed and her hand twitched a little. I could not see any guards. Perhaps there were too many people between us and them. She walked me down Bornholmer Straße and all the way to our street. She looked neither left nor right.

When we reached our front door she said: 'Now slip inside as quietly as you can. Let's hope they're still asleep. And tomorrow when they ask you, say… actually, tell them the truth. Tell them what you did. And tell them that I send my love, and that I hope to see them very soon, tomorrow if possible. Ask Oma to take you over if the border is still open; and if she absolutely refuses to, ask Opa Horst.'

'Don't you want to come in and say hello?'

She shook her head. 'I can't go into that building. I can't even be in this street. I'm done with this country. Go in there now, my love.'

She watched me open the door, then turned around and ran the other way, as if chased by dogs.

AFTER THAT NIGHT, EVERYTHING changed once again. Tobi and I went to see our mother together. Opa Horst took us to West Berlin the next day. He even collected his welcome money from a West German bank and queued with us for hamburgers at McDonald's, which were free if you showed your East German passport; and he bought us two cans of Coca-Cola as well.

The drink was not all that special, just sweet fizzy water really, though there was something pleasantly dark to the taste, like burnt caramel. The hamburger looked more or less like a normal Berliner patty in a bun. But after my first bite I decided it was quite different from a normal patty and actually very good, dense and savoury with a sweetness from the tomato ketchup. When I reached the gherkin in the middle, my tongue flinched at the sudden floppy sourness. I did not want to upset Opa and ate my way through it without making a fuss. Then I looked up and saw Opa's nose crinkle, and I knew he too had reached the gherkin. Like me, he bravely chewed his way past it.

'*Igitt!*' Tobi shouted. He opened his mouth and spat a green mess into his hand. Opa scolded him, worried that the workers at McDonald's would think us ungrateful.

'You didn't like it either,' I said to Opa.

'But I didn't spit it out.' He put his arms around us. 'Now remember what we said about the hamburgers. Not a word to Oma.'

—

My mother took us to the KaDeWe, the Kaufhaus des Westens, and bought clothes for us, bags and bags of well-fitting clothes. I could not believe how many things there were: how many lipsticks in how many colours, how many perfumes, shoes, toys. All around us were East Germans shopping with their welcome money from the West German government. Later, Oma said that was the Wessis' way of speeding up the takeover: get our people hooked on baubles and trinkets. 'Glass beads', she called the gifts. 'Look how they're coming over with their glass beads, ready to take our land.'

The pavements in Prenzlauer Berg filled up with old toys: hand-sewn rag dolls, rocking horses made from chairs, little trains carved from wood. No one wanted this old rubbish any more. New toys sat proudly on shelves and beds: Barbie dolls, superheroes, colourful plastic trains.

Children's books and board games piled up on the pavements, too. *Erika the Electrician; Come, Let's Build a Children's Home; Kolya the Brave Soldier.* The book that had taught me to read and write, *Our Spelling Book*, was reissued as *My Spelling Book*. Gone were the old illustrations, the flags of our Brother Countries, the tanks and guns. Gone was the story of Soldier Heinz and his sister Helga.

We had been taught badly, it emerged; we had been taught to think too much of the group and too little of the individual person, and there was a sudden effort to rectify that mistake with these new books. It was remarkable how swiftly that change took place, how swiftly guns were turned into flowers, and soldiers into little girls with pigtails. And just as swiftly, the new books in our schools also became obsolete. *My Spelling Book* lasted less than a year. Oma had been right, our country was not just being reformed. It was not just a question of changing a few words and pictures in our books – no, the whole country was deemed such a complete failure that it was better to scrap it altogether.

The German Democratic Republic vanished, and we became part of West Germany, of the Federal Republic, which was the only Germany now.

Oma and her comrades were not the only ones who struggled with this. The dogs in our neighbourhood were terribly, terribly confused by the change in their territory. Their masters now wanted to go over to the Mauerpark, stroll about in Wedding, expand their range a little. Occasionally they might forget for a moment that a street that had been shut off was now open, that a new shortcut could take you straight across where before you had to make a detour. We all took a little time to adjust to that, to redraw our mental maps, but eventually most of us did. The dogs, however, respected where the old division had been. I once spotted Frau Pietsch trying to tug her little yapper down a street, and he dug his claws in and absolutely refused. '*Komm,*' she called out, '*komm, komm!*' No use. He would not go left where he had always gone right. She gave in and let him continue along his familiar route a safe distance from the phantom wall.

Speaking of Frau Pietsch – the neighbours and friends who had discreetly shunned us after my father's death, who had pretended not to see me in the queue, who had stopped ringing the doorbell to ask for salt or butter – those people now told me how sorry they had felt for us, and how in their hearts they had always been on our side.

'There were some who talked very badly about your family,' perky Frau Minsky said to me one day, in her tight skirt and blouse, her bottom sticking out. 'But I always stood up for you.'

She straightened her blouse with fussy righteousness and gave me an expectant look, waiting for me to thank her, perhaps, or tell her that she was a good person. I did not know what to say and stared at her, wordless, until she said she'd better go and check how her roast chicken was coming along, Herr Minsky was very particular about his dinner.

The only one who continued as before was Frau Rachmann, the revered translator. She shuffled down the pavement in her soiled nightie, oblivious to the crates of Coca-Cola and the big Mercedes cars. Did not care at all. Was gently rounded up and led back to her flat. Smiled at me. Smiled at the sky. Did not care at all.

⁓

For the first few days, Mama burst into tears every time she looked at us. She could not believe how much we had grown.

She remained a little shy with us in the months that followed, was reluctant to tell us off, seemed uncertain of our needs and habits. We moved out of Prenzlauer Berg and into her tiny flat in Wedding. She had been unable to find a job at a university and was working as a cleaner. Once we began living with her, we noticed her strange aversions, her tremors, her fear of small closed rooms, of loud male voices, of basements.

—

Oma caved in and came over to West Berlin, because my mother absolutely refused to go to Prenzlauer Berg. Their reunion was not without its complications. Oma immediately tried to tell my mother that she should find a better job, that surely the West German government would help her.

'The Wessis already splashed out fifty thousand Deutsch-marks on me,' my mother said. 'I was a top East German export, right? So I don't think I can hope for much more from them. I don't think they want to throw even more money down this particular drain.'

'There's no need to bring up the past,' my grandmother retorted, as if she had not been the one who started it.

I went to a school in Wedding, and met Turkish children for the first time in my life. Everyone seemed to recognise me as an Ossi, even in my Western clothes. I was better at sports than most of the other children, even though I had been considered absolutely hopeless back home, and that, I suppose, was the only thing that saved me from being mercilessly bullied.

Slowly I eased into this new life, this life where my mother was a cleaner and my father had died in a tragic accident. And then, just after reunification, Mama sat us down and said she had some good news. A famous institute of art history, part of a big university in London, had set up a fellowship for East German academics. She had applied, and for once, her time in prison had actually counted in her favour. They *liked* dissidents over there. They had even offered additional support so she could take the two of us along.

'What about Heiko?' I asked.

'It's difficult,' my mother said. 'I'm doing all I can to find him. But I don't think being stuck here as a cleaner helps. I think if I had a more prestigious job, if I made a name for myself again, maybe even internationally, it would be easier.'

What had happened, she explained, was that the two Germanies had negotiated a contract for their reunification. The four victors of the Second World War – France, Britain, the Soviet Union and the United States – were part of those negotiations. The talks were about the big things, about the borders of the reunified Germany, about the weapons it was allowed to have, about the withdrawal of the Soviet troops. But smaller things, like the status of very small children who were taken away from their parents by the state – those things had not been negotiated.

As it stood, no one was obliged to return Heiko to us.

Even worse, it was likely that he had been adopted by another family. Their claim would now stand against ours, and theirs would win, because we had no right to get him back; no

East German dissidents had the right to get their children back. The adoptions had been lawful under East German law, and therefore remained valid.

And anyway, who would listen to my mother now? Who cared about the opinion of a woman whose last major published work examined the role of the Expressionists in the history of Class Struggle? She was a single mother, a cleaning lady; her books on art were as obsolete as *Our Spelling Book*. She had no legal right to Heiko, and the only other way to exert pressure was through opinion pieces and newspaper articles, through petitions and books. That avenue was not promising now, because she was a nobody. However, if she managed to climb back to some sort of status in this new world, if she won the backing of a renowned foreign university for example – well, maybe that would help.

'How would you feel about moving to London?' my mother asked.

I did not know what to say. She had never consulted me on any important decisions before. I felt a new sense of responsibility, of maturity.

My instinct was of course to stay, because then we would be closer to Heiko. But when I thought about it, I realised I did not even know where Heiko was. He might be anywhere in East Germany – he might be tucked away right by the Polish border for all I knew. He might have been adopted by Russians: that happened – no one was supposed to talk about it but it happened. Being close or not close was not the question. The question was how we could get him back. And I had already noticed that in West Berlin as in East Berlin, it helped if you had an impressive title and an impressive job.

Still, I asked: 'Can you really not get a job in Berlin?'

I was thinking of Oma and Opa, and how much I would miss them.

'It's not just that, Ella. I never feel quite comfortable here. I always have this sense of confinement, this fear that I'll wake up in the morning and they'll have put the wall back up. My health isn't what it used to be, and it's getting worse. I don't think I'll get any better if we stay in Berlin. Everything here reminds me of your father, everything reminds me of Heiko, everything reminds me of the past. I shouldn't burden you with this, but that's how it is.'

I nodded. I did understand.

'Do you think you'll feel better in London?' I asked.

She thought about it for a while. 'Well, I've never lived any-where but Germany, so I don't really know. We'd all have to learn English, and for me that would be harder than for you and Tobi, because I'm older.' Something stopped her. She thought again, and continued: 'Yes, I think you and Tobi would become English very quickly.'

'But not too English,' I said anxiously, aware that Heiko, wherever he was, would remain German.

'Not too English,' she agreed. 'But to answer your question – it'll be an adventure. I can't promise that it'll turn out right. We may not like it in London. The thing is, the only way to find out is to go there. And who knows, we may like it so much that we'll stay there forever.'

'And Heiko will join us?'

'Of course he will. It's all so chaotic now, but it won't stay like this. We'll just keep fighting and eventually they'll have to return all the children. You'll see, we'll get him back sooner than you think.'

'Then we should go,' I said. And I wondered what life in London was going to be like – where we would live, what we would eat, and how it would feel to speak in a different language and become a different person, an English girl.

Aaron

Berlin 2010

IT WAS THE LAST day of Aaron's internship. Bernd had brought in sparkling Sekt and *Bretzeln*. The other interns gathered around his desk and congratulated him on his work on the office evacuations and the metal workers. Several staff researchers had already shown an interest in the metal workers in particular, as part of an ongoing project on informal industrial action in the GDR.

Bernd had a new project, too – a big exhibition about artists and surveillance.

'It's going to be great,' he said. 'We've got a videographer and everything, interviews, films, paintings, archive stuff. *Stasi and the Art World* – that's just the working title. We'll think of something sexier, a bit more creative. *Framed: Artists in the Eyes of the Stasi.* That's pretty good, isn't it? *Self-portrait with Interrogator.* Something like that.'

Aaron reached for another *Bretzel*. '*Confession with Blue Horses?*'

'I like it! Why the blue horses though?'

'I don't know. It just popped into my head. Forget about it.'

'No, I really do like it. I'll check if any of the GDR's artists painted blue horses. It could work.'

Bernd typed the title into his phone. Later he gave a little farewell speech that summarised Aaron's achievements in verse.

Dr Licht gave a speech, too.

'The ancient Greeks,' Licht said in his ponderous way, 'believed that before crossing over into the next life, the dead souls had to drink from the Lethe, the river of oblivion, which runs through the underworld. Without forgetting about their past lives, they could not step into their new ones. But here, we don't drink from the Lethe, we refuse to even go near it. We've sworn allegiance to its opposite, to *a-letheia*, aletheia – un-forgetfulness – which is the Greek word for truth. Truth is the opposite of oblivion and the opposite of concealment. It's a state in which everything is known, everything is remembered, everything is brought to light and laid out in the open, and that's the state of being we aspire to here. To aletheia!'

'To aletheia!' Everyone raised their glasses.

How pleasant the dark gentle waters of the Lethe must feel, Aaron thought. Step in, let the water cool your sagging skin, let it wash away all your mistakes, all your regrets, all the accumulated failures of your little life. It was a wonderful vision, much more inviting than the cold, bright, brutal light of aletheia. There was a softness to the act of forgetting, a gentleness. Still, he raised his glass along with the others and thanked Licht for his trust and support.

'We'll take you back any time you want.' Licht raised his glass again. 'Come and apply for a job. We always need good researchers.'

'Thank you.' Aaron raised his own glass once more. 'It's been really fascinating, but I'm not really made for this sort of work. I'm not very good at compartmentalising.'

'Neither am I,' said Licht. 'I quite understand. It's difficult, isn't it?'

Bernd handed him a present from all the interns, a framed black-and-white photograph of the Stasi headquarters as they were being stormed by protesters, with shredded files and spools of tape all over the place. Aaron could hardly speak, so surprised was he by this outpouring of goodwill and warmth. They moved on to the bar with the cocktails in those silly teacups, and stayed there until Aaron staggered home in the early morning hours.

When he walked into the kitchen he found a cake covered in clingfilm, a mighty carrot cake with thick icing and marzipan carrots on top, and a card from his flatmates.

Hello Aaron! We hope you had a good LAST DAY AT WORK! Now you are free! Come to our performance tomorrow if you like, we will be dancing on a tightrope in the Tiergarten. Petra & Cem

Gosh, that was unexpected. Had they all co-ordinated this rush of love? Aaron ate one of the marzipan carrots, then some of the icing, then a slice of the actual cake, and then he went to bed.

The next morning, bludgeoned by a hangover, Aaron tried to tidy his room. He threw away redundant photocopies of the Valentin papers, stray bits of sticky tape, spent highlighters. Slowly the room returned to its original sparse state – the bare wooden floor, the bed, the glass desk.

On the desk was the page concerning *the child Ella Valentin*. Damn. He rubbed his face.

When he hazarded a visit to the bathroom – steadying himself against the walls – he caught Petra and Cem on their way out of the flat. They were wearing matching grey harem pants and black T-shirts. He thanked them for the cake and apologised for probably missing their performance. They laughed.

'There's a whole box of aspirin in the bathroom cabinet,' said Cem.

Petra pointed at a half-empty bottle of red on the kitchen table. 'Forget the aspirin, just have another drink.'

'I didn't know you were into tightrope walking.'

'We told you!' Petra smiled and shook her head. 'We even asked you if you wanted to join us, but you just gave us this blank stare and went back to your confetti.'

'Did you manage to patch it all together?' asked Cem.

'Yes. Yes, I did,' Aaron stammered, startled that they'd noticed. All that effort, for what? He'd have been better off learning to dance on a tightrope.

Later, over more carrot cake and strong coffee, Aaron weighed his options.

There was no way he could sneak back into the archive now and slip the page into the file; he had already handed in his security pass. The question was whether to hang on to it in the hope of returning it another time, or give it to Ella, which he should perhaps have done a long time ago.

He could recite the page almost by heart:

INFORMATION

The following has come to our knowledge through IM Erna:

The child Ella Valentin, b. 4.2.1979, regularly brings objects (toys, colouring books, illustrated art books, crayons) from the capitalist exterior (Federal Republic of Germany) to her primary school, the Clara-Zetkin-Schule in Berlin-Prenzlauer Berg.

Questioned about their provenance by IM Erna after class, the child stated that the objects were gifts from 'family friends' in the West. The child's family live in close proximity to the border, in particular the border crossing at Bornholmer Straße/Bösebrücke. The child appeared unusually interested in this border crossing. She also took an unusually strong interest in incident 4091/5 (attempted flight by a GDR citizen) at the Bösebrücke.

On a separate occasion, IM Erna overheard the child tell her friends that her mother often went to artistic gatherings and exhibitions in the neighbourhood. When pressed, the child revealed to IM Erna that those gatherings took place in attics and private apartments. It can therefore be concluded that the mother is somewhat active in the unregulated art scene. The child's mother and father are both art historians.

The mother of the child is Regine Valentin, b. 6.1.1947, employed as a lecturer in art history at the Humboldt Universität, ID no. —

The father of the child is Jochen Valentin, b. 21.11.1944, employed as a professor of art history at the Humboldt Universität, ID no. —

This situation bears certain similarities to the recent case of Professor Heiner Laut, an art historian in Leipzig who used his position to broker deals with foreign buyers and eventually absconded to the West on a research trip (report 676/5).

It is possible that the 'family friends' mentioned by the child Ella Valentin are West German art experts or dealers. If this is the case, Regine and Jochen Valentin may be selling works of art to West Berlin, possibly to build up a reserve of foreign currency. Combined with the child's strong interest in the border, presumably sparked by conversations overheard between her parents, this raises the possibility that the family may be preparing to flee the Republic.

With a view to this evidence, I recommend adding Jochen and Regine Valentin to the central registry of personal surveillance. Given the couple's professional renown, special care must be taken not to invite them in for questioning before sufficient evidence has been assembled.

Unit 7

Lieutenant —

Aaron cut off another slice of carrot cake. It would be easy enough to get rid of the page; paper was not stone. But even if he did, it would still be on his mind, and getting it out of *there* would be much trickier. And was it not a bit patronising to assume that Ella was better off not knowing this fact about her past? She trusted him, she would expect him to show this to her. What if she saw it and shrugged it off, quite rightly concluding that she hardly ought to feel guilty for bringing a toy to school as a child? He licked the icing off his fingers. Too much cake. He felt a bit sick. Or maybe it was still the booze.

The thing was, Ella would torture herself over something like this. Wouldn't see it with the right sense of distance and perspective. Ah, it was difficult. And with a head like this, he wasn't going to decide on it any time soon.

III

A More Permanent Obstacle

Our Spelling Book, Volk und Wissen Verlag, 1968
(Courtesy of the Baltzer family)

Ella

Homecoming

Berlin 2010

IT WAS A SUNNY afternoon and Aaron and I were walking along the Landwehrkanal, past cafes where people drank beer and Apfelschorle in the shade of big trees. Berlin was so spacious compared to London, as if someone had taken the city and stretched it out like dough.

'I would be pleased if someone spat at something I made,' I said. 'It would show they cared.'

'I'd prefer quiet disapproval.' Aaron took off his jacket and slung it over his shoulder. 'Or false praise. False praise is so underrated.'

'The point is that it's a visceral, physical reaction, and it doesn't actually matter whether it's positive or negative. The strength of the reaction alone is a good thing.'

'Not for the cleaning lady.' He stopped to drop a coin into the hat of a busker playing Pachelbel's Canon in D. Aaron was the only person I knew who always gave money to buskers. We stayed there for a while, listening to the music.

'When the Expressionists had their very first show at a gallery in Munich, they had to wipe down their paintings every night after closing time,' I said. 'Every night.'

'And you think they liked that?'

'I think they knew they were on to something very powerful.'

We walked on.

'I haven't made anything in a long time,' I continued. 'I used to think that it was all the art market's fault, that my work wasn't taking off because it didn't cater to trendy ideas of boldness or wall power or whatever. But to be honest, it probably just wasn't very good.'

'Wall power?'

'It's something gallerists say. When a work of art is so compelling that you walk into a room and are transfixed by it.'

'What's the worst that could happen if you started making something again?'

'It could be shit?'

'Fair enough.'

We laughed, and suddenly the idea of making things didn't seem quite so frightening anymore. People had made bad art in the past. People would make bad art in the future. What was wrong with contributing to that particular creative tradition?

We sat down by the canal. A cyclist with a trailer full of children passed us on the wide pavement, and a man with a pig on a leash. The water sparkled in the sunlight. Around us, people in shorts and T-shirts were eating ice cream from a van on the corner. It felt like all of Berlin was on holiday.

I began to hum a tune I remembered from Oma, and to my surprise, Aaron recognised it and sang along: '*In einer kleinen Konditorei, da saßen wir zwei, bei Kuchen und Tee…*'

When he'd finished, I asked: 'Did you learn this from your Berliner granny?'

'Ha, no, she's more into Chopin. She's coming to Berlin next month, have I told you? The director of the zoo is giving her a private tour. She was a big fan of the zoo as a child.'

'That's nice. I'm assuming the director didn't just send her that letter out of the blue?'

'I may have encouraged him a bit.' He said it with a sweet note of pride. It reminded me of the time we went to that *Kneipe* in Mitte, and he told me about his work on the file. He's someone who likes to fix things, I thought.

He opened two bottles of beer and passed me one. I took a sip.

'I'm going to see Kuboweit tomorrow.'

'Tomorrow? Have you spoken to him?'

'No. Look, that was the problem with Frau Jankowitz and Frau Benedikt and even your beloved Dr Licht. I did what they expected me to do. I gave them plenty of advance warning, and all they had to do was prepare their version of the story and stick to it.'

He coughed. 'You think they were dishonest with you?'

'Not dishonest, not exactly. But they were on-message, if you want. They knew what they were going to say. They'd had time to think about it.'

Aaron had the kind of face that was completely open, like a screen displaying his thoughts. Right now, he looked distinctly shifty.

'What's the matter?'

'Nothing, nothing.' He coughed again. 'Do you want me to come with you?'

'Thank you, but I should probably meet him alone.'

I did feel nervous about meeting Kuboweit. Not because I thought he would be dangerous, but because he might tell me things I was better off not knowing. Aaron seemed to be nervous, too, as if he was withholding something.

'Seriously, what's on your mind?'

'Nothing,' he repeated. 'Maybe I'm a bit worried for you, that's all. What if he slams the door in your face?'

'I've thought of that,' I said. 'I'm going to tell him I'm doing a survey. And then, when we're sitting down and he's feeling comfortable, I'm going to tell him who I am.'

'A survey.' Aaron looked unconvinced.

'Well, something along those lines. I'll play it by ear.'

We finished our beers, and I got up to buy us ice creams from the van.

K UBOWEIT LIVED IN MARZAHN, a neighbourhood of prefab tower blocks on the eastern fringes of Berlin. The streets were named after Communist resistance fighters and Russian space explorers: Martha-Arendsee-Straße, Allee der Kosmonauten. The atmosphere reminded me of the Berlin of my childhood. Women with tired perms were smoking outside darkly curtained pubs with names like Imma Uff ('Always Open'). The supermarkets advertised strawberries and asparagus, but the people inside were stocking up on beer and cigarettes. Nobody smiled at me, nobody wished me an excellent day. I felt at home.

I left the prefab high-rises behind and entered a quieter part of the neighbourhood, where whitewashed family homes with red-shingled roofs showed off their perfect front gardens. Here the streets were named after apple varieties: Jonathanweg, Herbstgoldweg, Honigrotstraße. And the houses and gardens were in fact a little like apples – wholesome, neat and glossy. I walked past elaborate displays of plastic windmills, bird baths, garden gnomes, or a combination of all three: a garden gnome sitting on the edge of a bird bath in the shape of a mill.

Kuboweit's house looked like all the others, same bird bath, same red roof. A cat-shaped mat in front of the door. I wanted it to look more threatening, but it was just an ordinary house, and the man living inside it was probably just an ordinary man who remembered only rather dimly (if at all) where he had been and what he had done in the summer, autumn and winter of 1987.

When I rang the doorbell, a grey security camera zoomed in on me from above with a quiet whirring sound. The door opened, and a stocky little man of about sixty stepped out onto the mat, dressed in a cable-knit jumper and grey corduroy trousers.

'Kuboweit.' He stretched out his hand. 'And you must be Ella. I've been expecting you.'

I stared at him, speechless.

'You look very much like your mother,' he said. He took my hand and shook it.

—

I followed him into a room at the back of the house, feeling rather stunned. The room was furnished sparsely with a desk, a sofa and a glass cabinet filled with Meissen figurines. On the window sill, a drab plant gathered dust. I could hear a clock ticking in the corridor.

'Water?' He opened a bottle of Selters. I thought of Frau Jankowitz and her biscuits. Perhaps this was a known technique, giving people food and water so they forgot to be hostile. He screwed the bottle top back on very slowly and carefully and placed the bottle in a drinks cabinet by his desk.

'Your mother came to see me a couple of years ago,' he said. 'I'm sorry about your loss.'

I was about to ask him how he knew, then realised that was exactly what he wanted me to do. No, I would not give him the satisfaction. He handed me my glass, and I caught his scent. Not Privileg, of course not, they no longer manufactured it. A light, modern scent.

I studied Kuboweit's face, trying to see the younger, stronger man who had interrogated my mother. Smoother skin, fuller hair. Angular glasses. Perhaps a military side parting. Dressed in a grey Stasi uniform, the type I had seen for sale in hipster antique shops here – with braided golden epaulettes, a hammer-and-sickle badge, a wide grey cap, a brown leather belt. He would have exuded a sense of unchallengeable authority, not only personal authority but the authority of an entire state.

When we are done with you, there will be no corner of your mind we won't know. We will be completely at home in your mind, we will be there always.

He looked at me with open curiosity. 'You're much calmer than I thought, you know? Your mother wasn't calm. I didn't expect you to be calm.'

'I don't know how else to be,' I said and felt a strange sense of embarrassment, as if he had diagnosed a crucial flaw in my character.

'No, you don't, do you?' He studied my face. His voice was pleasant, deep and unhurried. This was the only voice my mother had heard during her months of solitary confinement, when even her guards had not been allowed to communicate with her. He had bullied her, he had charmed her. He had told her about her little darlings, Ella, Tobi and Heiko, and what they were all up to. How little Heiko was being force-fed by his carers.

Kuboweit leaned against his desk. 'Do sit down.'

'I'd rather stand.'

'As you wish. At least you came through the front door. Your mother climbed over the garden fence. My wife and I were having lunch outside. She needn't have bothered, there was nothing I could tell her that she didn't know already.'

'Did she…' I began.

'I'll have to tell you the same thing I told her. I have no idea where your brother is.' He took a sip of water.

'You *must* know. You were the one who told her that all of us would be taken away.'

He snorted. 'So they've put the file back together, have they? I suppose it's one way to pass the time. Is Licht still there?'

I nodded, and didn't quite dare ask how they knew each other. Licht, who always kept his door open, just like my mother. Who had been in the shower when they came to arrest him. Who was no doubt still hoping to discover his own file one day.

Kuboweit continued: 'Poor man. He'll still be there in thirty years' time, hooked up to an oxygen tank, going through the shredded files at night. Did you know he does that, stays in there overnight? He locks himself into the store room after everyone else has left for the day, and then he burrows through the paper bags. And I thought *our* work was tedious.'

Tedious. Could he not show at least a little remorse? I thought of Katia, with her little boy in the crawl space that smelled of fuel. How she didn't even run to him when they pulled him out of the car; how she waited in her flat until they came for her.

Men like Kuboweit had owned our lives; we had obeyed them even when they had been nowhere near us. And we obeyed them still; we kept that instinct not to stand out, not to attract the wrong sort of attention, not to ask the wrong kind of questions. His pleasant voice had been the one that my mother heard when she screamed at night, when she fell out of her bed, when she wet her bed and then had to hose down the mattress in the morning, telling us she had spilled juice on it, because she felt so ashamed.

Shame was one of the most noble human feelings, I thought. It was a really important feeling. The fact that I felt ashamed now – ashamed of our failure to keep Heiko, ashamed of my fear, ashamed of all our embarrassing secrets – should be a source of strength, not weakness.

'You terrorised my mother.' I could hear my voice waver, but persisted. 'You accused her of trying to murder us. You humiliated her. You destroyed our family, you completely destroyed us. You destroyed our lives, our home, you destroyed everything we had.'

'Oh please!' He shook his head. 'Your mother sedated her own children. You may not want to hear this, but she could have killed you all.'

'You took away my brother and told her that if she didn't behave, you'd take away the others, too.'

'I didn't take him away. She gave him up for adoption long after she was transferred to another prison. I had no hand in that.'

'You did nothing to prevent it, either.'

'It was not within my power, but even if it had been – the adoption was ultimately in the boy's best interest.'

'How? How could taking him away possibly have been in his best interest?'

'Because it gave your brother the chance of growing up in a proper home.'

'We *had* a proper home!'

'A proper home? Oh yes, a delightful home. What a bunch of model citizens you all were. And after reunification, your side really rose to the occasion. Did your mother ever tell you what her friends got up to then? I had shit thrown at my windows. People poisoned my dog. My son was beaten up at school, my daughter was held down and had her hair cut off. There are still lists circulating on the internet, vicious little vigilante lists that made life hell for anyone related to me. There aren't many families called Kuboweit, you know.'

I felt my face grow warm. 'I had nothing to do with that. I'm here for my brother.'

'And as I said...'

'You must know where he was taken.'

'I don't.' He finished his water and poured himself another glass.

I tried a different tactic: 'Look at it this way, this is your chance to make up for some of the things you did.'

'Make up for what? I served my country, I helped prosecute criminals, I protected our loyal citizens. I have nothing to apologise for.' He smiled. 'How about you, Fräulein Valentin? You were in the Young Pioneers, weren't you? *We the Young Pioneers love the German Democratic Republic.* When exactly do you think you would have started to rebel? At university? Or later, when you had a job? A family? Would you have risked all that?'

'My parents did.'

'And you're grateful to them, are you?'

'They had the right intentions.' I wished I sounded more convincing.

'Yes, the right intentions.' He nodded, satisfied. 'I had the right intentions, too.'

'I'm not going to leave until you tell me. I'll stay here for as long as it takes. I'll be here when your wife comes home. When your son comes over, your daughter, your friends. If you throw me out, I'll just come back. I'll drill my way into your life.'

'Oh, stop it.'

'Tell me where he is.'

He smiled. 'Fine, of course I know where your brother is. And your mother knew – that surprises you, doesn't it? Are you sure you want me to go on? Yes? Because you want to know everything, everything, don't you; you people want to know everything, everything, everything. And you think that once you know absolutely everything, then – then what? Then you'll be at peace? Then you'll have us all beheaded? Fine, fine! You want to know what I told your mother. Well, I told her about your brother's adoptive family.'

'My mother knew where Heiko was?'

'Yes. And she decided to leave it at that. You didn't expect that, did you? Your mother could have contacted your brother, but she decided not to.'

'Why?'

'Because she saw him. I took her to see him. His mother – his adoptive mother if you want to call her that – had a stroke a few years ago. She's in a retirement home now. He goes to visit her whenever he can; apparently he's a wonderful son. He thinks his birth parents died in an accident, and by the way, he never spent a single night in a children's home, he was fostered by this lovely couple and then adopted, but did that count for anything with your mother? No, she still insisted on seeing him. Anyway, I took your mother there, we sat in the park where they always went for a walk – I'd asked around, I knew their habits. We had to try a few times, but the third or fourth time, we spotted them. The mother's in a wheelchair now; your brother was pushing her, they were chatting about something and laughing, the father was there as well. The mother was one of us, of course—'

'What do you mean, one of you?'

'Well, she worked for some ministry or other. They were loyal party members, otherwise they wouldn't have been able to adopt a child like that in the first place. I told your mother that. She wanted to know everything, didn't she? I told her not to expect some sort of junior dissident. I told her your brother was quite loyal to the old guard. I had my sources. Anyway, she insisted on going to see him, but when we finally spotted them, she suddenly went very quiet. She just watched them for a bit. I think she went back a few more times, but eventually I got a phone call from her – she said she'd changed her mind, she wasn't going to reveal herself to him. She wasn't going to tell him, and she asked me not to tell anyone, either.'

'Did she say why?'

'Do you want to know?'

I nodded.

'She said he looked so happy. She said he looked so much happier than her other children, the children she had raised herself.' He looked at me. 'I'm sorry, Fräulein Valentin. But you did say you wanted to know.'

'She didn't say that. She can't have said that.'

'She did.'

'He looked so happy,' I repeated numbly. 'He *is* happy.'

'They certainly seem like a very close and contented family, yes.' His tone softened a little. 'Before you allow yourself to get angry with your mother, consider that...'

'I'm not angry with her.' My hands were shaking. 'Of course I'm not angry with her.'

He looked happy. So much happier than her own children. That was how my mother had perceived us, that was how she had judged her influence on us. As if she had infected us. As if staying away from Heiko could protect him from the same disappointing fate.

'If you ask me, your mother did something very noble, very selfless, very...'

'I didn't ask you,' I said. 'And I don't care what you think.'

'Of course you don't.' He folded his hands. I turned around and left the house. Outside, the air seemed colder than before.

'Fräulein Valentin.'

I looked back. He stood under the grey security camera, one hand on the door frame. 'There are some things, maybe... I did tell your mother... when she came here, I did tell her that there were some things one wished one had done differently. But isn't that the case for all of us?'

THAT NIGHT I TOSSED and turned in bed. I opened the window and breathed in the cold night air, I fetched a glass of water from the kitchen and downed it, wide awake and yet so tired I could hardly stand. I looked at the transcript, the one I'd so foolishly set apart to remind myself of why I had to find Heiko. The interrogator's threat of force-feeding him. *Kuboweit's* threat of force-feeding him. All the while knowing that this was a lie, that Heiko was not even in a children's home; he was with foster parents – loving foster parents.

I lay back down and stared at the ceiling. I closed my eyes and thought of the blue horses.

Once upon a time there was a woman who lived… somewhere… with her three children… but the sorcerer took them away… and the grandmother came and killed the sorcerer and rescued all three of them. And they lived… happily ever after. In their flat in Berlin. With the bathtub.

It was not like that at all. It was much more complicated. Heiko had been rescued by a loving couple, and had become deeply attached to them. They had raised him as their own. He had prospered in their care.

He looked so happy.

Kuboweit was a liar. That thing about Heiko looking happier than the rest of us: now that I thought about it, it did not sound convincing. I might be a disappointment, yes, but Tobi was not. He was a successful garden designer who'd planted many a fine feature tree. Mama had always, always been proud of him. And she'd been proud of me, too, I knew that. Kuboweit had lied so much in his life that he did not even know how to tell the truth. Perhaps he was not even aware that he was lying; perhaps factual accuracy had become impossible for him. I usually jumped at the chance to tear into myself, to find yet another reason why my life was worthless and without meaning, but this time I thought: no.

I thought: Mama decided to leave Heiko alone, not because he looked happier than us, but because he looked happy. That was enough.

And I also thought: Kuboweit made up that bit about him looking happier than us because he wanted me to stay away from Heiko. He's still up to his old tricks. It's easier for him this way. Keep everyone nicely apart, don't ruffle any feathers.

And then I thought: he said the adoptive parents were – what were his words? – part of the old guard. Ex-Stasi, basically. But what if they weren't? What if they were just decent people who'd been told that Heiko was an orphan? Then Kuboweit would be in trouble, wouldn't he? If he'd known them all this time and not told them the truth.

I thought: I'm really glad they took him in. I'm really glad they gave him love and comfort and a home.

And finally I thought: Kuboweit is such an *Arschloch*.

I fell asleep, and woke up again in the early morning hours. The question remained of what to do about Heiko.

Was it right to drag him from this cosy home, this warm embrace, to remind him of a meadow in Hungary, of gunshots in the dark, of a dead man and an imprisoned woman? The thoughts were merging and blurring in my tired mind, the horses, the little boy, my dead father in the grass, the smell of grass, the smell of earth, the smell of metal, my father's chest rising and falling, the sticky wetness under my fingertips, the border guard with a face like a boy. The pale little boys walking out of the forest, hand in hand.

I did not know if this was something I had seen, or if I was only imagining it, but I had a clear picture of Tobi and Heiko holding hands as they came towards us. Trying to give each other courage, willing each other along. And then I felt as if it was my own hand that was holding one of those little hands. It was a strong physical sensation, of a little boy's hand in my own, a sticky, damp, warm little hand. I gripped it and held it tight.

I fell asleep again.

The next morning I woke up with a hot, heavy head and aching limbs. My sheet was soaked in sweat. I felt as I had felt on that flight back from Hungary: that all this was a nightmare, that I had to do something to end it, that I had to stop it from getting worse. But I had already made it worse – everything I had done had made things worse. I could not bring myself to follow my mother's example, I could not let go of that hand.

I thought: this was never about Heiko, this whole search was never about him, it was about me, and my need to hold on; and I knew that this was bad, and very selfish. The wet sheet clung to my skin. It would be best to get up and take a shower – clear the head, cool the brain – but my body would not move as I wanted it to.

'MY MOTHER DIDN'T WANT me to look for Heiko.' Aaron and I were sitting by the canal again, this time in a cafe. It was a cool day, and the waiter brought us two blankets with our drinks and sandwiches.

'I haven't told Tobi yet,' I continued, 'but I'm going to. She made me promise not to look for him. She didn't even want me to find out the name of the traitor.'

Aaron looked as if he'd just bitten into a dodgy pickle.

'Is something the matter?' I asked.

'What makes you say that?' He took another bite of his sandwich.

'There's something you're not telling me.'

'No! Of course not.' He smiled, but in a lopsided and tortured way, as if he had a toothache.

'What I'm saying is, it's an impossible choice. Do I follow my mum's wishes and give up on my brother, or do I contact him – and not only go against what she wanted, but also potentially make his life worse than it has to be?'

'Is that your own dilemma, or one that Kuboweit has planted in your head?'

'Fair point. You know, the weirdest thing was, while I was talking to him, I actually believed him. I believed him! Even though he'd just lied to me about a dozen times. "I don't know where he is, I really don't. Oh actually, I do."'

'Well, he's a pro. For what it's worth, I think it's highly unlikely that your mother would have told her former interrogator that one of her children, the one who was kidnapped, looked happier than the rest. It's just not something one would say.'

'My mum was odd. I do have to admit that. She was pretty odd. And I guess there's a version of this in which she said something, and Kuboweit interpreted it his own way.'

Aaron thought about this for a few moments. I bit into my own sandwich – goat's cheese and rocket – and thought how none of this had been around when I was little, not this sort of cheese, not the rocket, not the multigrain artisan sourdough loaf. It was tasty, though.

'I think you can discount Kuboweit,' he said, and his voice was firm and decisive, like when he talked about his archive work. 'Take the details he gave you, the address and so on, and ignore the rest. Totally irrelevant. May his name be deleted from history.'

'OK. I scatter his name to the winds. Done. That still leaves me with the fact that my mother was against all this.'

'But you said she changed her mind many times. And anyway, you're not your mother, you're you. She couldn't actually make that decision for you.'

'Do you think I should contact Heiko?'

'It doesn't matter what I think. I'm not his sister, or his brother, for that matter. What do *you* want, Ella?'

This was a good question, an excellent question. I took several more bites of my sandwich before I felt able to answer it.

'I want to meet him. I want him to know that I love him, and that I've missed him, and that I wish I could have seen him grow up, and been a proper big sister to him. And I think – I think he should also know how much our parents loved him, and that whatever they did, they did it because they believed in a better future.'

'Then that's what you should do.'

'Regardless of whether it's in his best interest?'

'You can't try and guess what is or isn't in his interest. If he doesn't want to see you, he'll tell you, right?'

What he said sounded so plain and sensible. I looked out at the Landwehrkanal, which was brown and heavy with rain from the night before. It reminded me of the creek back home. Back home! So London was back home. But Berlin was also back home. Maybe one could have two home cities, maybe one could have two true families, maybe it wasn't either/or.

I finished my sandwich and wiped my fingers on a napkin. 'Your turn. What's this secret you're keeping from me?'

'What secret?'

'Don't lie. You're a terrible liar.'

'Have you ever heard of an ancient Greek river called the Lethe?'

'No, and I'd rather hear what you've been hiding.'

'Fine. There *is* something.' He sighed. 'I don't know what to do with this. It's… well, it's this.'

He opened his bag, took out a taped-together letter and

placed it on the table, as if he did not want to give it to me directly. It took me a few reads to even understand what it was.

IM Erna...

The child Ella Valentin, b. 4.2.1979, regularly brings objects from the capitalist exterior to her primary school...

The mother of the child is Regine Valentin...

The father of the child is Jochen Valentin...

I recommend adding Jochen and Regine Valentin to the central registry of personal surveillance...

I laughed with bitterness. My mother had been right. Heiko was better off without us, without me. We were rotten through and through, the whole Valentin family – we were like a log that fell apart as soon as you picked it up. We were unhappy, we were disappointing, we were failures, and as for me, well, I was a traitor. A child traitor! My doll, my books, my bragging. My incessant need to show off. What an insufferable little brat I had been. Why had I not for once managed to keep my mouth shut? Why had I not left my bloody toys at home?

As for IM Erna – that could have been any of my teachers. There were plenty of obvious candidates, the type who never shut up about community and solidarity and the goodness of the party. The teacher who taught us songs from the Spanish revolution, or the one who made us write a huge collective birthday card to Margot Honecker with all our hand-prints on it. My thoughts settled on Frau Obst, my art teacher. She had been there one morning when Sandy and I had talked about the man at the Bösebrücke. She had asked me about my West German doll. And after Hungary, she had avoided me – because she was disappointed in me, I had thought at the time; but perhaps it had been out of guilt.

Frau Obst, with her dangling plastic earrings and her quirky assignments. It cut me more than I would have expected. I'd always enjoyed her lessons. She'd been kind to me. I did not want to hate her. And in any case, Frau Obst was just a teacher who had written a report about a bunch of strangers. I was the one who had betrayed my own family.

'You can look up IM Erna at the archive,' Aaron said. 'They'll probably have her real name.'

'No, I don't want to. I think I know who it was. And I don't want to stand in that reading room and go, ah, OK, yeah, it really was Frau Obst. You know what I mean?'

'I know what you mean.'

'At least it wasn't Oma who betrayed us,' I said.

'It wasn't you, either.'

'Of course it was. You don't know what I was like. I was such a pest. Look at what the letter says: *the child Ella Valentin, star informant on her own parents.*' The couple at the next table stopped talking and glanced our way, and I lowered my voice: 'What I'm saying is, I knew it was wrong, but I did it anyway.'

'You brought a doll to school. If someone turns that into a crime, it's their fault, not yours.'

'But everyone told me to keep all my West German things at home – everyone. My parents, my grandparents. We weren't stupid, Aaron. We were pretty clued up, we knew what was going on, even the children.'

'You were, what, eight? No one would blame you for this, certainly not your parents.'

'No, they wouldn't, because they would have blamed themselves instead.'

'Exactly, so don't go and blame yourself, too. Look, it says right here, they were already suspicious of the whole art thing. They would have spied on your parents sooner or later anyway; you couldn't have stopped it.'

'It's not guilt, not really. It's more like… there's something foul and rotten in those files, and now that foulness is part of me. Maybe it always was.'

'I shouldn't have shown this to you.'

'I'm glad you did. I'd rather it was me than Oma.'

Aaron shook his head. 'The important thing is that you're going to see Heiko. That's much more important than some file from a thousand years ago.'

'I haven't decided yet if I'm going to see him.' I put the letter back into the envelope and slipped it into my pocket. We paid, left the cafe, crossed the canal. I needed to walk, to feel a physical sensation of distance and tired legs and getting away from it all.

'I'm sorry I dragged you into all this,' I said. 'It just gets worse and worse, doesn't it?'

'No.' Aaron put his hand on my arm. We stopped. 'This is all there is, Ella. There's no more, do you understand? The worst thing, that thing you were always afraid of, that's out in the open now.'

'Why would Heiko even want to know someone like me?'

'Because you're the only sister he's got.'

'I was hoping you'd say, because you're amazing.' I picked up a twig and snapped it. 'It's just, I wouldn't exactly bring a bagful of fun to his life.'

'You've brought a bagful of fun to mine.' He coughed. 'Well, OK, fun might be the wrong word, but...'

'No, I liked fun. Can we keep fun?'

'It's better to have a sister than not to have a sister, that's what I'm saying.'

'It's better to have a sister than not to have a sister,' I repeated. It sounded reassuring, solid. Heiko had a mother, an adoptive mother, a mother he loved. But he didn't have an adoptive sister. I wasn't taking anyone's place, I wasn't challenging anyone's position. I was just his sister.

'Anyway, if I do meet him, and if it's a total disaster...'

'... which it won't be...'

'... if it's a disaster, I might just board the next flight out.'

We sat down on a bench.

'And if it goes well with Heiko,' Aaron asked cautiously, 'you'll stay?'

'At least for a while, I think. They've offered me a job at the artists' residence where I'm staying, nothing special, but it would pay the bills, and I like it there. It's been ages since I last saw a slug, and I have to say, I don't miss them.' I hesitated. 'And I'm working on something.'

'But that's fantastic!' He beamed with delight, and I was moved by his enthusiasm.

'You haven't seen it yet.'

'Doesn't matter, it's just great that you're making something.'

'I'll show it to you when it's finished. That is, if you're interested.' I suddenly felt rather awkward. 'It would be nice to stay in touch, right?'

'Of course – if you need any help at all with the files…'

'No, not because of the files.' Neither of us said anything for a while, and then I took his hand, because we were both quite shy people, and one of us had to make a start.

I CALLED TOBI, AND he said I should meet Heiko first. It was touching. My little brother, sending me ahead to scout out the terrain. Hiding behind his big sister.

Even with Tobi's backing, it took me a few days to work up the courage. Several times I picked up the phone, my thumb hovering above the screen, only to put it down again. And when I finally made the call, it was strangely dreamlike. Later, I could not recall the exact sequence. Who said what, and how. Only fragments remained:

'Ella?' said in a sampling, questioning, curious way, as if he was trying out the sound of it, as if it stirred some faint memory. *Eyya! Eyya!*

He spoke in a broad, earthy Berliner dialect. So rooted here.

He said: 'Yes, that's where I live now. It's a long story.'

I held back the things I wanted to ask. You moved back? So you do remember us? What do you remember? The smell of burnt pancakes? The West German nappies? Mama shouting at Oma? Your bee toy? The forest in Hungary?

Have you missed us?

That was another thing I did not ask.

At one point the line crackled and I was terrified I would lose him.

Towards the end he said cautiously: 'It would be nice to meet you.'

But we have already met, I wanted to say but did not. I am your sister. We are not strangers. We are kin.

Afterwards, I resisted the urge to call him back. I wanted to hear more of that voice, to fill myself up with it, to let it become familiar until it was my brother's voice again. Not a stranger's voice, but one that belonged to Mama, Papa, Tobi and myself. Perhaps Heiko was doing something similar, staring at his phone and trying to picture a body that would fit that unfamiliar Anglo-German voice, trying to find a connection.

It would be nice to meet you.

I was early. I went round the block once, twice, three times, then found myself walking into a second-hand bookshop. I had avoided this particular kind of bookshop since arriving in Berlin – small, cosy, with an ironic print of Lenin on the wall, and a well-stocked section on art history. I scanned the shelves for non-fiction, for history, for art history, for V, for Valentin.

There she was. *Expressionism and Class Struggle*, by Regine Valentin. Her regime-friendly book from the seventies, in which she argued that the Expressionists were decadent layabouts who were ultimately overtaken by true revolutionary artists with a Greater Purpose.

It was a handsome book, a light orange paperback with the title and my mother's name in black. The font was the GDR version of Garamond, produced by the collective enterprise VEB Typoart. It is still the most beautiful Garamond around; yes, we did manage to make some things that lasted. I leafed through the book. In the footnotes, I found a reference to my father, a little spousal wink from one art historian to another:

1) See also: Valentin, Jochen. *Die Avant-garde im Spiegel der Zeiten.* Aufbau Verlag, 1975.

Regine and Jochen Valentin. Two people from very different families who merged their life stories and left behind three footnotes: the Ella footnote, the Tobi footnote and the Heiko footnote.

2) See also: Valentin, Ella. *It Took Me a Long Time to Come Back, Mama, But Look, I Am Here Now.* Berlin, 2010.

I ran my finger along the spines of the books. Startled, I spotted another book by my mother. It was slightly mis-shelved, wedged between Volcker and Voss. I had not even known about this one; I had never heard or seen the title: *Not Nearly Close Enough: The Avant-garde's Legacy in the Divided Germany.* By Regine Valentin.

I pulled it out and opened the cover, checked the edition and publication date. It had come out in 1994! We were already in London then. I would have been fifteen. I had no idea she had been working on a book at the time; I had no idea she was in contact with editors in Berlin. Why had she never mentioned it? Had she thought we would hold it against her, that we would accuse her of forgetting about Heiko, of pressing on with her career?

I closed my eyes and remembered a scent. It was the scent of a rainy English summer – of plum cake, ink and grass – and all of us sitting on a blanket on the wet grass and eating cake while my mother marked up her pages. Maybe she had mentioned a book. Maybe I had simply not been interested. Maybe I had cared more about what we were having for dinner that night, and whose turn it was to empty the dishwasher. I turned around and there she was, tilting her head to read the titles on the spines, with that pinched, concentrated look on her face. Then she was gone. I leaned against the wall of the bookshop, knocked a few books off a shelf, had to crouch to pick them up. The woman behind the counter rushed over to help me.

'You're lucky, that one gets snapped up quite quickly,' she said and pointed to *Not Nearly Close Enough*.

'Does it?'

'It's a wonderful book, and I think people take to her personal story. She was in prison, you know. She composed the whole thing in her head, and when she came out, she wrote it down.'

'I knew she was in prison,' I said. 'But I didn't know about the book.'

I bought *Not Nearly Close Enough*, and then I turned back to the other, earlier book, *Expressionism and Class Struggle*. I read the introduction. The final paragraph said:

In the 1950s, some of these East German artists left for West Germany, lured by the promise of wealth and comfort. The majority, however, stayed and threw themselves into the construction of a new country. They streamed into the collective farms and factories, willing to forgo an easy life for the deep certainty that all their sacrifices would be worth it in the end.

'I'll buy this one, too.'

All their sacrifices would be worth it in the end. Were they, Mama? Was it all worth it in the end?

—

I was still half an hour early, but I could not wait any longer. I stuffed my mother's books into the pockets of my gaberdine coat and walked towards our street. The neighbourhood was mine again, the old map in my mind overlaid with a new one. The children in their yellow helmets, the restaurants with the mezze platters, even the British and Australian waiters had come to feel almost as familiar as the old people and landmarks. A neighbourhood became part of you quickly, if you let it.

There it was, our old front door. But it was not an old front door: it was new, painted cadmium yellow. Our entire building had grown younger. The stonework had been restored, the windows replaced. The bullet holes from 1945 had been filled in and painted over.

It had been quite a shock to hear Heiko give me his address. He was now living in the building where we had grown up; not the same flat, not even the same wing, but still, the same building. What I had really wanted to ask was: *Did you move back so we could find you?* But I had not dared to, on the phone. I had been afraid of saying the wrong thing, of scaring him off.

Heiko's name was the first on the brass plate by the doorbell. The brass plate was new, the intercom was new. The door was new, the paint was new. The people were new, their habits were new. No one in this building bathed children in a kitchen drawer any more. No one hung up furry Russian hats and gaberdine coats on hooks by the door. No one peeled potatoes with one hand. No one talked about winters in the camp. No one made foaming pancakes with cherries. No one defended falling balconies. No one traded sloe vodka for car parts. No one sighed and said building a country from scratch was hard, but look at what we had already achieved. No one was waiting for me behind one of those doors inside the building with her arms stretched out wide for a hug. No, that was wrong. Someone was waiting for me inside that building, behind one of those doors, and maybe his arms were stretched out wide, and maybe they were not, but there he was, waiting for me.

⌒

I rang the doorbell. Behind one of the ground-floor windows the curtains moved, thin white gauze curtains. I caught a glimpse of a room with bookshelves and a painting on the wall, then the curtain fell back again. It could not possibly be the same painting – no, the painting in my mind was larger than the span of my arms, overpowering almost, three big horses massing against a storm, tucking their hind legs under and curving their necks, comforting and threatening at once; and the painting I had spotted on the wall of this ground-floor flat was hardly larger than a doormat; the horses in it looked quite gentle and there was no sign of a storm. I was about to ring the doorbell again when the buzzer went. I pushed open the door. How easy it was to push open a big door when you were a grown-up. I used to have to push this door with my shoulder. This door that was not this door. The hallway smelled of soap and cabbage. In a minute Frau Rachmann would shuffle towards me and touch me with her papery hand, and from upstairs I would hear my mother call out and ask if I could bring up a bucket of coal.

'Come in,' a voice said. 'I'm right here.'

Author's note

THE STASI ARCHIVE IN this novel was loosely inspired by the work of the Stasi records agency in Berlin, which has undertaken the enormous task of safeguarding and providing access to the records of the former East German secret service. However, the archive where Aaron and Ella meet is ultimately a work of fiction. None of the characters or events there are based on real life. The same goes for everything else in this novel, including places such as Hohenschönhausen prison that were also broadly inspired by historical sites, but then fictionalised to fit the story.

Acknowledgements

I WOULD LIKE TO thank my editors, Helen Francis and Neil Belton, and my agent, Mark "Stan" Stanton, for their sharp-eyed comments, brilliant edits and unwavering enthusiasm. I am also very grateful to Eleanor Rees for her excellent copy-editing. Goldsmiths College and the German Academic Exchange Service kindly funded research trips to Berlin for this novel. The Goldsmiths community, especially Naomi Wood, Adam Mars-Jones and Andreas Kramer, provided much-appreciated insight and advice, as did Benjamin Markovits and Jo Catling. The Baltzer family generously allowed me to use a beautiful illustration by Hans Baltzer, which helped a generation of schoolchildren learn to read.

Sophia Tobin, Ceri Radford, Türküler Isiksel and many other dear friends inspired and encouraged me from draft to draft. The Bensimon-Lerner family provided warmth, support and laughter, and my son, Aaron, brightened my days throughout the writing process. Iwona Wysocka looked after him while I was writing; working on this book would not have been possible without her. Finally, I would like to thank my beloved husband, Dan Lerner, for believing in this book and its author.

About the author

SOPHIE HARDACH is the author of two novels, *The Registrar's Manual for Detecting Forced Marriages*, and *Of Love and Other Wars*. Also a journalist, she writes about subjects from multilingualism to child development for a range of publications.